THE HIRED GUN

THE HIRED GUN

A Novel

MATTHEW BRANTON

JUSTIN, CHARLES & CO., PUBLISHERS
BOSTON

FIRST U.S. EDITION 2003

Originally published in 2001 by Bloomsbury Publishing, Plc.

Library of Congress Cataloging-in-Publication Data

Branton, Matthew.
  The hired gun / Matthew Branton. — 1st U.S. ed.
    p. cm.
  ISBN 1-932112-03-0
  1. Murder for hire — Fiction. I. Title.

  PR6052.R278 H5 2003
  823'.92—dc21

Published in the United States by Justin, Charles & Co., Publishers, 20 Park Plaza, Boston, Masschusetts 02116
www.justincharlesbooks.com

Distributed by National Book Network, Lanham, Maryland
www.nbnbooks.com

10 9 8 7 6 5 4 3 2 1

PRINTED IN THE UNITED STATES OF AMERICA

The thing which
I greatly feared is come upon me,
and that which I was afraid of
is come unto me.
I was not in safely, neither
had I rest, neither was I quiet;
yet trouble came.

— Job 3: 25–26

THE HIRED GUN

1

AT MIDNIGHT, EVERYONE IN the sultry city had been level-pegging; two hours later, Decker had joined the wide-eyed crew who were going to have a lousy week.

Searching with his temple for a cool part of the pillow, his pilot-light consciousness pulled compatriots from the shrouded city. A bathrobed father, maybe, sitting up for his daughter, curfewed for eleven but still necking some pimply streak of piss, her cellphone voicemail innocently taunting him every time he hit the speed-dial. A supervisor from an over-stretched office, wakeful after sex while her husband slept and shifted, wondering if this would be the week that the temp would get tired of plugging the dyke and quit, go paint henna tattoos on tourists up in the Castro as she'd let slip she had last summer. A cop, knowing that every minute lost now would come back doubled in tomorrow's sweltering cruiser. A college student, wondering if a love pledged in dorm-room campus certainty would last out the studio-share, blue-collar vacation; a mortuary attendant, thinking how the blue fluid would smell after five hours' sleep, but unable to summon it nonetheless. Decker shifted over to the other side of the bed. Practitioners of his own profession were popularly understood not to sleep, or to do so in straight-backed chairs, four-square with the door; he knew different. Like the cop and the student, the supervisor and the orderly, he knew two missed hours on Sunday night meant a mis-step on Monday, with a nagging sense of catch-up all week; the feeling of having lost a point before play had started was the same for Decker as for anyone else.

The other side of dawn was time to focus and forget about it. There'd been a Decker once who could sleep on the fly, could fire on all cylinders as long as he had to; running on reserve and, when that was drained, running on fumes till the job was done. His body had changed on him somewhere in his thirties. He could still kick it when he had to, but the last few years even missing his window for a crap left him naggingly off-rhythm for days on end. He'd try a hot bath – maybe a herbal gel cap – when this was done, he thought, making the last turn in the labyrinth of Gallops, Drives, Meadows and Paddocks. Thirty yards from the turn he backed the rental into the realtor's drive, killed the engine, turned down the volume and shut it all out.

Two hours ten to go. The house across the street was booting up on schedule. Lights were on in bathrooms and hallways. Figures were discernible through the kitchen window, above the neat shrub border: the Kurtz's wife and daughter, moving between the refrigerator, the tea kettle and the counter. The drapes were still drawn behind the master bedroom's leaded window: textbook Kurtz, thought Decker, shifting his seat back and folding his arms. When they lost the plot, they stopped getting out of bed in the morning. It occurred to him that he should've added the Kurtz to his cadre of wakeful *compadres*, as he'd lain awake earlier; the guy hunched under hi-watt halogen against the dark of his den, plying an Exact-o-Knife under an ID laminate or whatever he did these days. Decker flicked his eyes up and down the suburban street reflexively, saw the same pattern of drapes and lights in every double-garaged, redwood-trimmed, half-mil-plus property. The same striped protective covers on every lawn chair and swing seat, the Kurtz's too. No one planning on going anywhere. He checked the time: two hours and five. It was a drag, but watch-and-wait intel was the only real route into the frame.

The paperboy hove into view down the street: 6.54 by the dash LCD, bang on the button. Little-league suburbs were a good place to work: routine-heavy, no surprises. His clients tended to live there for that reason: each unfamiliar car would catch an idle eye, and a strange pedestrian would have the dispatcher at neighbourhood security working through her break. Decker didn't plan to upset her routine this morning. The driveway he was backed into fronted the four-bed, two-bath estate of a realtor with four full days left on Maui. The rental he sat in was an Acura, blue-gray; same year, model and spec as the realtor drove, along with most people around here. It was a two-piece suit, a collar and rep tie, a pair of black Oxfords on wheels.

It wasn't Decker's choice. They were apt to shed tires when rammed a certain way, and the beverage holder, when he located it, was too small to take the cup from his brushed-steel Thermos. He poured out coffee anyway, balanced the cup on the dash and noted the mailman in the distance making his honeybee progress from one sunflower- or daisy-painted box to the next. As a kid Decker'd loved the mail, the whole round of daily renewables, reassuring you that you were part of something bigger, that there was a game plan in operation, that the machine was doing what it said on the box. The sight now made Decker think, as it always did, of 16 June 1980: *Time* magazine, an auto-insurance coupon and a credit-card statement. He could remember his name buzz-printed on the labels, ripping the wrappers, the different gives and textures, heat-sealed polythene, buff and white paper, not knowing this was the last. As a kid he'd loved the mail: forty years later he had five apartments but not one mailbox that wasn't bolted shut.

Hour and forty. He finished up the coffee. The air-con was too noisy to operate without drawing attention to himself in the quiet, dew-wet street, so he had to crack a window, let the car warm up at the same pace as the late-June morning. The Kurtz's drapes were pulled back now, and his shape occasionally darkened the frosted glass of the en suite. Below it, the kitchen was still now, the women gone to dress. A movement to Decker's left made him take the clipboard from the passenger seat, rest it on the steering wheel, make movements with his right fist over it as though checking off a list. The sound of a car door opening gave him the opportunity to look up, make eye contact with the neighbour who was staring at him with a 'Help you?' look on his face. Decker smiled, motioned to his watch and the clipboard, a nonsense gesture, but one that made the neighbour nod, half-smile, get into his car and back out into the street. It was all in the forehead, the neck and the teeth, a PhD hired by the Kurtz had told Decker two decades before. You bounced them back at themselves, like the burglar at the dressing table closing his eyes as the head lifts from the pillow.

When the daughter's ride arrived Decker was ready to do it again, but it wasn't necessary. The driver stared at the bonnet as her Beetle chugged at the kerb; the daughter came out, greeting the street with the high-eyebrow sweep of a fitness instructor, the kind whose job entails making sure that anyone looking up from spinning gets the eye contact they need. Decker watched her closely for a moment. She was sure of her place in the world, and she was about to find out it was all shit. In twenty years' time she'd be offering what happened today as a credential to strangers at parties. Not unattractive, if you went for that type. The fact that there was a kid here

4

didn't bother Decker, though he wouldn't have said that it was the best thing to see them immediately before. Mistresses say they never think of the wife, not the first few times; and since Decker's were strictly one-shot deals, he was never around to be reminded. As it was, the Beetle pulled away before the passenger door was even shut.

The maid arrived and the wife left with a little under an hour to go. The wife looked every inch the woman who'd been screwing her boss long-term until eight months ago and now wasn't sure where she stood. She carried a purse, a notebook case and an antiqued leather satchel; drove the black Lexus that she'd reversed into the drive the night before. The maid looked like a maid and drove a Honda. Decker slipped the seven-shot .22 from where it had been warmed by his armpit. The bore was flyweight, but a small cartridge meant less trauma in the morgue's ID room. He popped the rounds, ran the action, put them back in the order they came out. Lights came on and off as the maid worked the house. With twenty minutes to go, the drapes opened in the Kurtz's study, and Decker caught a flash of the white hand that had signed the paper that had put him in this car today, a quarter-century later. When the maid left for her next job, he opened the glove compartment, took out the cellphone he'd stolen the night before, slipped it into his pocket and opened the door.

The Kurtz was watching him as he crossed the street and strode briskly up the walk. Decker knew it, but neither man gave any sign. The lock on the front door was considerably better than standard issue, and took Decker four seconds instead of two. Inside, the smell got him, as it always did: not just the blend of floor cleaner, laundry soap and soft-furnishing decay that was unique to every house, but the smell of the two women: their skin, their hair, their cosmetics and their sex, raising Decker's pulse rate a fraction as he crossed

5

the hall. Pre-menopause women who lived together found their cycles swinging into sync, he remembered from somewhere as he took the carpeted stairs soundlessly, two at a time. The weapon remained holstered as he crossed the landing to the Kurtz's study, unbuttoning his suit coat as he went. He was about to push open the dark-wood door when it swung open from inside, and there was Miller, there was the Kurtz, in an open-neck dress shirt and sweatpants, grinning sourly at him.

'Decker,' he said. 'Boy. I must've fucked up good to get you.'

Decker stepped into the tiny office and swept it with his eyes. He hadn't been sure how the room would be: whether the loss of control in Miller's life would be projected in an obsessive neatness of in-tray, or whether it would look as if a first-year drama student had dressed it for sophomore symbolism. Decker had seen a lot of middle-age treehouses – in a dacha on the Black Sea, in a farmhouse outside Lucca, in a Westminster pied-à-terre – and they tended to fall to either extreme. This was somewhere between the two: steel filing cabinets flanking the door, pinboards covering the walls; worktops on three sides of the room piled with paper, toolboxes, technology and bastardized kit. A pre-Celeron PC hummed beside the window opposite the door, monitor on top of the box; fixed just right so Miller's line of sight would never be wide of the street outside.

'Coffee?' Miller asked, settling into his swivel chair and gesturing to a thermal pitcher sharing space on the mouse mat. Decker didn't respond. 'Mind if I do?' He unscrewed the cap a little, poured into an oversize mug with a marlin stencilled on it. 'Salud,' he said and raised the mug to his lips, holding eye contact over the rim, swallowed. 'Not the time-honoured shrimp platter and pie à la mode,' he said, cupping the mug in both hands, 'but like they say. Good cup of coffee – meal in itself. You sure?'

He took another sip, watching Decker over the rim. Decker shook his head.

'You look like you could use it,' Miller said, setting the mug down on a pile of fading, coffee-ringed faxes. 'You're what, forty-six?'

'Seven,' Decker said.

'You look ten years older,' said Miller, tilting his head. 'That postman of yours must think it every time he sees you.'

Decker kept his neck in line with his spine.

'Yeah, you must think it, huh? Every time you look in a mirror,' Miller went on, settling back in the leather-padded semi-recliner, finding the hollows his shoulders and buttocks had moulded already in the couple of thousand hours since he'd puzzled over the assembly instructions last Christmas. 'Never thought you'd still be working at your age, did you? Bet your postman never did either.' Miller's eyes narrowed. 'Though I bet his idea of where you'd wind up is pretty different to yours. Bet he –'

The phone cut him off. He turned to his desk, checked the caller-ID display and flinched – almost imperceptibly, but Decker saw it. It rang four more times before he picked up the receiver.

'Sweetheart?' He listened for a long moment. 'Daddy's busy, honey. Can't your mom do it?' His eyes relaxed focus to a point in space hanging in the morning air outside the window. 'How about if I call the store, give them my Visa number?' Decker could hear the girl's voice, faint but like a dry blade on a windshield. 'I see. So what's wrong with your debit card?' Miller listened, rolled his eyes. 'Okay, okay. I'll be there in a half-hour,' he said, checking his watch. 'With the money. There's only one of those stores in that mall, right? Okay. I said okay. Don't be that way. I love you.' He hung up, sat looking at the phone a moment, his hands in his lap. Then he swung round till he was almost facing Decker.

7

'My daughter,' he said, his expression only partially falling into line with his matter-of-fact tone. 'Her period started early, she's spotted the seat of her slacks. When this is done you're to call a cab, give the driver an envelope with seventy bucks in, have him drive it to the mall by exit 34 and deliver it to my daughter, who'll be waiting outside the Foot Locker franchise there. She'll think I'm a jerk for sending a cab, but she thinks I'm a jerk already. You want to ask, don't you.'

It wasn't a question, but Decker responded anyway. 'Ask what?'

'Whether it's been good to have a child,' Miller replied. 'I didn't have to. I could've faked infertility. I could've faked a lot of things.'

Decker held the man's steel-ball stare.

'The answer, anyway, is no,' Miller said, and broke it. 'They expect it of you – one, at least, to help fit your cover – but they give you no fucking backup whatsoever. That's her.' He nodded at a framed snapshot; the girl with the high eyebrows maybe ten years before, arms round her father's neck, grinning over his shoulder. 'But then you know that, don't you?' Miller's voice could've been giving a departmental briefing. 'Despises me. I would, if I were her. Dad who spends fourteen hours a day shut in his office. Running the precious consultancy that never makes any more than it did the year before. Or ten years before.' He took off his half-moon glasses and rubbed his eyes. Then he put them back on, looked up at Decker.

'But then we don't care, do we? We accept from the start that we drink the champagne alone, inside ourselves. It fits with how we think we ought to be. You can't anticipate how much it's gonna hurt, having your kid look at you like you're a loser, but you turn it around. You make it work for you. Up till this morning, I was even counting on it. Her –' he smiled, mouth only – 'how do we put this? Her low regard for me was what was going to take her up through the tax bands. Do better than her old dad to get back at him. But that's busted now, isn't it? You don't need to think about this, Decker, but I'm going to tell you. She's going to spend the next twenty years screwing losers to get what happened today out of her system. And then it'll be too late for her. You want to remember that? If you live that long, which frankly I doubt.'

'You had a choice,' said Decker.

'You still run yourself that line?' said Miller, disgusted. 'You know it like I do. None of us have a choice.'

'You could have chosen to follow orders.'

'I haven't had orders in twenty-five years, soldier, and you know it.' This was the old Miller, the pre-Kurtz Miller, and Decker's back straightened involuntarily.

'You're aware of what I'm referring to, sir.'

'I am, huh? Some careerist fuck calls time out, and I'm supposed to shut down my life's work overnight? Rule fucking one: you become a postman, you're on your own. The Depot wants control back, too bad. Too late. I'm on my rounds. Delivering the fucking mail, Decker. You understand me?'

'Yes, sir. But you know why I'm here.'

'I do. Certainly I do. But tell me something, doughboy. Do you?'

Decker took it, flexing his bicep against the bulge beneath it, feeling the good weapon press into his side.

'Do you, Decker?' Miller continued. 'I think I know better than you. Twenty-five years ago I told you to put a bridle on the bad thing inside you, you remember it? That thing that was fucking up your life. I told you to put it in a harness and make the sonofabitch work for you. And you did it. Yes fucking sir. You remember what it was?' He snarl-grinned. 'I don't think you do, soldier. C'mon, tell me.'

In Decker's experience, it was best to let them take the ball and run with it. They tired eventually.

'Mommy's too busy,' Miller taunted. 'And Daddy's eyes are for Jim and Jack, not Johnny. Johnny wants to play, but Daddy's in the bag . . . you know where they are now?'

'You don't have to do this with me.'

'Oh, but I do. Because you don't feel anything any more, do you? You don't feel for them because I wiped it. *I* did, and now there's just a fucking hole, Decker. And you know what? I'm not going to plug it. I'm not gonna give it back to you. It goes with me. Is that okay with you, Decker? Is that cool? Is that fucking-A, man?'

Decker stood straight and square.

'I took away a part of you and I'm not giving it back,' Miller said, eyes slotted, teeth bared. 'But I wouldn't fret, Decker. What you can't remember, you can't miss. That doesn't change where it'll take you, if you give it time. And you've given it plenty. The question is, how much longer till it's over? Is that what you ask yourself when you lie awake at night?'

'I sleep all right,' Decker said, without inflection. Miller didn't seem to hear it.

'And it isn't even your call, it's your postman's,' he said. 'What's come to me is coming to you, man. And it's coming when he says so. You ever think of that, you self-deluding shit?' Miller's eyes were bright behind his glasses. 'You ever think he might want to get out himself? He's fifty-fucking-six. You think he's going to go on for ever? Because you know they're not going to let him retire. And when they come for him, they'll come for you first.' He ran his tongue over his lower lip as though he were tasting it. 'Man, if you're thinking that having less than me means you'll have less to lose when your time comes, you're wrong,' he went on, shifting pace. 'I'm here and I know. It doesn't matter what you have, it's the same.' His eyes seemed to falter a moment, but Decker saw the man wrench control back. It wasn't good to watch: there was something left in there somewhere, but it had been pushed too far for too long. Miller's voice had dropped to a snarl. 'And it's already happening for you, Decker. The bird is on the wire. I could give you a date and a time, you sorry sack of shit. It's already *started*.' Miller held it a moment, chin down, mouth drawn back; then he laughed. It was the forced laugh of a poorly briefed guest on a shock-jock show, and Decker had to wait, skin pricking, for the silence that followed it.

'Do you have a note, sir?' he asked.

'You'd like it if I did, wouldn't you? Well, maybe I do, maybe I don't. Would you read it if I did? Say it was on this desk. Would you have the respect not to check I didn't say anything I shouldn't?'

'You ought to tell me.'

'If I had, you wouldn't find it,' said Miller, all Kurtz now. 'I watched you for an hour before you came in. I could've sent a little press release down the wire. Set some Bernstein on the start of the trail. Not much of a victory, but you find them where you can.' His voice had lifted, but Decker – whose ear had been tutored for such things – could hear the fight going out of it. The Kurtz seemed to sense it in himself; his teeth glistened. 'Where do you find your victories, Decker?' he spat.

The answer pulsed through twenty years, from one of Miller's own far-off tutorials.

'Where we always did, sir,' Decker answered, taking out the .22. 'In the absence of defeat.' He took two steps towards the seated man and offered him the weapon grip-first. The Kurtz took the little gun, weighed it in his hands a moment. Then he thumbed off the safety and raised his arm.

'You know there's no note,' he said and grinned. Decker ducked his head sharply, turning away. When it was done he reached into his breast pocket for a plain white sachet, tore it open and took out a pre-moistened towelette. He took the gun by the muzzle, finger and thumb, and wiped it down. Then he put it back in Miller's hand, dialed 911 on the stolen cellphone and reported the sound of gunshots at 237 Riverhead Drive. When the operator asked him who he was, he snapped the phone shut. It wasn't until he was out on the freeway and opening the Acura's window to toss it that he remembered the daughter, the seventy dollars, the Foot Locker store. He considered it a moment, then let the lightweight Motorola fall from his hand into the slipstream. Maybe it would do her good. She wasn't going to have the best day, anyway.

Fourth of July. Decker sat in the grey space of his Detroit apartment. A recliner and a TV were the only furniture in the room, positioned in line with the window so that Decker could see the entrance to the building without getting up.

The TV gave off a hot-wire smell. The woman on the screen said 'I need to pee' and moved her hand faster. Decker sat in front of her, sipping a Cuba Libre, his one drink of the year. His eyes focused on a point three feet beyond the screen.

'The wife put the house on the market,' the Postman said. 'Waited three days, then went to Cancun, left the keys with the realtors. Daughter's with her.'

Decker wondered how much the Postman's own house was worth. He'd never seen it, didn't know where it was, but he knew it would be a lot. Postmen's houses were their insurance policies, because if a postman died with his boots on, chances were it'd be suicide. Especially when it wasn't.

'It was a nice place,' Decker said.

'God bless the suburbs,' said the Postman. 'Room to maneuver. You catch that new John Woo tape? Helicopters and gas tanks and office blocks exploding.' He ticked them off on his fingers. 'Somebody should tell Hollywood where the shit of the last forty years really went down. Behind dwarf columns and carriage lamps, on streets called Greenacres and Fairlawne. Save them a lot of dough.'

'You didn't call me out here to debrief me on a Kurtz,' Decker said.

'I didn't,' said the Postman, and signalled through the windshield to the driver of his idling Lincoln, parked nose to nose with Decker's truck. Behind it was a boarded-up diner with 24–7 WE NEVER CLOSE in six-foot neon letters, turned off. The Lincoln reversed slowly, then snuffled away on heavy treads to join the backup car blocking the truck-stop access ramp.

'Did he mention me?' the Postman said. He might have been asking after an ex.

'He made the most of his fifteen minutes,' said Decker.

The Postman looked round sharply. 'What's the thing you have that he doesn't?'

'A heartbeat,' Decker said.

'Don't you forget it.'

'You didn't call me out here to debrief me on a Kurtz.'

The Postman stared straight ahead a moment. Decker followed his line of sight. This was his sixth meeting in two decades with the man who controlled his life, and he was hoping for a reward, a survey-and-set-up, maybe; something to get his teeth into, to take away the taste.

'There's no good way to put this,' the Postman said, and for a second Decker looked to the positioned cars with something worse than panic. No exit, except feet first. But he would have seen that coming; and then he saw what it was.

'A contender?' he said, with something close to wonder. The Postman looked away. 'You got a name?'

The Postman shook his head almost imperceptibly. 'But we wouldn't be here if I wasn't sure.'

'How serious?'

The Postman turned back to face him for a second. 'Did you hear what I just said?'

Decker looked away.

'You want a cigarette?' said the Postman. 'I have a pack in the glovebox out there.'

Decker shook his head, irritated. The Postman twisted his pinkie ring while he waited for the other man to speak, fooling with the weird grey stone set aslant in heavy gold.

'So which?' said Decker. 'Revenge? Pre-emptive? A rival?'

'I bid on a big Miami gun shill last summer; no take-up, and two months later he ODs. Okay. Then February I bid for a Korean trader, washing yen through San Francisco. Guess the rest.'

'What do you think? I mean, really.'

'We don't rule anything out. But get this: I bought the autopsy tapes. They were suicides.'

'Then he's a player,' Decker said. 'So where?'

'Wherever you go.'

'Do I get a team?'

'I'm sorry,' the Postman said. 'I'll do what I can otherwise. But at this stage he could be after closing me down too. I commit men in the field with you, it's making his job easier.'

'You have a lot of faith in me.'

The Postman looked him in the eye. 'John, I have faith in you doing what you do.'

Decker looked down.

'You're welcome,' said the Postman dryly. 'Is there anything else?'

'I guess not. I'll need the usual arrangements.'

'The new drops are as follows.' The Postman reeled off a list of grid references – the location of bridges, trash cans, ducts and culverts in seven North American cities – and Decker jotted them down into the palm of his hand.

'Why don't you take an extra fifty?' the Postman said when he was done.

'I got forty Gs two months ago.'

'I have it here.'

14

'When I need, I'll ask.'

The Postman looked over sharply. 'For what it's worth, everyone that matters wants to see you come out of this,' he said.

Decker registered that, stored it away. It mattered. For twenty years the Postman's job had been a three-hander: to feed Decker work; to be his eyes and ears so the man could sleep at night; and to persuade all interested parties that Decker was worth more to them alive than dead. If he hadn't done the last, he would have become as dispensable as Decker swiftly after. But that didn't change the way it was between them.

'I think the home stadium,' Decker said.

'Good man.'

'But no cities. The rolling road.'

'Of course.'

'Not till I have the sheet on him that he has on me.'

'You'll be the first. As and when.'

There was an awkward silence that, if they hadn't been in the Life, they might've filled with sports. But once the Life was in you, guy talk could give away where you lived, where you came from. You never did it. Decker searched his mind for something to take it down.

'Tell me,' he asked. 'You know I don't smoke cigarettes. But you always offer me one. You always tell me there's a pack in the glovebox.'

The Postman looked out the windshield. 'I knew a guy on death row once, three-packs-a-day man,' he said. 'You can smoke as much as you want there. You're locked down twenty-three hours a day, there's nothing else to do, but most guys still quit there. As did mine. Everyone knows, the ones who keep smoking don't get the last-minute call from the governor. Deep down, they don't expect to.'

'I never smoked,' said Decker.

The Postman glanced to his own car. 'One thing you learn, you work with people their whole life,' he said, 'is that they change. Even when they think they can't.' He leaned over to the steering column, flashed the headlights once: the Lincoln began rolling towards them almost instantaneously. The Postman looked back over his shoulder at Decker, one hand on the door release.

'I don't change,' said Decker.

'Then let's put the world back how it was,' said the Postman.

And Decker got the full taste of how it was now. 'Yes, sir,' he said.

'You know where I am,' said the Postman and got out.

Decker watched him walk across the hot asphalt to his car, a man in Nikes and a sixty-dollar sports shirt, a man who might once have been an athlete, a man you might mistake for a film-school professor were it not for the set of his shoulders. And that pinkie ring. The Lincoln's rear door was opened from inside, and he got in; one car followed the other, textbook-style, back to the highway; and then there was just Decker, the deserted truck stop and the dead neon, silhouetted against the boundless sky.

2

SEE THE WORLD, the first billboard read. FROM THE BOTTOM OF THE FOOD CHAIN read the next, two hundred yards later. Decker had to wait another quarter of a mile for the pay-off: OR GET AN ANIWA, which turned out to be a dash-mount GPS that could call for help with a grid ref if you broke down outside cellphone range.

Decker experienced a good feeling for the copywriter, the kind that comes when we register – with a measure of disbelief, in countries where the consequence of incompetence is rarely starvation and death – a job reasonably done. But he wouldn't be buying any Aniwa. Though a wrong turn here could lead to a dirt road that would beach any road vehicle before a driver thought to reverse, leaving him spinning his wheels in a place where his sixteen valves and passenger airbag and side-impact protection system couldn't save him from exposure and a slow death, to Decker it was a kind of home. The road he drove cut through clean white space on civilian maps, but to Decker's eye the landscape broadcast a rolling story of the strategic interplay between terrain and weapons. For as far as he could focus, game plans were mapped all over the dry, yellow land; this was military country, and he was closer to his own kind here than in the city.

He was heading back west already because it felt good to

have the sun behind him in the mornings. In a few days that would have to change, but Decker wasn't counting on it taking that long. He was doing everything he could to draw the Contender, to bring this on: driving a rental registered to a firm he'd used before, keeping his cellphone charged and poling, paying for gas and motel rooms with a Mastercard that had a year left on it. In the trunk were two gallons of water, six gallons of gas, a Mossberg shotgun optimized with the pistol grip and a laser scope he didn't plan to use; within fast reach were a three-eighty Sig, a Heckler & Koch P7, and a hunk of ten-mil that could punch through a moose. There wasn't a moose, however, for a thousand miles or more, and as for the Contender, Decker'd had nothing to tell him they were in the same hemisphere yet, let alone the same time zone.

It was the second Friday in July. Like the rest of us, Decker spent most of his life respinning shit into . . . not sugar, not always, but something he could live with, and road movies had always woken something real in him. In another life he'd flunked history, but since then he'd read about the Anasazi pueblos, first-millennium apartment blocks hacked into the cliffs between Santa Fe and Flagstaff. By Sunday he planned to hit Taos, one-time home to Georgia O'Keeffe and her celebrated beaver shots, and then he'd push on over the border. See Arizona and die, he thought. The sun broiled in his rearview. There was no signal on the stereo from one end of the dial to the other.

Decker was heading north-east in the mornings, east in the afternoons. It kept the sun out of his eyes. He'd read that you couldn't get cancer through windshield glass but he'd passed a Greyhound the week before, going wide on an empty road, and had glanced over to see a heavy-set white guy asleep against a window, the flesh on Decker's side livid red. He played it safe, slathering on SPF-15 first thing and at noon, paying special attention to his neck and ears.

His plan was to make the big loop round and head south again. The world was too modern north of the desert: motels standing adrift in lagoons of zoned blacktop, with annexes and wings and five or more entrances, impossible to monitor from one window. In a diner the fourth night he heard a man at the next table say to a puffy-lipped woman, 'What we agreed was you took it in your mouth, then spit it out. That's not what I saw in there today, is what I'm saying to you, Leana.' He felt out of water somehow and his sixth night out he broke his m.o. to stay at a Comfort Inn. The sounds of abuse in the next room that started up soon after Letterman he ignored as none of his business. It went on all night. Next morning he promised himself that was the last time, drove out of his way instead to the mom-'n'-pop motels he'd always favoured, the old-fashioned horseshoe of cabins grouped around a central parking lot, where no one could pull in without everyone else knowing about it. They rarely carried cable, but most nights he'd put in an extra hour or two to find one. It was a shock to find what a dying breed such places were, even in kissing-cousin country. It'd been too long since he was out here.

After ten days he'd clocked up close to six thousand miles. The lack of so much as a sniff was a mind-fuck, but if he'd been the Contender he'd have hung back exactly the same. In the meantime Decker was replaying the same audiobook for the second time, that summer's bestseller, but he still wasn't getting it. It sounded like a pile of half-assed lame crap to him, but the chattering classes chattered about it nonetheless. Books and music, people will make their minds up to like if they're told to like it hard enough, he concluded, remembering the effort he'd made to like June Tabor a long time back. A girl he'd been after had liked her. Give a person enough pressure to stay in the loop and they'll make themselves like anything, he concluded, and tried to find a reason to like the bestseller. Somewhere on the fringe of the Cibola National Forest he wound down the window and tossed the tape out, feeling bad about littering but not wanting to share space with the piece of crap any more.

Five waitresses had come on to him in the first week, of whom he'd have gone with two if he'd thought he'd be able to come. He hadn't so much as jacked off since the Kurtz. But in a tailback by the business spur of a mediocre city a short-haired exec in a low-slung coupe shot the look with him, crossing her legs in the dead traffic to make the skirt of her suit ride up to the weave of her pantyhose. He tailed her when the lanes opened up but she passed the gas-food-lodging exits and headed for I-70 towards Denver; he took that as a woman's prerogative and dropped back. That night she featured in a dream, giving a flipchart presentation he didn't understand, her skirt hiked up on her powerful hips. He woke with his hand on his gun, thinking this is the day it will happen.

He'd thought that most days so far. But this time he felt it in his piss: a thick ropy cable with his balls behind it, not a mutter from his prostate as his drill bit into the white china. Hadn't pissed like that in weeks. He'd read a book by a PhD who'd proved that dogs go to the window when their owners leave work, even when the owner breaks with routine. There were things you couldn't explain that you could trust, and Decker tried to remember that.

It was going to happen today, and it was going to be revenge, he knew it. No way was this a rival: in the dry American desert he smelled lemon trees and kerosene, olive bark and black tobacco, goat shit jewelled with flies. This was a son, a cousin, a brother: someone who'd watched him do a job one time while he was just trying to get through his day.

Someone who'd changed the course of their life just to pay that day back. Maybe Decker had even felt it as he did it, eight, twelve, fifteen years before – this is the one that will bring it down upon me. Sometimes you knew you were closing a book, other times it felt more like turning a page.

There was a twenty-mile straight up towards the state line. He'd driven it in the dark two nights before, the road so straight and the air so clear that he'd been able to see needlepoint headlights coming at him twenty miles away or more. It had made him think of fibreoptics, synthetics so conductible that you could see a candle flame through a mile-wide hunk of the stuff. He'd tried to guess the model of car from the shape of the lights, ducking behind some swell in the road between them, then cresting it, reappearing in the dark below him. That would be a good place, Decker thought, blacktop and sand, and he headed back for it as soon as he had dressed in his good suit and stripped, dry-fired and loaded his weapons.

There was nothing on the road when he reached it just after noon, but he could feel eyes on him; eyes searching a dark monitor and finding him, Decker, a moving pinpoint in the centre of it. He pulled off the road on to the cracked playa, unlocked the trunk and stood in the centre of the road, the ten-mil in his left hand and the Sig in his pit.

The road ran east–west and he faced east, the sun overhead fixing him to the spot. Nothing let you down out here. In Paris, Vienna, London, you got dumpsters competing with your thousand-dollar-an-ounce cologne. Here, you could button the coat of your suit, push your Ray-Bans up to your eyes, stand straight and tall with the desert wind whipping your hair back. In Baltimore, Vancouver, Diego, people filled their spaces with acid-bathed wood, with antiqued implements, with markers of the simple life; here it was just you, America and your thousand-yard stare. Decker ran his centre of gravity through his coccyx, and waited.

Waiting was what he did; waiting was a click off one hundred per cent of the job. Waiting was what he'd done in the ranks, knowing that he'd be discussed over a board table, and then in idling town cars. Waiting was what he'd learned as a boy, shivering in the rain hours after track practice, trying to sift from the traffic's strobing beams the familiar squared headlamps of a wood-trim station wagon: are these lights the ones? Are these? It was how you waited that made you, that meant you were still alive at forty-five when the other guys you started out with were in the ground with their pricks still smooth. It was how you waited that set down how ready you were when you had to be.

Decker was ready, standing in the road at one. He was ready, sitting in the car at two. He was ready, leaning on the hood at four. And he was ready, the sun broiling the sky behind him, when the Contender showed, eight to ten away, closing the gap with an hour of daylight left.

When the car was twenty yards distant it halted, sizzling on the blacktop like it was seizing the ground beneath it. It was a Mustang, black, with baked-on dust visible in swathes from where Decker stood. The windshield was cake mix around a fat rainbow decal of cleared glass, but the chromed grille below was a snarl of grit teeth. Decker held the ten on the car, shifted his consciousness through his shoulders. The engine growled again, and the Mustang swung a fishtail off the road, side on to Decker. The door opened and the Contender got out and, with the door open wide, pushed the seat down to show the empty back. Then he walked up to the road, Decker tracking him all the way, and stood facing his quarry, his hands by his sides.

Decker stood in the road with the sun backdropping him, the roiling sky indicating to the other man where the gods' fury lay. The Contender kept his wraparounds on his nose.

He was young, as Decker had known; twenty-six, twenty-seven, six dead, hundred and sixty pounds. A dirty blond rash of goatee stubble framed the mouth that opened and said:

'Decker.'

The accent could've been any place, but he looked straight-A American and it threw Decker a little. Revenge you expected from eastern, maybe Mediterranean, Europeans; not from SoDak Swedes with a service look to the sit of their jaw. There was a chance he could be Adriatic – you got those fair-haired north Italians working all the way over to the Caucasus sometimes, and Decker tried to remember what he'd done in the region as he swapped the ten for the Sig in one clean move and haired the three-eighty on the bridge of the Contender's nose.

'The shades,' Decker ordered, his voice this side of a shout. The Contender obeyed, slipping them into his hip pocket with mime-show care, aware of the Sig putting a bindi between his brows, unwavering in its focus while Decker's eyes followed his hands. He let them hang by his sides and squinted into the lowering sun.

If he so much as breathed wrong Decker could kill him straight, or maybe make him dance in the road first while he shot bits off him. An elbow, a kneecap, a few fingers: sometimes it behoved a man in his position to do these things. He was almost mad enough. Twelve days out of his life, for some blue-eyed swimsuit model.

'So,' he said, the Sig in both hands. 'You gonna kill me, you little shit?'

'No, sir.'

The only thing he could be working was a partner with a high-velocity rifle; but the sands stretched for miles on both sides, lone and level. He had to be planning something else, which made him even crazier than Decker had anticipated.

'I switch your daddy, boy? And you're gonna make me hurt your mama again?'

Decker knew the type. Their father gets his head opened; so they drop out of college, enter the service, get pulled for special ops, wetwork; listen, learn, drop out and pursue. Spend ten years working up to revenge but when the moment comes they don't know what to do with it.

The Contender looked him in the eye and said, 'No, sir.'

'So this is a message? Your boss thought he'd find me before I find him? Who sent you, boy?'

'No one sent me, sir.'

Decker's finger tightened. Two minutes before he had felt the gates to his life start to open; now this guy was jamming them halfway.

'You want your brains on the road, soldier?'

'No, sir.'

'You want to die in the desert? You keep fucking with me and I'll cut you off at the shins, leave you alive for the coyotes.'

'I don't mean to fuck with you, sir.'

'Then what the christ do you want here, soldier?'

'Parlay,' the Contender said. He gave it a moment to register, then took off his suitcoat and tossed it on the hood, showing a clean white shirt uncrossed with black webbing. He put his hands on his hips and waited. Decker held the Sig steady as he flashed the jut of his chin to the other man; the Contender commenced walking over the sand-blown hot-top towards him.

Decker waited, legs apart, on the balls of his feet. Both men watched each other's eyes. When they were close enough to kiss, Decker stuck the barrel of the Sig into the soft flesh under the blond man's chin and patted him down with one hand and one leg, not taking his eyes off the pristine whites between the sandy blond lashes. He was clean. Decker pushed him away with the weapon, motioned him to back off till he was ten feet away. The Sig stayed centred on the bridge of the Contender's nose.

'I said parlay,' he said.

Decker kept the weapon where it was. 'Give me a reason not to kill you,' he said. 'Now.'

'My name is Jake Olsen,' the Contender said. 'Seals ninety-four to seven, three years' Agency, taken from the rank's two thousand.'

Decker eased the hammer back. A pretender, then, closing him down. Part of a team: he didn't look like he could've done the other jobs alone. He was too young, too pumped; he could've got lucky, but luck counted for dick in this business. If this Olsen was involved, he wasn't alone. He'd have to go after all of them, but at least he had a place to start.

'You die now,' he said, officer to grunt. 'You understand this? You've disrupted my operation, and my postman's. That does not happen. Make this clean, soldier, and tell me who's next up the line. If you know who I am, then you know I'll find out by morning.'

'There is no next up the line, sir.'

'Don't fuck with me, boy –'

'Not any more,' Olsen went on. 'I'm on my own.'

'You are, huh? So how'd you find me, "on your own"?'

'I know how to look, sir,' Olsen said.

'You know how to get yourself killed,' said Decker, pulling back the hammer. 'Who sent you?'

'No one sent me.'

'You found me. Who's feeding you?'

'No one's helping me now, sir.'

The gap opened. 'But someone did,' said Decker, hearing it a second before it came.

'Miller,' Olsen said. 'Miller was my postman. I came out of

25

the ranks for him, and now I don't exist. You've orphaned me, Decker, and now you owe me.'

Olsen was on his knees in the road, looking up at Decker, gunmetal indenting his forehead.

'The reason you can't place me on Miller's team is the reason you took Miller out, man.' Olsen said it urgently, his eyes searching the other man's. 'He was a Kurtz, for christsake. It's what they *do*.'

'You want me to hurt you first?' asked Decker.

Olsen's face was pressed into the hood of the Mustang, his arms spread wide across it. Decker was between his legs doggy-style, the .38's muzzle dug under the back of Olsen's skull.

'Put yourself where I am,' Olsen shouted against the hot metal. 'He pulls me out, he sends me under, and when it's too late to get back I find out he's a Kurtz? I had no *choice*, man!'

'I want to hurt you first,' said Decker.

The Sig was inside Olsen's mouth, pushing up against his soft palate, making him gag around it. One eye was closing and there was blood in the corner of his mouth. He spat the gun out, retched, brought up dark bile, ropes of mucus hanging down into the road.

'Kill me then,' he said wearily. 'Kill me if you're sure.'

He had the look then, and Decker had seen it too often to think it faked.

They sat in Decker's rental, the desert night rolling up around them.

'I've been living it the last eighteen months,' Olsen said. 'I tried to get picked up, but Miller had me too far under the line. No one knew except me and him.'

If he was telling the truth, then he was in a worse position than Decker. Decker didn't want to believe this was possible.

'My postman sent you,' he said. 'Thought I needed a little backup on this game. Isn't that right?' He reached under the dash, pulled out a cellphone for a weapon. 'I can call him right now. You may as well tell me.'

'I swear,' Olsen said.

'You want me to call him?' Decker demanded. 'Because I tell you, I haven't broken protocol in twenty years. I have to do it now, I'm taking it out of your hide.'

'You don't need to call anyone.'

'Then tell me who told you.'

'No one told me anything,' Olsen said. 'I knew it was coming from six, eight months ago. When I saw how far Miller was gone.'

'So you watched his house?'

'I paid neighbourhood security to. Told them I was gathering divorce submissions for a woman whose man was gay for Miller. Told them to page me if they saw a strange guy drive on his street, and I'd come with a camera. You drove by different times for four days, then parked early morning on the fifth. You used a grey Acura, put it in a driveway opposite. The resident was on vacation in Maui.'

'You were there.'

'Yes, sir.'

'I didn't see you.'

Olsen didn't answer. Decker exhaled.

'So what did Miller have you doing, that you could spend eight months waiting for him to get switched?'

'I can't tell you that, sir.'

It was obvious anyway: nothing. Bullshit assignments. Busy work. Which was what had told Olsen his boss was a Kurtz.

'Why should I keep talking to you?' Decker said.

'Because if you let me go, you won't know what you're starting. I know you don't work like that.'

'What else do you know?'

'Nothing, sir,' said Olsen. 'I want you to teach me. I've proved I'm worth taking on by finding you.'

Decker narrowed his eyes. 'You know how to drill to French? Field-strip FN-3s, Austrian Steyrs, the Russian and the Chinese AK?'

'Sir yes sir.'

'Then go to Africa, boy,' said Decker. 'Go to Africa and find yourself a war.'

'Dollar-soldiering's for shitkickers got the death wish, sir.'

'And the Life isn't for guys like you,' Decker snapped. 'Go. Get out. Have a future.'

'Miller erased my past. And my present, sir. I have nothing to go back to.'

He wasn't as dumb as he made out, working a number on Decker even as he spoke, picking up on his tone, his posture, establishing an alpha/beta thing.

'So you want to be like me?' said Decker, switch-hitting where he best-guessed it might hurt. 'You want the most human contact you have to be when you're getting your change at the market? You want sex to mean some hard-faced old hooker? And even her, she turns out to be good and you use her a second time, you can swallow the barrel soon as you're finished.' It was the stuff nobody told you that hurt. 'You're not in so deep that you can't get out. Do it. Be a man. Choose life. Fuck off.'

'I appreciate how you feel, sir.' Still doing those beta-male moves he'd learned in some workshop. 'I've watched you for eight days. You're trying to pull a contender.'

Decker should've seen it coming. 'You don't understand anything,' he said, looking away.

'I can help you,' Olsen urged, then checked himself. 'I

appreciate this is tough to accept, but I can be the thing he doesn't expect. I know you'd be using a team if anyone'd commit one.'

'You don't know anything.' Still looking away.

'I know one thing,' said Olsen, leaning in for attention. 'He doesn't know I exist. No one does. Only Miller, me, and now you. But no one else on the planet. I could be your fire in the hole. If I get switched I get switched, but I don't mean for that to happen. I mean for us to come out of this, so you can teach me what you know.' Olsen took a breath, looked him in the eye. 'You're the best in the business. You've got to be. Mailmen don't live past forty, I know that much.'

'And you won't live past midnight 'less you get out now.' Decker showed him the ten a second time.

'Let me talk to your postman. I'll take any deal you cut me.'

'Go.' Decker pushed the ten's barrel into Olsen's temple.

'I'll work for expenses.'

Decker ground the muzzle into the swelling flesh by his eye. The tendons on Olsen's neck stood out as he kept his head straight and fought the pain. Decker put his shoulder behind it, gave the other man the chance to forget what this was about, have his present become the pain and his future a way to stop it.

It worked. Olsen's hand found the door release and he rolled shoulder-first into the road, hunkered on all fours, his eye closing all the way now. Decker reached over and got his hand on the door as Olsen looked up at him. Then he swung it, knocking the other man flat in the road, and gunned the engine, threw the transmission into drive, put the boy in his mirror and the plains on his grille. Decker watched him rise, groggy, to his knees as he receded in the mirror, then put the pedal on the floor, his eyes on the road ahead. It would be hours before he could sleep. The Contender was still out there, a red pulse in the gathering darkness, and Decker had never felt older in his life.

He called the Postman first thing next morning, breaking protocol from a payphone. He should've driven twelve hours straight but the game was beyond basics now.

The Postman denied he'd sent Olsen as backup, said he'd check him out, see if he could place him in Miami or Seoul when it went down there. There was nothing more Decker could ask him to do, and it made him feel like he was the only prisoner in the world. He didn't have to ask to know the Postman was hurting from this too; the world they moved in was small enough for this episode to cause a major rearrangement of pieces on the board. Decker drove back the way he'd come the week before, appetite for the horizon all gone now.

That afternoon he stopped at a back-road motel, still standing somehow, despite the state putting the highway through six miles north three decades before. A hand-lettered sign read *Ice, Bait, Chainsaw Art*. In the office a girl with metal stuck in her face lit a roach from the dirty ashtray and watched him through her smoke while he filled out a fading pink card.

She slipped her sandal off one foot while he wrote, swung it back and forth, and Decker saw she had a blood blister under the nail of her big toe, right under the moon. One Friday night a quarter-century before, Decker had stepped his big parade boot on his girl's foot while their mouths locked together and her hands tore at his belt; all that summer he'd watched the dark blemish advance, a tiny fraction of an inch each weekend leave, thinking that he'd never see her foot perfect again; and he was right, he didn't. Later, Miller taught him the construction worker's method of dealing with them: drill through the nail with a $\frac{1}{32}$ bit to relieve the pressure. The pierced girl gave him the cabin opposite the one they stood in and he didn't ask for another.

That night she fucked the chainsaw artist with the drapes open, straddling him with her ass to the window and her head back. She knew Decker was watching, and he knew she was getting off on it as she poled in place. She turned and squatted, facing Decker, and he watched slumped in a broken-backed armchair while she gave the guy the whole menu plus a couple of tastes from the dessert cart. That night Decker dreamed of the janitor who taught him to smoke in the furnace room of his grade school, dreamed the old shitheap was there at the motel, unlocking doors with a home-made cigarette stuck to his lip. He woke up with the pillow wet, left just after dawn without coffee.

He passed the white geodesic dome of an observatory before the sun was all the way up, and accepted that he was probably heading for a city now. He didn't want to be where the air was so clear of emissions and light interference; he needed the mess, the jumbled signals of a crowd. It was right to go with his instinct on this one. The Contender would wait until he was out in the open again, and Decker needed to regroup.

He needed to deep-six the sense that the world began and ended with the blurred road, with the sun suspended so close above his hood ornament that he felt like he was driving into it, like the Solar off-ramp would loom on his right any mile now. He needed a break from space. Two days in a city would mean time out with the pressure turned down: two more days alive and nothing asking questions.

He drove fast now, anxious to get across a landscape that anyone with a choice would fly over. He'd only ventured into it before to do his job and get back out, and looping aimlessly around was the difference between having groceries to buy and driving to the store for the sake of it. He took the toll roads now, grateful for the company, grateful for the cable in the franchise motels he slept at. If the ceiling was false or the windows weren't welded shut he checked straight back out, but most were good enough in a pinch, solid handles to the doors he could prop a chair under, sleep with a semi-automatic in each hand. He saw himself as he tossed and twisted: forty-seven, tooled up and constipated, jerking awake in his clothes on a mattress where couples made the windows rattle every day except this.

Mornings he shipped out when he woke, under purple dawn skies that gave the lie to July till the overnight cloud burned off. He'd be on automatic – nosing back to the turnpike past road-ups and bottlenecks, traffic signals swinging on their cables, entering the slipstream of the commuter flow, brake lights flashing ahead as a donut shop's Bottomless Breakfast caught a driver's eye – and would have to remind himself what he was doing there. He drove through the kind of anywheres where things happened, cable panic-porn stuff, streetscapes that took a lick while the tornado chaser's videotape rolled, 'pikes that the daytime nation had seen cleared for the chase from live-feed helicopters. At night he ached for bars – it was like being pregnant, his new state bringing with it new crav-ings – but in this kind of country, bars were where guys who had no other way to compete in their lives went to compete. He knew he wouldn't get the Lite to his lips before some bonehead called him out. Instead he made shame-faced meals from gas-station pickings, cross-legged on his motel counter-pane; drapes drawn, a chair propped under the door handle, the cable switched to the porn or the news channel because you didn't have to follow it to watch.

And then his last night before Denver he'd gone to bed early in anticipation, thinking about a friendly hooker the next day if the gods were smiling on him, an unfriendly one if they weren't; he was woken by the neighbouring room coming back, a quarter before two, commotion in the corridor and probably all the way up from the desk, getting the gist of it even before they were inside: some wife-swap thing gone real-shaped, morphed from faceless fantasy to four unhappy people in a lived-in room. He pulled the pillow over his head as he heard it carry on inside next door, recognizing the signs as the man's voice got lower and the woman stood her ground, wincing already at the first sick thud, counting four beats of silence before the woman began to sob and the man moved in for more.

Something that had been pulling for weeks in Decker snapped now. He was out of bed and in his pants by the fourth blow, rapping with one knuckle on their door by the ninth. The guy opened the door and Decker put him down directly to save chatter, stepped over him and found the woman on the carpet by the bed, checked her pulse and gave her an airway. He was standing over the guy when he came round, his nose spread wide across his face, ready to give him the option of sincere, heartfelt apology or the short-cut to the parking lot below the window, when the guy held up his arms, wrists together, and said, 'Take me in. Please,' through the blood and snot.

'I'm not a cop,' said Decker.

'I need help,' the guy said, struggling to his knees on the floor. 'I'm only hurting myself.' He knelt in a prayer posture, wrists still clamped together like he was expecting Decker to cuff him.

'Please help us,' the woman said. Decker turned to see a pair of sad Onassis eyes looking back, ringed with run mascara, wanting more from him than he could possibly hope to give. Walking out on them felt like the worst thing he'd done and he'd done plenty.

He got his weekend in the city but didn't step out of his suite at the Sheraton, thinking fuck the Contender, let him worry about what Decker might be pulling. He opened the *Yellow*

Pages to E for Escorts but left it there, fooled with the DreamCast that rolled out from under the wide-screen TV, ate canned chilli heated in the steaming washbowl because an ordered-in meal could be his last one if the Contender was there too. Still not knowing what kind of a man he was dealing with. To fuck with someone's food was not Decker's style, but he couldn't know what this guy might stoop to: whether he'd want to get close enough to make sure the client knew why this was happening, or whether he'd hang back, do it like a kid deploying icons on a screen. If Decker had precedent it would've been different; a few had dared over the years, but the Postman had picked them up and taken them out long before Decker needed concern himself. This time had been exceptional from when the Postman told him he was on his own. All Decker had to go on was that the guy was serious enough to shake up the board like this; and that he could make a suicide look like a suicide, at autopsy level to boot. Decker had to assume the worst: that he was as good, and that he operated outside the code. Whether this made him better in the short or long run was academic; in the real world there was only the present to live in.

He called Dollar at eight forty on Monday, had them deliver a Sunfire directly so he wouldn't need to check the valet-parked Hertz for plastics there in front of the lobby. It was the first time he'd had clothes on in three days and they were all clean, starched and pressed from the bowels of the Sheraton the way only hotel laundries make them. It should have been a boost, heading west on I-70 with his Samsonite full of fresh clothes, but it just made him feel he was starting out again, as if the twenty days gone by had been for nothing.

It was a bad feeling to be leaving the city for the food chain again and when he saw a sign to LA he thought, Screw it. Feeling like the done-to and not the doer was not a good thing for a man to support and he'd gone the extra mile already. If he was going to bring it on this late in the day he could do it from one of his apartments, where he could take a crap in the morning at his own pace, not be forced to try and get the mail moving before check-out time. Some things weren't right for the soul.

Driving with a destination felt better, screwed the cap down on what'd been seeping at the rim since the greenhorn, maybe even before. Decker's job was tough enough without the pressure of being at the top of the tree, having to feel every scramble on the branches below. He never meant it that way, he just stayed alive and there was nothing weird about that; so had a bunch of others. But then shit happened and kept on happening and he exhaled each time he heard, until Calhoun got unlucky the week George W. scraped in and Decker was out in front by six years. Or rather, Decker was the bar that everyone else felt they could better, given his run-up. He hadn't meant it to happen. He didn't think about death any more than the next guy. Like a smoker en route to the chest ward, he could see that two and two might combine in theory but four remained hard to visualize. Decker concentrated on his stopping distances, let an eighteen-wheeler pass him, flashed to let the guy back in lane. He was going to have a hooker that night whether he felt like it or not. Sometimes the ones you forced yourself to call, making a decision about what you could and could not stand, sometimes they surprised you. There had been a Michigan girl with DETROIT across the top of her tail in four-inch gothic letters, one of the best he ever had and the hardest to forget her number. The tattoo was so truckers could look down and see where they were at, she told him over her shoulder as he worked her, taking her hips in his hands and pulling her heart-shaped heinie back on him. Man, I could use some a that, he thought, one hand guiding the well of the wheel between the line on the left and the line on the right.

Later, an RV made him pull out and pass, a top-whack job with a satellite dish and a bumper sticker that read, *We're spending our children's inheritance.* Two old coots in the cab, sold for a quarter-mil what they paid fifty for in the seventies, still riding the boom they'd left school into: Decker waved to the wife and she gave him the finger. He chuckled, checked the mirror and then checked it again. A black Jeep Cherokee eight vehicles back. He pulled a fast pass on a Neon compact, slipped back sharp, watched the mirror: the Cherokee moved one space in its own configuration. Decker sped up behind a station wagon, made to move out and pass but pulled back sharply. He heard a horn blare eight cars back as the Cherokee made the same feint and drop, an outraged Dodge sedan forced back behind it. Sweet son of a gun, thought Decker, he was on.

The game was on, west on I-70 out of the blue August sky. Decker went through some opening moves and the Cherokee followed, holding him two lanes back like he was being towed on a wide cable, textbook moves, his intention so clear now that he might just as well have covered the Cherokee with Grim Reaper decals, maybe a parade-float skull on the hood. He wanted Decker to know and that was something.

Decker reached in back as he switched lanes with one hand, pulled the Rand McNally from his laptop bag, put it between his hands on the wheel so he could look for an exit to some place where they could expedite this or move it into the next phase. The guy's visor was down behind his glare strip and Decker couldn't see his face. All that mattered was to take this off the highway, get it in a zone where no one could get hurt but the two of them, and as if by common consent both cars signalled smartly, turned responsibly and filed down an off-ramp. Where the civility ended.

Decker shot the lights at the bottom, sending a pickup broadsiding across the access road he'd been headed for. A glance back showed the Cherokee rounding the stalled truck at speed, lurching down hard on its outside wheels but all four holding the road. There was no way for Decker to know the driver wasn't barking orders into a hands-free. It looked like a team job and that meant that it was a team job until Decker proved otherwise.

He made a hard right on to straight, empty blacktop, kicked down and floored it, putting another sixty yards in the gap while the Cherokee was making the corner, pushing ninety, ninety-five, the Sunfire flying after the swell of a culvert but Decker's eyes remaining locked to the mirror. The Cherokee could only hold the gap and that was no good; Decker gave his full attention to the windshield, the straight road ahead and the camber to each side, then dropped suddenly into third, stabbed at the safety-belt release and fishtailed viciously into reverse.

His car only just held its integrity – the edge of the blacktop deteriorated worse than he'd been able to tell as it flashed past – but his hand was yanking the door release while it was still biting for purchase and he was out, swarming over the open door with the ten-mil in both hands, about to punch out the Cherokee's windshield when it flashed its brights at him. Decker kept the muzzle on the Jeep and whirled, the Sig materializing in his free hand, but there was nothing behind him. He straightened, mad now at such a baby trick, and put both weapons square on the windshield as the Cherokee rolled up, thirty yards, twenty-five, feeling the twin recoils in his wrists already as he made the triangle on the figure at the wheel.

But then he heard the Cherokee drop into neutral; he saw white palms flash up close behind the windshield and stay there as the driver trod down on the footbrake. The Jeep pulled to the right a little as it rolled to a hands-free stop but Decker stayed put, waiting for the rear doors to angle open and a couple jackboys with Tec-9s roll out underneath and bring fire upon him. He was planning to shoot for their shoulders, leave them alive just long enough to find out who set this up and for whom, but nothing happened. The doors stayed closed, the palms stayed raised, and Decker had to take a second to come out of it, to shift down a level before he could accept the evidence of his eyes.

3

THE CONTENDER PLACED THE pinkie ring with the weird grey stone on the Jeep's dash between them.

'You understand this?' he said.

Decker did. Twenty years was wrenched out from under him in that short moment, and he understood.

'And this?'

The Contender put a gold watch next to the ring, the ugly kind sold as retirement gifts. As Decker watched, he turned it over. Engraved on the back were Decker's initials.

'Stuffed into his mouth,' the Contender said. 'I'm serious.' He reached under his jacket, unholstered a .38 Special and placed it next to the ring and the watch.

'Your call,' he said.

Decker couldn't believe how wrong he'd been; if anyone ever could, when their time came. He looked at the weapon, made himself do it. This had started with him laying down a pistol for another man to use. What you sow you reap and he'd lived that for twenty years. It was his time now and he wasn't ready. But that was as ready as he'd ever imagined he might be.

Decker reached out to the .38, touched the metal warm from the other man's body, moulded his palm around it. It ripped at him, tore at something deep inside him, how unfamiliar the other man's piece felt in his hand. But he accepted it. It was the way it went, that it shouldn't be your own. It was the final insult, the one you had to take, and the fact that you could take it meant you where ready to go.

He lifted the gun, his head down, and took one last breath. He felt the world in that moment, felt it run on, inside and around him, what he'd given his life to maintain and to protect. There had been no final catastrophe, the justice and the injustice rolled on; and he'd helped to achieve that, and was proud of it. But now he had to go, loving the world and afraid for it. He couldn't exhale, but he brought the gun up anyway.

'I had no choice, man,' said the Contender, in the driver's seat. 'You sent me back out there, you left me no choice. I had to try and get hired.'

Decker looked up, stared into Jake Olsen's blue cornbelt eyes.

'I let your postman know I was looking,' Olsen said. 'But he came to me, I swear. He sent word: a meet, Friday afternoon. Get a look at me, find out what I could do. I show up, I drive into the lot, there's no security and I'm about to get out of there fast when I see why. He's dead on the ground. His men are dead on the ground. I swear, all I was trying to do was stay alive. Please don't kill me.'

Decker raised the barrel.

'I could smell the cordite, man,' Olsen said, whites of his eyes showing around his irises. 'I picked up a cartridge and it was warm. He was *there*. I was watching my future bleed away into the ground, and he was there, getting off on it. He was enjoying the expression on my face.' He flicked his eyes to the gun and said, 'Please don't.'

His eyes locked back on Decker's and Decker couldn't stand it. He brought the muzzle of the Special slowly to Olsen's right eye, covered the iris with it. Olsen's left eye tried hard to hold

40

steady but it was no use; it crept towards the barrel as well, and Decker exhaled, finally, when it did.

'Pull that trigger and you're doing what he wants, man!' Olsen couldn't get the words out of his mouth fast enough. 'He knew I was on to you and you bet he knows I want to work for you 'n' why. He knew I could be a use to you so he kills your postman two minutes before I meet him. He wants me out of the picture, man, he wants you isolated. Pull the trigger and you're doing what he wants. Please.'

Decker looked wonderingly at the younger man. The last thing his postman had done was to go after this chicken, this twenty-five-year-old piece, without telling him. And now his postman was dead, he was alone in the world, and he envied the Kurtz's widow for everything she had. Even if she'd loved the Kurtz once. He drew back the hammer with his thumb, put a fat round in the chamber.

'You think I'm him?' Olsen's voice was thinner than it'd probably ever been in his whole adult life. Decker had listened to this happen many times; you could hear the life fading out of them. 'You think I'm the Contender? So shoot me. And go back to jumping at shadows. He's out there. Fuck, he's here now. Laughing at you, man. So do it. Do what he wants.'

Olsen took the last breath, held it; and Decker understood in that moment that he couldn't kill him. He'd heard it said that if you got too close yourself you couldn't do it and he'd scorned it; you were a professional, you could always do it. But he saw in Olsen's face what he'd felt eighty seconds before. He took the gun out of the other man's eye, brought it down to the crook of his arm.

'Shit,' Olsen said.

'He contacted you,' Decker said coldly, keeping Olsen's weapon on him. 'The Postman called you.'

'Yeah,' said Olsen, nodding reluctantly, a man confessing to his buddy that it was his wife made the first move.

41

'Tell me how.'

'Give yourself a moment. You don't have to know now.'

'Tell me.'

Olsen dropped his eyes, exhaled. 'Miller and me, we used dead drops,' he said, looking up at Decker like he was telling him they used the marital bed. 'I like encryption, but Miller was old-school.'

Decker had only ever used dead drops. 'Go on,' he said.

'I went home after you were done with me, got in around dawn and the milk was sour. I was driving down to the all-night 76 to get a quart, maybe a pack of cigarettes too. I gave up last year but I'm thinking I'm dead now anyway 'less I can think. And, like, I can't think, but maybe a cigarette's gonna unblock me. You ever quit smoking? Then you know what it's like. So I'm driving down there, get milk and a pack of Luckies, time out, not thinking about much except the cigarettes; I glance out the side window just from habit, and there's a chalk mark where it always was, blue mailbox by the corner. And I'm thinking it must be an old one or maybe some kid did it, but I go check the drop anyway, mostly to put off buying the cigarettes. And inside the drop there's a sticky in six-five code saying 4 p.m. Friday and a grid reference.'

'A sticky,' said Decker. The Postman wrote on stickies since they first came out, used to drive him crazy.

'Yeah, a sticky, a yellow, uh, Post-it note. Is that weird?'

'Go on,' said Decker.

Olsen searched his face a moment but found nothing. 'Okay,' he said. 'I make the grid ref and go straight there, check it out: a brownfield, middle of a tyre dump. One way in, one way out. A pro set-up, no messing. And I'm like, maybe I'm dead if I go in, but maybe – just maybe – Decker got his boss to check me out. Maybe he did, and maybe he liked what he saw; maybe this is a way out for me. So I went, expecting to die or get hired there. And that's what I found.' His eyes clouded over. 'It was horrible, man, fucking horrible. A Lincoln with more bullet holes than body, four switched security, and your postman with the wristwatch in his mouth.' He looked down at his own gun, looking back at him. 'I swear.'

'You didn't buy the cigarettes?'

Olsen looked up from the muzzle. 'No.'

'You want one now?' said Decker. 'There's a pack in the glovebox.'

4

IN A RIPTIDE, YOU swim to the side, Decker was thinking as he drove. Try to swim back in and it might play with you all day. The trick was to swim to the side or, better, out into the ocean, though it was the last thing you'd want to do. In deep water you could float, save your energy, not throw it away fighting something stronger than you. But from where he was, treading water, fighting to stay in one place, he couldn't see the shore and he couldn't tell the open sea from the rest of the blue around him.

From the first day a postman took you on you were bound to him in a grotesque embrace. You couldn't let him go because he was your eyes and ears, the hand that fed you and the arm that locked. He couldn't let you go because you depended on him and would switch him or die trying the moment he tried to drop you. Now he was dead, and Decker was free to die himself. He wouldn't be letting anyone down now.

If the Postman used other mailmen, then Decker didn't know about it. They'd always told him there were two code fours, him and some other guy; it was either true or a playground psych-out, there was no way of knowing for sure. If there was another guy – or guys, even – out there in the field, hearing this news or about to hear it, he had no way of knowing. There could be four other Deckers wondering why their drops had gone cold of a sudden, or he could be the only one. It was a fact of the Life that you didn't know.

It was something you could think about, but not something you could ask. A man could think about his woman with her exes, but even if he liked the idea it wouldn't do him any good to get details. Decker had never liked the idea. He needed to believe that he was too big to juggle, and the stature of his targets seemed to confirm that. So what had the Postman been doing, setting up a meet with Olsen? Decker wanted to believe he'd gone there to switch the guy, to finish the job with Miller's stable that Decker had begun; but the Contender had got to him first.

Unless this gel-haired little greenhorn was a lot more than he looked.

Decker checked him in the rear-view, Olsen sitting tall and tight behind the wheel of the Cherokee, tailing him back to the city. It was hard to believe. If Olsen was the Contender, then he'd know the way it worked. He'd know that keeping Decker alive couldn't help him. Postmen sorted and mailmen just delivered. They were functionaries, nothing more: that was part of the tie that bound them to their postmen. The Contender would know that Decker couldn't lead him to anything: that anything he might've wanted from him would be switched with the Postman.

So if Olsen was the Contender, the only thing that made sense was that he was completing Decker's humiliation. He was killing the greybeard and pissing on the corpse, making sure everyone saw him do it. If Olsen was the Contender playing some sick sadistic game, then Decker would be dead inside a week and he wouldn't have to worry any longer. Even a psycho would get impatient and cut his losses after a few days. And then Decker would be free: free to stop swimming, let the water close over his head, fold him into the swell like he never existed. Until then, he had to work out which direction was land and which was ocean. He pushed the car on through the cracked desert, thinking about deep blue water, thinking about the end of him.

When they'd slept off the straight drive, Decker sent Olsen out for groceries – milk, juice, coffee, yogurt, fruit, Portuguese sausage, tomatoes, pasta. He brought back a package of Armor bacon too and Decker told him that if he wanted to fry that shit he could do it outside. After they'd eaten breakfast, Decker sat Olsen down on the recliner he'd slept on. It was the only piece of furniture besides the bed in the apartment: the other fixtures were a refrigerator, a washer, a cooker, a TV/VCR and an industrial-size air-conditioner on wheels that had been running since they arrived.

'We got a situation,' said Decker to the window, standing to one side of it. The mesh grilles he'd rigged himself were proof against most high-velocity rounds, but some things you didn't unlearn. He turned around. 'I never came across it before, but we still go back to the manual. What do you do when you're in a corner?'

Olsen raised an eyebrow at the question, reeled it off anyway. 'Take fire to the enemy.'

Decker looked back over his shoulder. 'If you're playing some clown game with me you can quit it,' he said. 'Again. First rule of combat.'

'Take fire to the enemy.' There was nothing else Olsen could say. He knew better than to improvise against his training.

Decker rolled his eyes. Maybe that was what they taught them these days, now the assholes and the academics had to approve every line of the manual, make sure it didn't breach ethics or insult anyone. *Hold fire on Muslims until after dark*

46

during Ramadan. Kosher your hollow-points before gut-shooting Israelis . . .

'The first rule of combat,' Decker said, 'is to do something.'

'Do something?'

'Anything.'

'I don't follow.'

'When you don't know what to do, you do something,' said Decker patiently. 'And then you keep on doing things until you start a sequence of events. When you have a sequence of events, you have options. One of those options might be to take fire to the enemy. But if you don't know where or what the enemy is, you can't take fire to him. Kapeesh?'

'Sir yes sir.'

'You may be a grunt but this isn't a parade ground: don't say that again. What options do we have right now?'

'Run or fight.'

'And are we running?'

'No, sir.'

'Then how do we get options?'

'We start a sequence of events. We do something.'

'So hit me.'

Olsen looked up, a little warily, from the La-Z-Boy. 'I'm not trying to be smart, so don't shoot me down,' he said. 'I had the whole drive to think about this, you know? Trying to keep it simple. Not complicate stuff for the sake of it.'

'Okay,' said Decker patiently.

'What it comes back to is our biggest problem. That we don't have a postman. I came to you because I didn't have a postman. And now you don't have a postman either.'

'Go on,' Decker prompted.

'So what we should do, we should try to get hired. And then we've got an operation looking out for us again. We'll have a team, we'll have backers. And this other guy, he can know we're not running any more. He can know we're ready to hold terrain.'

'And how do we do that?' Decker asked. Trying to make it sound like if there was some basic he'd overlooked, then he genuinely wanted to hear it. 'How do we get hired?'

'We pull a job,' Olsen said. 'Something high-profile. Doesn't matter who, long as it's someone that's gonna get us noticed. A gangster, maybe. Someone the right people won't miss.'

'Uh-huh,' said Decker patiently, not wanting to crush the guy. 'So we hit a mobster. And say there's a postman out there, say he's been having guys work this *capo* for a year or two, putting him where he wants him, having the guy feed him his set-up, his contacts, till he can take down the whole operation with one order to his mailmen. Then we roll up out of nowhere and switch the guy: flush five years' work down the bowl. That's gonna get us hired?'

'So we choose carefully,' Olsen conceded. 'We check the ground.'

'And that could take a year,' said Decker. 'If someone was working the guy or not. You assume a basic level of competence. They're not going to be advertising it. It could take a year before we could be sure. And there's a guy out there who wants us dead every day in the meantime.'

'So you're saying –'

'I'm saying that you don't work a target for no reason. It's up to a postman to know if he's stepping on someone's ground. That's what they do. Us, unless we have a postman point us to a target, we don't touch it. Those are the rules.'

'So we have to get a new postman.'

'Except we can't,' said Decker. 'No one's going to touch us till this is over. This world of ours, it's not a big one. Everyone knows what the score is, and no one hires trouble. Same as with women: you're desperate, forget about it; you're getting plenty, every woman you see comes on to you. We have to lose the taint, we have to get this guy. But until we come out on top, we don't get any help.'

Olsen stared at the bare cement floor, not able to keep his eyes still.

'I've told you once,' said Decker, meaning to prompt him.

'What did I do now?' Olsen complained.

'Look, drop the fucking attitude,' Decker snapped. 'Okay? Either you want to learn from me or you can go.'

There was a silence, and Decker regretted it. This was hard enough anyway.

'I apologize,' he said. 'There was no call to take that tone. What I meant was, I've already told you what we have to do. "Unless you have a postman link you to a target, you can't touch it."'

'Okay,' said Olsen. Either he was an exceptional actor or the cogs were almost visibly turning.

'You have to understand this,' said Decker. 'The only targets we can work are those that we're linked to by a postman. We contravene that rule and everyone who's hanging back now is going to step in to stop us compounding the problem. So we play the game.'

'We're out of the game. Both our postmen are dead.'

'As you say. I killed yours; we don't know who killed mine. But we do have some of his cartridges,' Decker said, and watched Olsen's face register the thought. 'Don't we?' he prompted.

'No one's gonna stop us if we go after that guy?'

'Only the guy himself. And he's trying to switch us anyway. We go after him, we're inside the rules,' said Decker, thinking how the fucker might be looking at them right now. There was only one way to find out. 'You said you touched some shells at the scene, they were still warm,' he went on. 'I take it you took a few souvenirs?'

'From both sides,' said Olsen, brightening as he slipped back into a position he understood. 'But I stashed them.'

'Tell me they're this side of Denver.'

'They're this side of downtown.'

'Then let's go get them,' said Decker. 'Unless you don't want me seeing your cache.'

Olsen weighed it for a moment, then shrugged. 'I stashed them in a drop,' he said.

Before they were eight blocks away, Decker knew where they were going. Left, right, then right, right and left; pull into the lot by the Tastee-Freez, park in the far corner, slip out and over to the culvert behind the dumpsters. Decker cut the roar of the air-conditioner, watched Olsen take a brisk scope around, then crouch and shove his forearm into the pipe, feeling for the dry run-off that Decker's own fingers had scrabbled for a dozen or more times in the last decade. It was one of the Postman's drops; this was a mark in Olsen's favour.

But it was a twisted knife for Decker. All the time he was watching this greenhorn for the slip that would give him away, he could forget that twenty years of trying had been undone. He could forget that while he'd been out on the road playing at making some spectre materialize, a flesh-and-blood foe had cut his one rope to reality. And now he was floating free . . .

Olsen palmed something from the culvert and started back to the car. He knew the walk – the one that looked preoccupied and unselfconscious but was designed to maximize in-puts, gauge obstacles and threats, open up options – and he did it well. Decker almost smiled as Olsen got back into the car, but he was thinking that there was no way he could put it off any longer. He had to decide whether to kill him anyway, and decide quickly.

He gave it headspace as they drove back. He was used to

working alone, almost never had the encumbrance of a partner or team. But then he'd never been without a postman before. Olsen wouldn't be a partner, but the extra pair of eyes he sorely needed. The extra gun. Fine.

But what was that worth to him, if all the while Decker had to have one eye off the ball? Watching him, waiting for him to give himself away? There was no way to verify his story except to listen to what his mouth and his body said; it could take weeks before they said enough for Decker to be sure, and by then it would be academic. And in the meantime he had to train him to be at least as good as he was besides.

Decker took this seriously. The desire that had led him into this business – to maintain the greater good for the greater percentage – meant that teaching was a logical extension. He'd fantasized about running a program some day teaching strategy, survival, psychology as well as network. He'd always thought he'd be good at it, but he didn't seem to be doing so good this far. Was there any use trying to teach him what he knew, all the time he was looking for excuses to pop him?

He was tempted to tell himself there was no way he could be watching the guy for giveaways and still give 100 per cent as a teacher, but he knew that was just what his own teachers had done, Miller included. All the way through his training, in the first months after he'd ceased to exist, he'd known that the same guy who was unselfishly passing on his skills at noon could be approving your termination at one because he didn't like the way you crossed your ankles when you sat. And that was twenty years ago: the world was a different place now. Decker hadn't had call to acknowledge this for a long time.

'You're quiet,' said Olsen, four blocks from home.

'Get used to it,' Decker said.

He left Olsen to make coffee and took the evidence into the bathroom. It had been pushing ninety-five outside but was bearable in here. The apartment could be a witch's tit in winter, but in summer you were grateful for the cement floor, the thick stone walls. He untied the condom in front of the mirror, switched on the brights, spilled the four spent cartridges on the rust-stained porcelain of the old laundry sink: an original, from when the building had been a garment factory way back. Decker'd discovered loft-living long before the yuppies: industrial spaces were cheap, out of the way, and only had one entrance once the loading-bay doors had clanked shut for the last time. There had to be realtors all over the developed world trying to evict long-term tenants from prime loft space, unaware they were boltholes for hitmen cooling their heels between the cold unrendered walls. The chill was something you got used to. Even so, Decker was perspiring as he fixed the jeweller's eyepiece and brought the first cartridge up to his eye.

He turned it over between his fingers, not sure if he could trust what he saw. But there it was: what he'd wanted to see, or a variation on it. He put his whole consciousness through the one pupil, but it didn't go away. The second cartridge was the same, and the third one. There was no doubt about it.

Decker glanced back through the door. The question was, should he tell the greenhorn yet? He could tell Olsen the shells bore a few marks, but they were inconclusive; that he'd have to send them to a lab, wait for the results. And while they were waiting, he could fill their time with something less critical, give him space to make up his mind about the rookie.

'They were doctored,' said Olsen behind him. Decker drew a breath as calmly as he could.

'Yeah,' he said.

Olsen stood in the doorway, filling the frame. 'I didn't have time to look too hard, but I could see someone's put a die-clamp on them. Removed the round, boosted the charge, replaced the slug and made good. They didn't plan to pussy around.'

'As you say,' said Decker, thinking about what a pumped charge behind a fat slug could do to flesh and bone that a regular one couldn't.

'So we know we're dealing with psychos,' Olsen said. 'We knew that already.'

'We know we're dealing with careless psychos,' Decker corrected, dropping the shells back into the Trojan and retying the neck. 'Ones who leave their signature all over a scene.'

'So we go after them?'

'Yeah, I think so,' said Decker. 'C'mon. Let's go for a drive.'

At the first drop, Decker sat in the car while Olsen put the message in place under a footbridge. While he waited, he took the Postman's ring from his wallet, turned it over in his fingers. The right thing to do was to get it to the widow and the kids, but he didn't know if either existed.

Olsen ducked his head under one of the bridge's struts, then looked back to the car. Decker gave him the thumbs-up, and Olsen put his arm up into the gap, fixing the note. Decker slipped the ring over his own pinkie, then quickly slipped it off. So what he should really do was throw it away. It was a death warrant, right there in his pocket, and not just for him either. If the right person found it on his body, then it would be a link: the *raison d'être* of his business was that there were no links. It had been that way since way before Watergate, but Woodward and Bernstein sealed the deal. Men were chosen for their ability to serve their country in autonomous cells, without orders, without chains of command. Men were chosen for their capacity to wear the medals on the inside, to accept victory as the absence of defeat. They were chosen for their loyalty to principles, to value systems, not to people. But

Decker wanted to get the ring to his postman's wife and kids. If they existed.

Driving from the third to the fourth drop, Olsen said, 'You and Miller went back, didn't you?'

'He taught me,' said Decker, pulling out into traffic. 'But you knew that.'

'I knew you'd have something on him. I knew with a Kurtz, they like to make it personal.'

Decker shrugged, changed up.

'I thought of going back to one of my old tutors,' said Olsen, looking out the window. 'No one tells you what you ought to do if you're cut free. But they told us at the time: if we ever looked them up, didn't matter why, they'd switch us on sight.'

'They told us that too,' said Decker. 'It's how it works.'

'Then why didn't Miller switch you?'

'Because he was still a postman,' Decker said. 'He was a Kurtz, but he believed he was doing his job. When I showed up, it was the first signal he'd had that the Consensus didn't share that view. He accepted that.'

'And that's who we're calling now? The Consensus?'

'If they're listening.'

Olsen exhaled. 'Man, I'd sooner just go for it. Find this die-clamp motherfucker, put that clamp to his johnson.'

'We do this first. If there are people out there want to help us, we give them the chance.'

'For how long?

'A week. We check each drop every day, morning and night. If there's a response, then someone's looking out for us. We know we're not alone.'

'And if there's nothing?'

'Then it's die-clamp time.'

*   *   *

Pulling into the fifth drop, Olsen said, 'I was using this drop once, an old broken commode on the edge of a landfill. I get the signal one day, go directly there to collect and – get this.'

'There was some wino taking a dump in it,' said Decker. 'I heard about that.'

'Really?' said Olsen, grinning. 'That got around?'

Decker shrugged, turned down the corners of his mouth.

'Man,' said Olsen, pleased. 'I said to him, you dirty-ass scumbag, why can'tcha just crap anywhere? This is a fuckin' garbage heap. He looks up at me and says –'

'"You don't happen to have any toilet paper, do you?"' Decker finished for him.

'Fuckin' toilet paper,' Olsen said. 'Twenty Gs stuffed into the U-bend and some guy with a nickel to his name taking a crap on it.'

Decker checked the mirror, pulled into the slot.

'I should've pulled a wad of twenties outta the commode,' Olsen went on, filling the gap. 'Said, use a couple these, bro. But you never think till it's too late.'

Decker cut the engine.

At the second-last drop, Olsen said, 'So who was your post-man?'

'Code three,' said Decker.

Olsen looked up sharply. 'No shit,' he said.

'No shit.'

Olsen pulled out the last clot of leaves and bagged them. 'So what?' he said. 'He was Agency? Blue-hat?'

'Doesn't matter,' said Decker. 'Nationhood is a PR concept at code three and above, nothing more.' He peeled the next note off the pad of Post-its and handed it to him. Like all the others, to the right eyes it would read: C741 REQ 50–218. It was 6 August, the two hundred and eighteenth day of the year.

Olsen looked up as he took the Post-it. 'Did you ever work down at my level?'

'Everybody starts somewhere,' said Decker.

Olsen put the note in a baggie and pushed it up into the pipe. 'Even a few months, it was getting samey,' he said. 'You're not much more than a cop who discharges his weapon every time out.'

'But the lines are clear,' said Decker. ' "I am the G-man, these are the pipe-hitting jackboy scumbags." The idea is you enjoy it while you can.'

Olsen straightened up, brushing off the knees of his pants. 'And then what?'

'And then there are no lines,' said Decker, needing to get this straight. 'Except the ones you draw yourself.'

They started back to the car.

Two miles away Olsen drew a chalk mark on a lampstand, indicating that the pipe was holding.

'So code four,' he said when he was back in the car. 'No one ever mentioned anything above code seven. You just, y'know. Guessed there were higher numbers. What're two, one and zero?'

Decker made a right, heading back toward the freeway.

'God, the devil and the deep blue sea,' Olsen said, kidding. 'Right?'

'For all it matters,' Decker said.

'Code three,' Olsen repeated, looking out the window. 'That's how many postmen? I mean altogether?'

'How many balls you got,' said Decker, slowing for some children playing jumpball.

'You're kidding,' said Olsen.

'When I kid you, you'll know about it.'

The freeway was busy but they were only on for two exits. The last drop was through a canyon and out the other side, under a bridge over a creek. They stuck the note directly inside the lip of a girder. When they were back in the car, Olsen reached for the glovebox, flipped it open.

'You said there were cigarettes in here,' he complained.

'No kidding,' said Decker.

Decker wasn't used to having another guy in the same car, let alone the same apartment. But every morning he came out of the shower and found the guy rummaging in the fridge in his BVDs; every morning, that seemed to suggest that the guy was harmless, that the guy could be used.

'Why don't we just start planning?' Olsen said the third morning. 'We're going after this gun shill in four days. We could figure how we're going to do it.'

'We work at this till I'm satisfied,' said Decker.

'I hear you in there, moaning and wailing. You'd sleep a lot better if we moved now.'

'We check the drops for seven days.'

'Why seven? Why not four? Or four hundred?'

'Seven days shows willing.'

'Shows you got the death wish,' Olsen muttered.

'We do it my way,' said Decker sharply. It didn't square with his perception of himself to act as fucking nursemaid. But if he was going to use the little crap-weasel, then he had to be sure of him. 'Again,' he said, and touched his nose.

Olsen sheeshed but spoke up, if flatly. 'Increase in hand-to-face contact combined with decrease in supportive gesticulation means the guy's shitting you.'

'Exceptions,' said Decker.

'Insults,' said Olsen. 'You're being insulted and you're trying to stay cool: but you can't help touching your nose as the first insult hits.'

'You're no rookie. You learned this already, didn't you?' said Decker.

Olsen touched his nose. 'The second exception is when you're responding calmly to a trick question,' he said calmly.

'Good,' said Decker. 'The exceptions say that nose-touching shows a split between inner thoughts and outer calm. Lying is just one example of that.'

'We did this already.'

'And we'll keep on doing it,' said Decker. 'Until I'm confident that when we go to face down this brother, you're thinking the same as I am.'

'Be simpler if you just gave me orders,'

'No,' Decker said. 'Either you're in the loop or you're no good to me. I can't be watching your back when I've got to watch my own. Now. Laughing.'

'Whole face or just one side?'

'Just one.'

'One side of the face is obeying the order to laugh, the other isn't. Trouble coming.'

'And the worst laugh?'

'The one this bastard's doing at us right now.'

'C'mon.'

Olsen sighed. 'Head thrown back. The jutting chin means fuck you.'

'And remember gaze direction,' Decker said. 'Humans are the only species to have evolved whites to their eyes, because we're the only species spends so much time trying to shit each other.'

Olsen rolled his eyes.

'Funny guy,' said Decker. 'Negotiating postures.'

'Copied body language indicates attempt to level the field,' said Olsen. 'He wants to play ball, or is trying to make you think he does.'

'What's the difference?'

Olsen knit his brows, flushed a little as the seconds passed.

When he looked up it was to look for the answer in Decker's face, but he didn't find it; until Decker touched his nose.

'Ah, *man*,' Olsen complained. Decker laughed, but kept his chin down.

He had him watching birds in the park, cats fighting in suburban streets. Man had spent too long on his own, in Olsen's opinion.

'There!' Decker said from the driver's seat. 'You see that? The gray one turned away and yawned?'

'I saw it,' said Olsen, looking in the general direction.

'That's the proof of what I'm saying,' Decker said.

Here it comes, thought Olsen.

'It's relic behaviour. The gray cat's about to get its ass kicked and subconsciously it knows it – see it walking away? – so its brain's trying to send the rest of it to sleep. Same in the field: you're ready to go over the top and risk your neck and your brain knows it. So it tries to shut you down before you can get in any worse trouble than you're in. That's why combat rations have that little package of trucker's speed.'

'I thought that was to keep you pushing through the night,' Olsen said.

'Well, it is,' said Decker. 'But you watch the hard-hands, the guys who've gone over the top a hundred times. They pop a couple tabs just before it kicks off. So all the rookies are yawning, these guys are pumped and ready.'

Always greenhorn this and rookie that. It was tough enough being in over his head without having to take insults twelve hours a day. What he needed was some time to think, something he should've done a little more of after Miller got switched. He'd been free then, if he'd known it, could've gone anywhere. But you don't spend ten years trying to get your head above the crowd, then forget it all overnight.

Out on the road, closing on Decker, Jake Olsen had felt his

59

one-way ticket to Palookaville turn into a passport to the future. And then watched it turn back when Decker sent him away, and then turn into something worse when he found Decker's boss whacked by the tyre dump. Knowing the guy who did it was watching him, waiting to see what he'd do next. He should've run then, got the fuck out, maybe gone to Africa like the man said. But he'd gone back to Decker instead, still thinking he wasn't so different – just older – not knowing how big-league he really was.

Now he was in over his head, and square in the Contender's sights. Instead of getting out, he'd put himself right in the cross-hairs, just making the guy's job easier for him. He needed to think, but shit, all this rookie and rabbit and tenderfoot crap. He didn't have anywhere else to go, but he didn't know how much longer he could put up with this.

'Where're we headed now?' said Olsen as Decker, apparently satisfied with watching cats fight instead of doing real work, pulled away from the curb.

'The Marriot, downtown,' Decker said. 'I want you to watch the desk clerks for a couple hours while people check in. See how they can tell which couples are there to fuck each other, which ones are really together. When you're done, maybe we'll drop by the airport. There's a traffic-controller dispute, should be interesting.'

'The airport?'

'Airports are machines designed to exploit the behaviour of crowds under stress,' said Decker. 'Anxious crowds are things you need to be able to read.'

'Ah, c'mon,' Olsen said, disgusted. 'Enough of this college-boy crap.'

'Not tough-guy enough for you, huh?' said Decker. 'Think a man doesn't use his mind?'

'I'm not saying –'

'Because you got a straight fucking choice here. You wanna

flex your mind, I'll drop you off in the real world. You wanna flex your shoulders, you can hitch back to the farm.'

Olsen was getting to know when not to push it. 'I could come with you instead,' he started.

'No. I got business.'

Business with some bitch, Olsen thought, but let himself be dropped at the Marriot anyway, where he spent two hours trading smart remarks with the girl making lattes for conference delegates. The man was going to make him sit still, he'd do it his way. Unwind a little, free his mind up.

When Decker picked him up, he said, 'So who was there just to fuck each other?'

'The ones who were making kissy at the desk,' replied Olsen smartly. 'And the ones who were acting like they were a couple of busy hotshots.'

'And who was real?'

'The ones who did stuff for each other without the other knowing.'

'Good,' said Decker. 'Real couples have a kind of terse synchrony to what they do. Neither wastes actions that don't get the job done. That's what we have to shoot for.'

'Well, we don't have to shoot for it tonight, do we?' said Olsen. 'It's Saturday.'

'So?' said Decker, slowing for a light.

'So it's time to get laid, man,' said Olsen. 'C'mon, we've played the game all week. We're giving anyone who's checking the drops plenty of time to get orders to us before we go it alone. We've done the right thing, now it's time to cut loose a little.'

'Aren't you forgetting something?' Decker said, waiting for the lights to change.

'We haven't seen anything,' Olsen persisted. 'Not a flicker. He's not here. The guy's probably got business of his own.' The traffic started to move; Decker shifted up, changed lanes.

'He's big enough to take you out, he didn't get that way sitting on his ass,' Olsen said. 'He hasn't brought it on with us yet, that's got to say something.'

'It says we don't know what we're dealing with,' said Decker, who'd enjoyed his two hours off from the other man. The whole evening off would be paradise. 'Until we do, we don't risk our necks.'

'Don't tell me you're gonna pull that Don King shit on me,' Olsen said, checking his watch surreptitiously. 'No fucks before the fight, gotta channel the energy. Channel my ass. A man needs a release, he's gonna be distracted till he gets one.' The girl from the Marriot got off at seven; it was five thirty-eight now.

'You're not going to give up on this,' said Decker. It'd been a long week; maybe it wouldn't be so bad to let Olsen have the evening off. And besides, Decker hadn't had a woman since he got the orders for the Kurtz: six weeks was a long time by anyone's reckoning, and this particular six weeks had felt like six months. If he could die any second of any day, to have a woman while he still could would be fine.

'Bet your butt I'm not,' said Olsen, knowing he'd got him.

'All right,' Decker said. 'We'll stop at the market, get the weekly paper.'

'The listings one?'

'That's where the hooker ads are. But I warn you, you're having yours in the TV room. My door stays closed: I don't go for that swapping crap.'

'Do what now?' asked Olsen. 'Just backpedal a second there. Where's this hooker bullshit coming from?'

'Whaddaya mean?' Decker glanced over.

'I don't go with no hooker, man,' said Olsen. 'Shit.'

'You've spent too long in the dorm room,' said Decker, turning back. 'Well, we can pick you up a strokebook at the store. Me, I could use the real thing.'

'You call a hooker the real thing?' Olsen looked at Decker like he was under glass in a museum. 'Was that, what, something you always did? Or just when you got, y'know? Old.'

Decker looked over. 'You want a punch in the mouth?' he said.

'I mean, in the field, okay,' Olsen said. 'I can see, for the sake of convenience. But fuck it, man, this is Saturday night, we're in the biggest city in the time zone. Gotta be ten thousand women in the bars tonight, screw either of us soon as look at us. Shit, you're not one of those guys think women don't *like* it, are you?'

'I'm one of those guys who like to stay alive,' said Decker. 'You call a hooker at random, you fuck her, and you make a note of her number so you never call it again by mistake.'

'They want the same as the rest of us,' continued Olsen. 'Work all week, go out, get laid. And do it all over again. Man, they don't expect you to *call* them.'

'What if they do?' said Decker absently, remembering the Kurtz's words for his daughter: *She'll fuck losers for twenty years to get this out of her system. And then it'll be too late.*

'You can smell 'em,' Olsen said, warming to it, 'the ones who want to talk. Give 'em a wide fuckin' ride, there's plenty of others. See, what you do is, you make a move early as you can. Put your hand where you shouldn't. Later it is, the sooner you do it. And say to them, Well? On balance yes or on balance no? Give them the decision, let them see how little they've got to lose: go home alone or have a fine fuckin' time, wake up feeling appreciated tomorrow and all week. I tellya, nine times out of ten.'

'You're not working for Miller now,' said Decker. 'Get in the loop. You really think we can afford to go to a bar? Have this guy watch us come back with a couple of women? What do you think he'll be thinking?'

'He'll be thinking, It's Saturday night, I'm gonna get me one of those too.'

'He'll be thinking, I walk in the door in ten minutes, both of them are gonna have their hands full of ass. We get hookers, and we take turns to watch the door.'

Olsen considered. 'At least let's go out and cruise for them. I don't want some old bag.'

'You take what comes.'

'Let me have the good-lookin' one, then. I've still got some taste left.'

'There's a convenience store behind the Arby's here,' said Decker, signalling to turn into a stripmall. 'Get the local paper, the one with the classifieds. And some rubbers. The thick ones.'

'Thick ones?' said Olsen, as they bumped into the lot.

'The ones that don't split.'

'Man, you may as well put a Hefty bag on it,' said Olsen, getting out. 'Maybe I'll get that strokebook after all.'

Olsen was up at seven next morning, but Decker's door stayed closed even after he'd made coffee and eggs, filling the grey unrendered space with the good smells of living, of routine. He had to dress without a shower, the scent of the girl still on him, but that was okay today. Let Decker kick back like a regular guy. Sleep off the strain a little, then maybe they could talk like real people. A couple of guys in a situation, not masters of the damn universe sounding off.

Olsen took his blanket, laid it out on the floor and commenced to strip his weapons as quietly as he could. Cleaning kit always felt good. Reminded you who you were and that what happened to you depended on what you did. That had been easy to forget this last week. He needed to get some control back. He needed to play it carefully. The sun patch from the window moved across his shoulders and he started to sweat, but he didn't notice; lost in the accustomed work, lost in it still when Decker came out, fresh from the shower with his collar unbuttoned and his shirtcuffs turned up.

'You ready?' Decker said.

'Yeah, reckon I am,' said Olsen, easy, guy to guy. The man was relaxed: hadn't even put on his webbing yet. 'So whaddaya say? We've got one more day. I could use a couple hours at the gun club.'

'You need to go to the gun club?' Decker said, taking a carton of juice from the refrigerator and sniffing it.

'It'd hit the spot,' Olsen said, letting the implication ride. 'I could use it.'

'You could use a couple of hours off is what you mean,' said Decker, taking a swig from the carton. 'If you can't shoot by now, then it's too late.'

Though he knew where the other man was coming from. Both men's blood was up from the sex, filling their veins, and another day of sitting around seemed like one too many that morning.

'Yeah but –'

'But nothing,' Decker said. 'We pick up where we left off.'

He got himself a cup of coffee, ignoring the way that Olsen was kneeling across the floorspace, looking to him, waiting. He'd get over it; just wasn't used to this. Decker used to spend too much time in gun clubs himself. The antidote to the waiting life was to allow yourself the kind of actions that delivered immediate results, and cutting shapes in paper targets with live rounds gave you an indisputable link between cause and effect – the absence of which a straw poll of hitmen would define as the biggest frustration of their job. The smart ones understood that it was exactly this that kept them sane, operational: the others liked to shoot things up. He turned back to the space and did the dribble-cup walk, sipping his good Colombian roast, through the shaft of sunlight to the window. Olsen looked down, busied himself, a groove appearing between his eyebrows as he worked.

'Enough sitting around, man, c'mon,' he said. 'It's messing with my mind.'

'Listen,' said Decker, putting his shoulders against the wall by the window grille. 'We don't get orders by tomorrow, then we've got to work together. We start with the first guy in the chain that ends with whoever put us in this position. Agreed? So when we walk in there, we've got to be on the same frequency. And that's my frequency, not yours.'

Olsen looked up. 'But all this theory shit, man . . .'

'This is my league, you hear me?' said Decker. 'This isn't taking potshots at jackboys. This is deep cover. We're gonna be facing down guys, serious guys with security to pat us down, take our weapons at the door. That leaves us our eyes and minds to fight with. I'm loading your magazine is what I'm doing and you better respect that.'

They faced each other down a moment, but Decker wasn't afraid to break it. There'd been two condoms floating in the bowl that morning, wouldn't flush; Olsen'd been unsettled by it, that was all.

'I'm just trying to make sure we come out of this,' he said, watching the other man dig in his heels with activity. 'This thing, this life of ours, we spend too much damn time on our own. You get used to being yourself, but when you're out in the field that won't cut it. You need to react on automatic, but if that reaction comes from the way you are 'stead of the role you're playing today, then you're dead meat on a hook. You need to switch from one self to another in a click of a second. And you got to know which self to switch to, is all I'm saying. If you pick the wrong one, it can get you killed.'

'I understand that,' Olsen said, thinking, I can't do this. Someone gives me a place and a time, I turn up, shoot and run; that I can do. But not this. Get out. 'You never saw me in the field,' he said. 'You don't need to worry about how I react.'

'But I will until I'm sure we're on the same channel,' said Decker. 'I need to know where you're gonna go, same as you do me. You know that feeling you used to get? When your squad works together like you're part of each other? You only get that with time – months on maneuver, living together, working together. We've only had a week. So we've had to short-circuit the process, decide up front where the lines get drawn.'

'I appreciate that,' said Olsen, waiting for the moment. 'But I think we're there. I think what we could use today is to get our fur up.'

Decker should've been proud at the way he was coming on. Olsen was copying his posture, the timbre of his voice, hitching what he wanted to the contrary desire, exactly the way they'd run through. He knew how to do it now, though maybe he'd just been hiding it before.

'I'm heading this up,' Decker said quietly. 'We do it my way.'

'Busy work,' muttered Olsen, working a swab inside the chamber of his nine.

'What did you say?'

'I said this is busy work,' Olsen said, thinking, Do it now. Make him push you, make it his decision. 'Why don't you admit it? You got yourself into a groove, you got jerked out of it, you don't know what the hell to do. So now you've got us doing busy work instead of squaring up to it.'

'You really think that?'

'I think,' said Olsen, 'that you need to look at where you are. I mean, I may be wrong, but sometimes it takes a fresh pair of eyes to tell you what's in front of your face. What I see is, you're an unknown quantity, okay? No one lived as long as you. Nobody has the experience you have. You don't know how you should feel about where you are because nobody got there before.'

'Go on,' said Decker.

'So there's no precedent,' Olsen continued, not sure how hard he could push. 'But what I see is, you've started to let things become more important than they should be. I know it's natural to try and bring as much to your job as you can. Even a fucking paperboy knows that: try and make it more than it is and it'll seem like less. But you don't want to let that take over. You can't let it take your eye off the ball.'

'So what you're saying,' Decker said, 'is that this guy is right to be trying to close me down.'

'Ah, yeah, turn it around,' snarled Olsen, getting up. 'I tellya, bro', you'd feel a sight fucking lighter if you could stop trying to do a thousand things at once. Can't you see that? We kill people, nothing more. We're not shrinks, we're not guys who go off in the jungle to watch, whatever, the tribesmen taking swings at each other's dicks. We put a nine-fucking-millimeter between some asshole's eyes and we blow him away. You need to remember that, man, forget all this bullshit.'

Decker checked the window before putting his cup on the ledge.

'Do you know what I do?' he said. 'Do you have the faintest fucking idea what level I work at? I do not put a nine between some guy's eyes and blow him away. One job, I have to take out some guy who spends his whole life planning against being taken out. The next week, I take out a guy who hasn't done anything yet. A civilian, you understand? Some guy who's gotta go for what he might do, not what he's done. You have to be a hundred per cent on why you're doing it or man, you're not gonna.'

Olsen popped a magazine, bent to it so Decker couldn't see his face, started counting out the rounds in a neat row.

'This is through the looking glass, you understand me?' Decker continued. 'Nothing you learned on the other side can help you here. Of *course* you're in over your head. That's why you have to listen to me. Because I'm not. This is what I do.'

Olsen slipped the rounds back into the mag one at a time, trying not to think about when they ran out.

'Up here, you don't get the luxury of blowing holes in jackboys with do-rags on their heads. Up here, your targets don't even look like you, they look like people you want to be. You have to know you're doing the right thing to be able to do it, because there's nothing else to tell you are. You listening to me? Or this sound like more bullshit to you?' Decker was getting riled now. 'You have to do it so no one can ever tell it was you,' he spat. 'You have to get inside their mind before you can close it down. That's what this *bullshit* is for. Did you understand Miller? *Huh?*' He pushed Olsen's shoulder with his foot.

Olsen flinched from it but kept his eyes on the floor. If he'd understood a thing about Miller, he'd never have got into this shitpile, and both of them knew it. He'd still be drawing his pay, taking his leave, thinking about the future. No, Olsen hadn't understood Miller.

'Well, I did,' Decker went on brutally. 'A Kurtz, he can send up a shitstorm before he goes, if that's what he wants. And Miller wanted it, I tell you. But I stopped him. And it was this bullshit that helped me do it.'

He stopped then, knew he didn't need to say more. Olsen popped out the last round, his gut sinking to see the bare, spring-loaded chamber staring up at him. How had he thought he could get out of this? How had he thought anyone would let him? Anger flared at the hopelessness of it.

'It was twenty years that helped you do it,' he said, pushing the first round back into the mag. 'If you hadn't gone back with him, you wouldn't have got the job.'

'Simple as that, huh?' said Decker.

'You ever think that it might be?' Olsen said angrily, getting up. It was time to quit fooling. If he couldn't get out, they could at least get it moving before the other guy did. He hurled the words at Decker, knowing he'd been an ordinary guy once, wanting to squeeze that part of him. 'But simple couldn't ever be enough for you, could it?'

'I've made twenty-five years of enemies, just doing my job,' Decker responded coldly. 'Until you have, don't tell me what is and what isn't.'

'You're dressing it up, man,' said Olsen. 'You shouldn't be obsessing on what you're doing, you should just fucking do it. I'm not trying to chip at your authority, I've got to say this. Because if you don't come out of this, then neither do I. We could just assume a level of competence in each other and go to fucking work, huh? Do what we do for a change, instead of writing the book on it.'

'What is this "we" shit?' Decker threw back. 'We're not doing what *we* do, we're doing what I do. I'm trying to teach you how to do it in a hundredth of the time it takes to learn, and you're throwing it back in my face. Damn.' He got up, pushed his hair back hard.

'We're wasting fucking *time*,' Olsen pleaded, 'can't you see that? We're sitting here doing nothing and he's out there, working better ways to fuck us up good. Fuck orders, man. Anyone who could give us orders is dead in the ground. I say we get our thumb out of our butts and go to it.'

'And I'm trying to tell you, this isn't about getting a line on some brother and pulling the trigger, okay?' barked Decker, his face draining colour as he squared up to the other man. 'Forget what you know; this is somewhere else. This is where the big boys play, where it takes months of work before you get close enough to do your job. And I'm trying to teach you how you get close to guys who spend their waking moment

70

waiting to get switched. Take it or fucking leave it, but don't tell me how to do my job.'

'Then maybe I'll leave it,' said Olsen. He knelt to his weapons and made to gather them up.

'Go on then, fuck off, I'm tired of it,' Decker said. He wasn't worth it, even as a decoy to draw fire. 'Go out there, see how long till he gets to you. He wants you as much as he wants me. He killed my postman before your fucking meet, remember? Let's see how long you last.'

'Oh, I'll last,' said Olsen, cramming metal back into metal. 'And I'll be watching when he comes for you, old man.'

'You little shit,' said Decker. He put one foot on Olsen's shoulder and pushed hard, sending him thumping down on his back, the nine still in his hand. He had it drawn on Decker before he knew what he was doing. Decker glared down at him, breathing hard.

'We're going crazy here,' Olsen said.

'Yeah,' Decker said, up on the balls of his feet, watching the gun, seeing his P-7 lying where he'd left it by his bed. They held it a moment, their faces drawn as they locked eyes over the younger man's weapon.

'Shit,' said Olsen, colour seeping back into his skin, and dropped his arm. Decker judged the distance instinctively, measuring the angle to break his elbow with one sharp kick before he even knew what he was doing.

'Forget it,' he said, to himself as much as the other man. He needed leverage, things the Contender hadn't got, and Olsen was his sum total so far. 'Here.' He gave him a hand to pull himself up on.

Olsen found his feet, but didn't move to brush at his pants with his free hand. He looked up at Decker.

'So,' he said. 'What?'

'Okay,' said Decker. 'Agreed. This can't go on.' It was the truth, one way or another.

'We go and check the drops now?'

'Yes.'

'And if there's nothing there?'

'If there's nothing there,' Decker said, 'then we're free.'

Free to get ourselves killed, thought Olsen. But anything had to be better than sitting still.

'Let's go then,' he said. 'And Decker?'

'Yeah?'

Olsen holstered the nine. 'You might want to put your gun on now,' he said.

5

THE TROUBLE WITH CHEFS was that you couldn't torture them, they wouldn't stand for it. Jimmy Noff poked with his fork at the prosciutto lying in slivers atop his sculpted melon and said, 'What is this shit?'

What it was was clear: raised on apples, cured with care, pink as a black girl you-know-where. What Noff meant was, what is it doing here? He pushed the plate away.

'This the new guy?'

'Uh-huh,' said Paulie Segotta, who knew all about Noff.

'Get him up here,' said Noff.

'Yes, boss,' said Segotta, leaving the office. When he came back, apron-boy in tow, there was maybe a third less prosciutto on the plate than before, rearranged to make it look like none was missing.

'Anthony,' Noff said. 'We have a misunderstanding.'

'Mr Noff?' said the chef.

Noff registered his goatee and his spiked black hair with distaste. He'd been told that the richer you got the more shit you had to swallow, but he'd never believed it until it happened to him.

'I want us to have a relationship, Anthony, a partnership. I want you to know that your expertise is appreciated. I want you to have the confidence to do your best work here.'

'Thank you, Mr Noff.' He shifted from foot to foot, looking as though he had more pressing things to do this morning than talk to the man who paid him fourteen hundred dollars a week.

'You're welcome, Anthony.' Noff only had to look at Segotta that certain way and he would drop the chef on the carpet, muss that clown-boy hair with a size-twelve loafer. But then Noff would be forced to order in for a month or two, Patricia giving him holy hell because their guests would know they could eat these appetizers anytime they wanted, just call up the caterer like their big-shot hosts had.

'Now,' Noff went on. 'I understand just where creativity comes from. You need the, uh, freedom to create, am I right? And I'm here to give you it. But Anthony, we need ground rules. You follow me? We need to mark out the territory.'

'Is there a problem, Mr Noff?' The tattooed little asshole seemed to be drawing himself up to stand his ground. Noff sighed. Why did they have to make it hard on him? He answered himself: because they knew they could. He had, at one time, ordered the dislocation of a promising young sous-chef's shoulders – just temporarily, he made sure they were popped back in after a minute or so – only to have his entire kitchen walk out on him. He'd spent the next four months choking down the slop of some frycook to whom Thai meant thai stick and Fusion was maybe a nightclub downtown. Patricia had come to bed in a ratty old T-shirt for the duration.

'A problem, yes, Anthony, a misunderstanding.'

'I'm sorry to hear that, Mr Noff.' Saying it like he could order a cab inside sixty seconds, negotiate a transfer fee within the hour.

'I'm sorry to say it, Anthony. But it's important that we're clear on this. I need you to be sure of your ground, not anxious about any gray areas. If you're going to make me proud. You follow?'

'Go on.'

Giving him direction now. Man, he'd like to put it to this little punk, have Segotta put it to him like he would with just one word. Restraint, thought Noff. Respect is self-respect.

'When we had our discussion last week, I thought I'd made myself clear,' Noff said, tenting his fingers on the desk he sat behind. 'I didn't want to tie you up in rules and red tape, I told you one thing. I told you no red meat.'

The spatula-boy frowned. 'I don't buy red meat, sir.'

Segotta stepped in. 'You put prosciutto on Mr Noff's breakfast,' he said, thinking that if only he'd waited five minutes before blundering into the office just now, Noff would've furtively gobbled it and he wouldn't be listening to this charade when there was business to take care of. Business that might mean business: that might mean mattresses on a warehouse floor and hiring jackboys as shooters type business. But that had to wait until the boss was finished jerking around over his damn breakfast.

'The *carpaccio*?' Anthony said, like he'd misheard.

'The garnish,' Noff confirmed. 'Now, if you mistook my direction then *mea culpa*, I wasn't clear enough. But when I say no red meat I mean none. If you thought I was talking about fi*let, pancetta, au jus* –' Noff rolled his tongue around them – 'then you were correct. But I was also talking about all other meat and meat products. No food in my kitchen – let's be clear on this – nothing in my kitchen with warm blood, you understand?'

'I see, sir,' said Anthony, thinking, Swallow it, choke it down: fourteen weeks and you're paid off, you're home free.

'Then we're clear,' said Noff, thinking about the Doberman's chunk steak in its stainless-steel bowl, tucked away on the top shelf of the third floor-to-ceiling refrigerator from the door. If he sacked this little fuck he could go directly down, slip six chunks into an envelope, come back and braise them on toothpicks over the aromatherapy-oil burner in his office. Patricia insisted he light the thing an hour each morning, but this was the first time he'd thought of a use for it.

'Shall I send up more melon?' said Anthony, testing the water from the door Segotta had opened.

'I can scrape it off,' said Noff, like he was a reasonable man, sitting back in his chair.

Great, thought Segotta. That's another twenty minutes. He sent Anthony on his way, went out to the sundeck while his boss ate the meat in his air-conditioned office.

Segotta smoked a cigarette among the climbing plants, wondering whether Anthony would last the debt or disappear first. He seemed to be coming round to the fact that he no longer lived in the real world; maybe he was getting smart.

He hadn't been before. Most of the patrons at Anthony's short-lived signature restaurant had looked like gangsters; and gangsters' wives were the only people who cared about being on the in-list enough to want napkins fluffed over their laps every single night by sexually deviant twenty-year-olds who looked down on them. But Anthony had welcomed the trade, seated everybody. Segotta suspected he hadn't had much money behind him, even at the start: and while artsy types were okay for lunch, he'd needed to cover his tables any way he could in the evenings. A bunch of rich guys competing with each other wasn't the worst way to do it, and Anthony had probably figured he didn't need to know where their money came from.

But the trouble with gangsters was that they liked to own a piece of everything they used. Soon Anthony was experiencing trouble with his suppliers, or rather his suppliers were experiencing troubles of their own. Inside eight months he was buying his whole inventory from guys whose names ended in vowels; inside fourteen he was signing up to work off his debt to Noff, and probably planning on taking himself and his coke-bum bitch Ariadne to Thailand for a couple of years when this was done. If he was smart now.

Segotta snubbed the stub in a dwarf magnolia, pushed it down into the peaty dirt, thought screw it, lit another. The meat thing was the beginning of the end, he knew it. Noff had taken this operation from the madness of the eighties, turned it around, made it smart, made it work money and not just accumulate it. But now he was starting to go at the edges. Segotta had seen it happen before. You got guys who went after success because it was the thing to do, always telling themselves they'd still be the same guy underneath when they were top of the tree. The trouble was, they were. They still wanted to live like they did twenty years ago, when they were worth twenty thousand times less: hustling, pushing, only stirring otherwise to chase after appetites. It was the pay-off they made to themselves, to remain the same guy in secret; it was how they handled the fact that none of it felt real. That none of it felt deserved.

With Noff it was manifesting in meat, red meat. Segotta had found it almost funny at first: guy wearing hundred-dollar hose sneaking weenies from the staff refrigerator. Wanting people to think he lived in another dimension from meat, from all meat, from the blackened round steak half-frozen in the pan as it smoked on the tenement stove to the sixty-buck *Steak hache a la McDonald's* at the latest irony-ridden restaurant. The sorry son-bitch couldn't go anywhere without his muscle; couldn't slip into a deli and scarf up a sloppy joe: instead he had to sneak it around the house like a kid with an underwear catalog. In public he was too good for meat, like all the other guys on the golf course: but in private he'd eat dog-dick if it was charbroiled with mesquite. Segotta had heard stories of other guys the same way, with narcotics, with sex. You didn't need to be a shrink to see why. It was as if the life they'd won was a dream for them; as though they only felt awake when they were feeding the old need. And if they never felt awake, then they never felt alive.

But then reality came home to them, and Segotta had a feeling today was the day for Noff. He put out the second cigarette early, mashing the long stub in after the first one, telling himself he hadn't really wanted it. Then he went back into the house to tell his boss about the call that had come through that morning.

Noff licked the last shred of flesh from his fingers, savouring his private moment at the start of the busy week. Then he swivelled his chair, selected the entertainment section from the crisp *Times* fanned out on the credenza, shovelled the melon into it and crammed the whole bundle down into the wastebasket.

Instantly the bundle started to expand again. It filled the basket: there'd be no room for anything else, unless he got the maid to come down now. But then she'd look in the bag as she took it to the kitchen, idly wondering why, he could see it clear as shine. He got out of his chair, stamped it down with one lizard-skin slip-on, standing in the basket up to his calf. The phone rang on his desktop and it brought him back, made him see how he must look. He removed his foot, kicked the wastebasket under his desk and hit the speakerphone irritably. Janine's voice apologetically identified the caller as the recently installed stock supervisor at one of his outlet warehouses. There was no need to but he took the call personally, reassured the guy, deflected the problem in hand to a series of lesser, more solvable problems, and hung up with the guy feeling valued, part of a team that got things done. Noff could do this, it was what he was good at. He punched the END button with satisfaction. Segotta's head came round the door almost immediately.

'Boss?' he said, and came in without waiting for an answer. He sat down in the chair in front of the desk, and Noff squared himself behind it. Paulie knew all about him, Noff suspected, though they'd never discuss it. Paulie understood why. Paulie would probably do it himself if he was Noff, if he was married to Patricia.

'We got a call this morning,' said Segotta. 'Couple of guys in town from Detroit.'

'Guys?' asked Noff.

'Guys,' said Segotta, and told him the score.

It was the *pizzo*, thought Noff as he listened, always the *pizzo*. The bills that trickled into his machine weekly from every operator on his territory, the tribute, the miserable *pizzo*. If it weren't for the *pizzo* he needn't be tied up with criminals. He'd have no connection with lowlife, with hustlers and junkies who thought they were as good as him deep down.

Because they weren't. The evidence was all around him. He ran businesses that made money: real money, no catch, money that was earned by working people and paid out to him for goods and services. He ran outlet stores: notebook PCs for the suburbs, cellphones for the city, call-bureau prepay cards for the immigrant neighbourhoods between. He hired staff, appointed supervisors, rented office space; he established relationships with start-up companies, negotiated discounts for massive promotions, spent money on leafleting, advertising, made orders for hundreds of thousands of units. Then he sold the stock out from under them, threw away their invoices, fired his staff and filed for bankruptcy. And by then his guys had already found new suppliers, new patsies to whom his sales promises were the big break they'd been waiting for, and he did it all over again.

He did it and he kept on doing it – there was always some

79

new angle to cut – but he had to accept the *pizzo* at the same time. If he didn't, he was dead. If he refused the *pizzo*, tried to let it slide, the guys who paid it would threaten to have him killed on the grounds of better-the-devil-they-knew. He'd have chaos on his hands, if the soldiers he paid to collect it didn't shoot him in the head already for making their jobs redundant. It made Noff sick to his stomach. The world was different now, there was money to be made almost anywhere; all you had to be was fly, fast and first. But if it was the Life got you in on it, you never got out. You were in the Life till you died, and that was the end of it. And here was the Life come to call, as it did. Without warning but you better be ready, every step of the way.

'What do you think they want?' he asked Segotta when he was done.

'They've been ripped off by a guy on our patch,' Segotta said simply. 'I guess they want their money back. And to teach the guy a lesson, make sure it doesn't happen again.'

'The guy is?'

'They don't know. They did it through a chain. But I'm thinking Moss.'

'That moron?' Noff snorted. 'You sure they're serious?'

'I made a few calls,' said Segotta. 'Many as I could. Couldn't get anyone with first-hand, but it seems our caller has a serious rep on him.'

'So what's he doing, making deals with pipe-boys?'

'My guess is he needed hardware for a job that's going to leave a mess. The kind where you can't clean up after. So he buys through a few guys, over a distance, from people's he's not concerned about the units getting traced to. My sense is, he got a guy down here to buy locally for him, ship it up to Detroit on the sly. I'm thinking Moss got wise to this halfway into the deal, tried to burn him on the margin, make the risk better worth his while.'

'So when'd the guy find out he'd been burned?'

'Didn't get that far. He didn't even take delivery yet. Just took some samples, got a quote for the rest,' said Segotta. 'The quote was high, he's come down with one of his guys to teach Moss some respect. If it is Moss.'

'He doesn't know?'

'He wants to run it through us first, Jimmy,' said Segotta patiently. 'He wants to do it right, spank the guy but make sure everyone knows it's at your behest.'

'And if I don't give my blessing?' The last thing Noff wanted was Moss's crew getting emotional. Segotta read his boss's mind.

'I think that on balance you'll choose to,' he said simply. Noff understood, and knit his brows gravely as Segotta continued. 'The guy's at the Sheraton. He's biked over some shells from the sample weapons, let us tell him who they came from. If they're from Moss, his boy will have left his signature all over them, no doubt about it. Kid's got two left hands.'

'Where are the shells?'

'I sent the bike straight to Adrian. He'll call us by eleven.'

'Fine,' said Noff. 'Okay. Get Janine to book us a table, that new place was in the paper yesterday. World Diner, World Café, something like that. She can look it up. Downtown.' The review had mentioned a lamb *shawarma* the guy could order, maybe share a taste of it if they got along. Why not? Two guys, same business, same pressures. He was a people person, that's what he did. It came with couscous and mint, the review had said.

By the time he was seated, Noff was ready to order it himself.

'You get what, lot of Greek, lot of spices in your meat up there?' he said over his menu as Decker signalled a waitress for a clean fork. 'Keep out the cold, huh?'

Decker turned down the corners of his mouth, shrugged.

81

'Same old same old,' he said, picking up his menu. 'You get tired of it. Greektown's mostly for the tourists. I find myself heading up to Royal Oak more often.'

'Royal Oak, that's wholefood joints, right? Black-bean stew, okra . . .'

'Keeps the mail moving.' Decker studied the menu.

'You said it,' said Noff. 'Man, if you only knew before it's too late. You're fucking, you're fighting, you're forking up whatever you damn want, any hour of the day, you think it's gonna last for ever.'

'Teaches you respect,' said Decker. 'You learn to respect yourself.'

'Brings you up short anyway,' Noff said as the waitress came for their order. 'But it does a man good, get a taste of those days once in a while. Nothing takes you back, you know what I'm saying? No other sense like smell and taste. Now. There's a lamb *shawarma* – you see it? On the entrees? – you gotta try it while you're here. Melt-in-the-mouth, ah, man. Like you wouldn't believe.'

'I'll take the chicken Caesar, bottle of water,' Decker said, handing his menu card back to the waitress.

'And for you?' She turned to Noff.

'The Waldorf salad, a little sesame in the dressing,' he said. 'And didn't I ask for the Ty Nant water already? Tell me, you make everybody ask twice, or am I the lucky guy today?'

'It's on its way,' she said, taking his menu from his hand and turning to relieve a neighbouring diner of the empty salt cellar he was waving it at her.

'Little bitch,' Noff said, loud enough for her to hear as she walked away. 'Service is for shit in these places, but you got to move with the changes, huh? Could spend your life in the joints you go back with, you know what I'm saying? Where you know the maitre d's kids, went to their confirmations, ate everything on the card a hundred times. But it makes a man lazy, you with me? You gotta keep going for what's out there or you die a little. Gotta keep pushing it out like the guy says. So no cigar with the lamb, huh?'

'Business travel,' said Decker, 'you know how it is.'

'Forget about it,' said Noff. 'Vacations, it's a different game. You want to try everything, you're out there, you're looking for new experiences. Business?' He flapped a hand dismissively. 'You gotta function. Your routine's gone, you're sleeping any chance you get, you gotta use a new bathroom three, four times a day. But no kidding, the *shawarma*'s worth just a taste. We could split one?'

'I'll stick with the salad,' said Decker.

'Wise man,' said Noff, waving a hand at the waitress. 'The way I always say it, it's the same with red meat as suntans. Used to be just the hicks, you follow me? The fuckin' farmboys. Wrecking their skin out in the field all day: you had a suntan, meant you slept six to a bed and married your sister. Fifty years later, a little colour, it means you got money for leisure, for a pool. Everyone else, they don't get outta the sweatshop long enough to freckle their nose. Now.' He put his elbows on the table, leaning in to Decker conspiratorially. 'Way I see it, we got the same thing going with meat today, red meat. Right now men like you and me, we leave it to the shmoes, y'know? Shovellin' down their burgers, their gyros, their cheese-steak fuckin' sandwich. But it takes eight hundred liters of water, you hear this? Eight hundred liters to grow the feed for the cattle, their hay and oats and crap, almost a thousand fucking liters of pure spring water to get you one eight-ounce steak for your table.' He leaned in further. 'Now. This shit in the 'Glades I read about. The run-off, the fuckin' algae. Same problem, world over. Ten, twenty years, clean water's the premium item. You think I'm kidding you? 'Cos looky here, this water on my table, you know what I'm saying?' He tilted the bottle back, one finger on the cap, so

Decker could admire its blue depths. 'Ty Nant fucking water, four-fifty the bottle, check it: there on the fucking menu. Ten years from now, that's what you're paying for your basic tap water. No one has that kind of money 'cept guys who made something outta themselves, you understand? Eight hundred liters, every time you sit down, not to mention dealing with the methane, the cow farts, the fucking emissions. Don't get me started on the emissions.' He quit fooling with the bottle, leaned in closer. 'What I'm saying to you is, it all adds up. And it's gonna hafta go like with suntans. Joe Shmoe, he'll be scarfin' down salad in front of the tube. The Afr-Ams, Cubanos, they want jerky, they can jerk their own. But you and me? White cloth on our table, good silver, good crystal, red meat all the way. Broiled, baked or fuckin' fried. Miss? Yeah, you, honey.' He leaned back. 'Bring the lamb *shawarma* for my friend here on the side, okay?' He winked at Decker. 'Believe me,' he said. 'Melts on your fucking tongue. Just a taste. You'll thank me.'

'I'm guessing you're a reading man,' Decker said.

'I keep my eyes open,' said Noff. 'I read, watch Discovery. Don't need a diploma to see the way the world turns, understand me? This show last night, for example: you guys catch it? The dolphins? The christing porpoises. And these fuckin' beach-bum so-call professors tryna speak with them, I tellya. They say there's five basic calls they understand, but everything else? The dolphin's talking, they don't know what he's saying. I turn to Patricia and I say to her, you know what the dolphin's saying? He's saying, Get the fucking hippy away from me. He's saying, Lemme talk with someone don't got his hair down to his ass. Guys like us, they think we count for shit, and you know what? Maybe we don't, maybe we do, the type circles these so-call brains-trust people move in.' Noff snatched a breath, let it out, leaned in closer. 'But this thing of ours, you understand? This life of ours: we know what it's about. The race to the swift. You keep your eyes open, listen to what the world's tellin' ya. You get there before the other guy or you float in the water.'

'Speaking of which,' said Decker, edgewise.

'You want me to turn up the air-con?' said Segotta in the car outside.

'Nah, I'm easy,' Olsen said, keeping his eyes on the plate-glass frontage of the restaurant. Decker and Noff were just about visible on the second open-plan floor, couple of tables in. 'Crack a window, if you want.'

'You like this heat of ours, heh?'

'Can't get enough,' said Olsen. 'You guys with your air quality, your UV index. You wanna freeze your balls off all winter, see how anxious a little sun makes you then.'

'Get cold enough for you up there?'

Olsen rolled his eyes, not overdoing it. 'Man, does it. Tellya, this trip coulda come off January, I'd a been a happy man.'

'You don't get used to it?'

'You never get used to it.'

'I woulda thought,' Segotta mused, studying him, 'a guy grows up there, I'd've thought he'd be, y'know. Acclimatized.'

Shit, thought Olsen, who thought he'd been doing pretty well up to that point. Shopping at the RenCen, Ford plant at Dearborn, casinos across the Detroit river in Windsor, Ontario. Did you have to be from a place to get made there? He didn't know. Decker would – he was the guy who'd gone undercover with these guys enough to pull this off – but Decker was inside the window there, feeding his face.

'My family moved north when I was in high school,' Olsen tried.

'Yeah?' said Segotta.

'Yeah,' said Olsen pointedly.

Segotta shrugged, looked out the window. 'All power to you. Does a man good, move around a little in his life.'

'Yeah, I guess,' said Olsen, trying to get off it. 'How 'bout you? You move around?'

'A little,' said Segotta. 'Been down here a long time now.'

'Letting the grass grow, huh?'

'It's been good to me,' said Segotta lightly. 'But I like to stay ready, you know what I'm saying?'

'Don't get tied down too far.'

'Could ship out tomorrow,' said Segotta, looking at him. 'If there was a reason to.'

'The way I see it,' said Decker, 'I'm containing a situation here. This guy – you gonna give me a name?'

'Moss,' said Jimmy Noff. 'My man checked out the work on your shells, only one guy on the east side supplies those signature rounds. Samuel Moss.'

'So this Moss guy,' said Decker, sawing at a piece of blackened chicken. 'He's running his operation on your turf, he's paying you for the privilege. Now my concern is, he's trying to stiff guys like us on the price – he doesn't know us, thinks we're nobody, thinks he can get away with it. If we'd paid up, you think he'd have passed on the percentage to you?'

'And I appreciate it,' Noff said, spearing a piece of lettuce on his fork, then stabbing at a strip of grilled lamb from the plate between them. 'Your bringing it to my attention. The man's a problem waiting to happen, no doubt about it.' He put the lettuce-hidden lamb away under his moustache and chewed. 'But you know, these fucking jackboys. Moss keeps 'em rocked up to their eyeballs, crazy like insane. And in this case, sitting on a heap of kit could dam the damn river. His crew only runs to half-dozen, maybe eight guys, but I'm not committing men to a firefight down there till he major-league pisses me off.'

'And this doesn't piss you off?' said Decker, but keeping it light, as if it was an intellectual game, nothing more. 'It's no big deal to you that he's quoting over the book, skimming on your take?'

'Look,' said Noff, laying down his fork, picking out a walnut with his fingers and popping it in his mouth. 'In fairness, you were shafting the guy. You had a man buy for you down here, I'm guessing because you weren't so particular about the kit being traced after use. If Moss found out you were shipping the invoice to use it up north, he's smarter than I thought he was. And if you had to come to me to find out exactly who you bought from, I'm thinking old Moss the Boss is operating pretty slick these days.' He popped another walnut into his mouth, chewed.

'Too slick for security, some guys might say,' said Decker.

Noff let it hang a moment. 'So what're you gonna do for me?' he said.

The guy was trying to get hired, Olsen thought, a little stunned. He was networking on him here, no doubt about it. Fuck it, why didn't he think of that?

'Hear what you're saying, bro',' he said, like they were just shooting the breeze. 'Gotta keep mixin' it up.'

'There's gotta be that challenge,' said Segotta. 'You don't got that challenge, you get sluggish, you know?'

'Fat birds don't fly,' said Olsen.

'My point exactly,' Segotta said. Just talking, just making time, that's all they were. 'Lotta guys, they'd think a guy'd got it pretty sweet down here. Good climate, good money, y'know? And jesus, Jimmy in there, he's no Bill Gates but he's coining it here. Lotta waves to ride. And nothing that'll get him more than four-to-six if it all falls down. Which it's not gonna.'

'Sweet,' said Olsen.

'You're telling me,' said Segotta. 'Between you and me, the old games, these staples of ours, he could let most of 'em slide and not take a hit where it hurts. You guys call up, say someone's screwing him on the *pizzo*, if it weren't for the principle he'd say fuck it.'

'But the principle.'

'You said it,' said Segotta distractedly. 'Now Jimmy, he's working a lot of good games, like I say. Man has his faults but he's an innovator. Opened up a bunch of new ball games down here. Games you guys up there might wanta think about. Sweet, like I say. Money so clean you could almost declare it. But I'm serious, man. Turned this joint around. And every time, every new game, I've been in on the ground, setting it up from dollar one.'

'Some valuable experience there,' said Olsen, thinking, Give the guy the wink, call him up to Detroit, shoot him in the head halfway. Then ride back on down here, say, I hear you're hiring.

'It's always good for a guy, feel that his expertise is valued,' said Segotta lightly.

'Ain't that the truth,' said Olsen, looking at the other man as he gazed off at the restaurant. Good climate, easy money. Live in a fortress with soldiers every fence post. Never go out without a car full of backup. The long arm of the lawless, cradled lovingly around him. Could be sweet.

'Any dessert? Any coffee for you folks today?'

'Decaf espresso,' said Jimmy Noff. Decker shook his head and the waitress left.

'My concern,' Decker said, 'my real concern is this. Forget the money, who needs it? But this Moss guy's making a monkey out of you.'

'The guy's a legacy,' said Noff. 'A hand-me-down from my predecessor. Been working this patch twelve years, and he was permitted, if I can say this, to get a little cocksure under the old administration. A little connected. Has himself a wide selection of clients, shall we say. From day one he's been – how do I put this? – too settled for me to take down 'less he was causing me a real headache. Which he hasn't yet.'

'He's ripping you off, Jimmy,' said Decker quietly. 'And if it came to our attention, it'll come to someone else's. We're concerned that the guy tried to rip us off, but most of all we're concerned that you've got a situation here.'

'A situation, that's a little harsh,' said Noff. 'A situation? Not yet. But if I personally took him down – maybe that would be a situation.'

'I understand you,' said Decker.

'But you, you guys, you're out of town and he's pulled one on you,' Noff said. 'If the way you like to work is to teach a little respect for good business practice, far be it from me.'

'I'll have to charge you consultancy,' said Decker. 'I can't work pro bono on this.'

Noff considered a moment. 'Close him clean, invoice me,' he said.

'Half up front,' said Decker.

'Forty-sixty, freelance rate per capita,' Noff said.

Decker held eye contact a moment.

'Agreed,' he said, and poured out the last of the water. 'Now tell me where.'

'You're gonna move now?'

'I'm not gonna hang around in this heat,' said Decker. 'Detroit, we like it this side of a hundred.'

'Made in the shade, huh?'

'Just tell me where, Jimmy.'

'The waitress brought the check,' said Segotta.

'Hallelujah,' said Olsen. 'Got a hole above my belt you could drive a truck through.'

'Four blocks –' Segotta pointed the way – 'Kaufmann's deli, it's on your way. Beef-hash sub like a baseball bat.'

'Yeah?' said Olsen.

'Bring the water to your eyes,' said Segotta. 'I could use one myself, but Jimmy don't like food in the car. Four blocks, next to the electrical store.'

'I'll check it out.'

'You do that. And if there's anything I can help you guys with. Paulie Segotta.'

'I appreciate that, Paulie.' One hand on the door.

'Maybe I'll see you some time.'

'Not if I see you first,' said Olsen, getting out. 'Take care, man.'

The Cherokee, though they'd left it in the shade, was like a furnace, and their guns were hot in their hands. It was good to get them back, had felt like being out without a wallet.

'He give you him?' said Olsen, in the driver's seat for appearances.

'Pretty much,' said Decker. 'Noff thinks we're gonna switch him.'

'And are we?'

'We'll see,' Decker said. 'Make a right. How'd you make out?'

'Good.' Olsen joined traffic. 'I mean, good as I could. Guy was pushing pretty hard.'

'And what'd you do?'

'Pushed him back. Here to do a job, not suck each other's dicks.'

'Okay,' said Decker. 'I think we need the freeway.'

Olsen checked the mirror, switched lanes.

'So, what,' he said, 'we headed there now?'

'It'll take a few hours to set up,' Decker said. 'We being followed?'

90

'Yeah. Blue Lincoln.'

'Fine. There's a mall coming up on the right. I'll drop you there, you can lose whoever's with you, pick up another car.'

'And you?'

'I'll take the Lincoln for a spin. This is it: come off this exit. And turn in just there. Okay. I'll lose the Lincoln, then do what I gotta do. You get a car, lose your tail, do whatever you like but meet me at the Sheraton, six thirty sharp.'

'Won't they be waiting for us there?'

'Sure,' said Decker. 'Doesn't mean we want them in our face all afternoon, though.'

'What're you gonna do?'

'Couple errands.'

'We go for the guy tonight?'

'Yes, we do,' Decker said. 'There, pull in there.'

Olsen did, reversing into the space. The Lincoln passed them, then turned at the end of the aisle.

'How many guys?' Olsen said as they got out.

'Later on? Don't worry about it,' said Decker, walking round. 'Tell you what, while you're losing your tail in there, find a hardware store, pick up some stuff for tonight.'

'What kind of stuff?'

Decker got in the driver's seat. 'You ever torture anyone?' he said.

Olsen shrugged, holding the door. 'Once or twice.'

'Then you know what kind of stuff,' said Decker, putting the seat back the way he liked it, gunning the engine. 'Sheraton, six thirty.'

'Uh-huh,' said Olsen, but Decker was already pulling away, his tyres squealing on the hot asphalt as he accelerated out of the slot, the tail-lights of the Cherokee flashing a split-split-second as he rounded the corner. The Lincoln streaked after it.

'Mess my paint job and die, motherfucker,' Olsen muttered,

watching them shriek up the on-ramp. He turned and headed into the cool depths of the mall.

But when Decker pulled up outside the Sheraton it was in a late powder-blue Merc.

'What happened to my Cherry?' Olsen demanded.

'Ask your mother,' said Decker. 'You get the stuff?'

Olsen hefted the backpack from the pavement at his feet.

'Put it in the trunk.' Decker popped it from under the dash, and Olsen walked round and dumped it in. There was an aluminum briefcase and another backpack in there, a roll of gray canvas plus an eight-disc CD changer. He whumped the trunk closed, walked round to the passenger door.

'Pretty slick,' he said, getting in

'Isn't she?' Decker grinned, knocked a knuckle against the polished wooden dash. It was immaculate save for the broken flaps where Decker had screwdrivered out the airbags.

'You paid for this, didn't you?' said Olsen. You could always tell.

Decker pulled away, maybe a touch of self-consciousness showing in his frown.

'You can't steal these,' he said.

'Why not? And where d'you get the money?'

'It fucks them up,' said Decker. 'And none of your business. Besides, we need her. Gotta blend in now, the plush neighborhoods and the pimps'.'

'Which one tonight?'

'The second,' said Decker, ignoring the freeway ramp and turning under the six-lane instead. 'What'd you get?'

'Nail gun, pliers, blowtorch. Duct tape and some rope.'

'Christ,' said Decker, looking over. 'Did you ask if they had a coupon on torture packs?'

'Now there's an idea.'

'Make your pile.'

'Specially this neighbourhood.' said Olsen, peering out. 'Jesus.'

They'd only gone a few blocks the other side of the freeway but already they were somewhere lost tourists told stories about when they were safely back home. Tenement buildings decayed between brownfields; the only businesses in evidence were the occasional heavily fortified loan shop or lotto-and-liquor store.

'The guy lives here?'

'Far edge,' Decker said. 'Brother likes to keep it real.'

'How real?' said Olsen, frowning as he ran the action on his nine.

'You're gonna like this,' said Decker.

They watched the girl go into Moss's building, short blond hair, make-up and nails, carrying a leather satchel the brother on the door had a fine time rooting through.

'What's in there?' asked Olsen.

'Tools of her trade.'

'She's a hooker?'

'I told you you'd like it,' Decker said. 'Only way we can get him alone. Noff says the guy's some hard-ass but partial to a session with this girl of Noff's once in a while. I had him send her over to Moss as sugar for keeping his nose clean, some raid the cops made last month. There was no raid that concerned him, but this moron's not gonna argue. The girl has a way with her, Noff says, charges top dollar, but she's being paid to make out this is pleasure, not business.'

'Noff thinks we're gonna switch the guy?'

'Yeah. But all we need to do is squeeze a name and number from him. Whoever ordered the hardware.'

'Then what?'

'Then we go after that guy, and the next one, and the next one if necessary. But remember, this is information the

Contender already has. He'll be waiting for us, could be here, could be the next stop on the line. Be ready. Here we go.'

'Son of a bitch,' said Olsen as Moss's crew filed out of the building: big guys, socks on their heads in the heat, batting each other and kidding as they crossed the street to the curiously unfortified barbershop opposite. 'He's alone in there?'

'Just beauty and the beast,' said Decker. 'Seems the guy likes to entertain alone. His crew can keep tabs from the barbershop but we're going in the back.'

'We gonna keep the girl there while we work?'

'Have to. She comes out, the brothers there go back in.'

'Man, I hope she's not squeamish,' said Olsen.

'Are you?' said Decker. 'Were you shitting me earlier? If you haven't done this before, you'd better be straight with me.'

'Like I said, no problem. I've leaned on plenty of guys –'

'You done it in a team? Because if I'm asking the questions and you're turning the screw, you need to know how hard to turn it. Too far, you can lose them.'

'Sure,' said Olsen, not sounding it.

'Look,' said Decker. 'Don't worry about it. The only trick with torture is that you've got to do it. You can't threaten twice. You say to the guy, Tell me or I'll break your arm, and he goes, Fuck you – that's when you break his arm, and I mean immediately. You don't, he knows you're full of shit.'

'Okay.'

Decker looked at him; he still didn't seem so sure of himself.

'I'll be the judge of how far,' he said. 'I'll give you very clear instructions. If he doesn't answer fast enough, I'll tell you to do something, and you just do it. Even if he starts answering while you're working on him, just keep doing it till it's done. You can handle that?'

Olsen nodded.

'Okay then. What do you say? Think they're comfortable in there yet?'

'I guess,' said Olsen, a little green around the gills in Decker's opinion. But it wasn't the time to pick him up on his attitude now.

'Then let's go,' he said. 'Get the bags from the trunk.'

The gray canvas Olsen'd seen there earlier turned out to be a steel-mesh weave, four feet wide by twenty long, weighted at each end with reinforced holes for footholds running between. Decker threw it over the back wall and they swarmed over the twelve feet of brick like it was topped with Doritos, not wicked shards of broken glass. Two more of the same and they were in Moss's yard, looking at ground-level door and windows hidden behind crack-house steel.

'How do we get through that?' whispered Olsen. He scanned the back wall and saw no unguarded opening save a dripping toilet overflow.

Decker pulled a crowbar from his backpack and inserted it behind the nearest heavy-grade window grille. 'Catch,' he said. The moment he braced, the whole thing came away, and Olsen had to lunge to grab it before it clattered to the ground.

'Shit,' breathed Olsen, looking at the rotted masonry the bolts had slid out of.

'Jackboys,' Decker muttered, nodding up to the dripping overflow as he put a slim-jim to the window catch. 'Spend their money on gold necklaces like a bunch of women, 'stead of looking to their damp course like a man. Here.' He slid the window up, climbed soundlessly over the frame, took the bags from Olsen and handed him in.

Inside was an office, or what passed for one: a few filing cabinets, a desk littered with ashtrays and scorched foil, a thumb-tacked map of the district on the wall with crude divisions etched on in red and blue marker.

'Where do they keep the hardware?' whispered Olsen.

Decker shrugged, took out his P-7, motioned to the door. They crept towards it, found a stale-smelling hallway beyond, and above it the staircase to the second floor. Sounds reached them as they proceeded, Fed-style, upwards: Celine Dion playing softly, a grunt over it, some kind of movement, another grunt, all of it muffled behind the door above. When they pushed it open they swept their weapons over a druglord lounge: black leather sofas, monster TV and sound system, zebra-skin rug on the floor. The smell of good weed hung in the air; the grunts were coming from behind a black-and-white door on the far side, louder now. Decker motioned and they slipped out of the backpacks, crept over, took a position on each side of the door: half turned, ready to roll, one high and one low, listening. Inside a throaty voice said:

'You like that?'

There was a deep chuckle, a wet rustle, then a hard-edged groan – of relief, of satisfaction, it was hard to tell over Celine's warble. Decker and Olsen flipped a glance, got nothing from each other, ducked their heads in closer to listen. The only sound now was slick and slow, some kind of lubricated friction, Decker couldn't tell where exactly. He was about to move when a woman's voice cut over the slick sound, clear as a bell.

'You ready for the Boss?'

They looked up at each other now, Olsen mouthing, 'Two girls?' Moss's nickname was the Boss: maybe he was sitting to one side, waiting, while one girl worked another; another girl who'd already been here. Maybe that was what he liked to do.

'Huh?' the voice demanded again, unmistakably female, sharp and stern. There was a brisk movement inside the door, a sudden, agonized yelp. 'You want the Boss, you bitch?'

Two girls. It didn't matter. They could shut them in the bathroom while they worked on Moss. Decker motioned to wait, wait until the Boss was *in situ*, get the guy while he was going to town in there.

They flanked the door, fixed in place, frowning hard, straining to make sense of what they heard below the music. The picture the sounds seemed to draw was of a girl on the bed, the hooker working her, Moss off to one side pulling himself ready. That was the most likely, Decker thought. They should wait till they heard Moss get on the girl and start going at her. Then bust in, pull him off her, start on him even as he detumesced before them; catch a ride on the disgust he'd be feeling as he deflated, the self-disgust at letting his hogleg ride over his horse sense. Make him feel like he'd let them all down, not just himself.

'Yeah, go 'head, lick it, bitch,' came the hooker's voice. 'You get the Boss wet 'n' ready.'

Decker motioned to Olsen, Olsen nodded back. Wait till he's in her. That was the thing to do, Decker was sure, but still something didn't click here. Decker knit his brows, turning his head this way and that trying to pick up more sound. The second woman, he figured, the one the hooker was calling 'bitch', that had to be Moss's woman, his permanent fixture. But if it was, then why the secrecy? Why had Moss sent his guys out while he did this?

It had to be that Moss didn't want his crew knowing how he liked his woman hurt and humiliated before he got it on with her. If this had been Jimmy Noff, Decker could understand that: Noff's wife would want to lord it over the help, certainly wouldn't want them privy to what she put up with in the bedroom. But Moss was in a different league, and so was his woman; Decker would've thought Moss'd be proud of the way he pushed her around, would want the other guys to know about it. He didn't understand it, he didn't like it.

But then there was a grunt – Moss's, too deep for a girl – a breath and a long, low moan.

'Take it,' the hooker urged. 'You take it all, you bitch!'

Moss cried out now, and the picture in Decker's mind morphed into Moss arching his back, pushing into the girl on the bed. The way he sounded, he was putting it somewhere she rarely let him and it was too much: he'd be pulling out, shooting over her back PDQ. Time to go, catch him as he came and fell back maybe. Decker held up his left hand to Olsen, fingers splayed, counted off five-four-three-two . . .

They burst into the bedroom, Decker going high, Olsen low, sweeping fast from wall to wall, closing on the bed where the figures were, where they'd expected the figures to be.

Where they'd expected three figures to be. Where only the hooker and Moss were. The hooker flattening herself against the wall, eyes wide, mouth open; Moss staying put, belly down on the bed, tied too tight to be going anywhere. Even as they covered the hooker, Olsen gaped and Decker blinked, their eyes drawn to Moss, barely able to believe what they saw.

He was tied face down on the bed in front of them, spreadeagled, wrists and ankles wound with silky white rope stretching out, taut as plucked strings, to the bedposts. His head whipped from side to side as he tried to get a look at them, heaving against the bonds, cords standing out in his arms and the backs of his legs as he strained to bring his head round, or at least to spit out the panties crammed into his mouth and held there with a gauzy white scarf. But he couldn't manage either. The salmon-coloured soles of his feet quivered towards them but their gaze was fixed, incredulous, a little horrified, further up the bed. Beside it, on the nightstand, stood a pump-bottle of lube and a selection of sex toys in black, fleshtone and candy-pink that brought water to the eyes just thinking what they might be for. But they were only appetizers, building up to the main course: which was, as they could both see, some kind of plug, injection-molded from solid black latex. The kind that would draw your eye in a sex-shop display case, make you wonder if anyone could possibly ever use a thing like that, or just bring it out for effect mid-session. It was huge, unfeasibly so: the width of the business end of a baseball bat, yet Moss the Boss had apparently been relishing it. Until the moment they walked in, at least.

'What do you call this?' Decker asked the hooker mildly.

'Special service, four hundred an hour,' she said. She didn't take her eyes off the gun, but her voice was easy, not about to be fazed by anything guys could do. 'Why, you interested, honey?'

Decker lowered his weapon and returned her flirty half-smile.

'Maybe I am,' he said. 'But what I meant was, what do you call *this*?' He motioned towards the thing, the monstrous object distending the man on the bed.

'That?' She grinned. 'That, baby, is what we call the Boss.'

The Boss wasn't Moss. The Boss was in Moss. Olsen let out a swift, incredulous hoot. Moss roiled against the ropes but it was no use; the girl knew her slipknots, evidently. Decker and Olsen exchanged a happy glance, nodded *go*. Olsen strode round the right side of the bed and jammed his gun into the hollow at the back of Moss's shaved skull, forcing his face down into the pillow. Decker opened the en-suite door for the hooker.

'I'm sorry to have to do this, miss,' he said.

'Yeah, yeah,' she said. 'But he's only paid up to the hour, understand? Over that, my meter's running.'

'I'm sure he'll be a good boy,' Decker said and motioned her inside. She gave him an inappropriate look but went along like she was told, heels clocking on the tile floor as she crossed to the toilet and sat down. Decker shut the door on her with an apologetic nod, then turned back to Olsen.

'Turn the music up,' he said and, as Olsen went back through to the stereo, he knelt down to the bed.

Moss's face was pressed into the pillows but his eyes glared up at Decker, showing white round the irises. Decker had to look away a moment, contain himself. Then he squatted down to bring his face level with Moss's.

'You saved us a lot of work, you know that?' he said, grinning into the other man's choking fury. 'You're a considerate man. Thought we were gonna have to torture you.'

'But looks like you saved us the trouble,' put in Olsen, behind them.

Decker straightened up. 'Push it in,' he ordered.

Olsen glanced at him. 'Do what now?'

'That.' Decker nodded towards it. 'Push it in.'

'Ah, *man*,' Olsen said. 'I'm not touchin' that.'

Decker glared at him and motioned him over to the far corner of the room.

'What did I say in the car?' Decker hissed under Celine, who was shrilling now concerning her right, as a free woman, to express that freedom.

'We were talking about breaking arms and such,' Olsen protested, 'not this.'

'Do it,' said Decker. 'You agreed.'

'No,' said Olsen, holding up his hands. 'Uh-uh, no way. I agreed to roughing the guy up, slapping him around a little, not this . . . jesus.' He made himself look at Moss, as if to be sure. 'This is some fucked-up repugnant shit. You want it, you do it.'

A muted roar from the bed made them both turn their heads. Decker strode over, yanked the panties out of his mouth – pink cotton, lace trim – and replaced them with the muzzle of his P-7.

'You say something, boy?'

Moss glared up at him.

'What's the problem, son?' Decker enquired innocently. 'Isn't this what you wanted just now?'

He gave the Boss a sideways backhander. Moss hauled against the ropes, every muscle in his panther's body bulging.

'Here, suck on this,' said Decker, easing the barrel further into his mouth. 'That's right. Just a big ol' pacifier, that's what we've got here. You suck it like a good boy. Uh-uh,' he warned as Moss strained up uselessly again. 'What's that you say?' He withdrew the barrel just enough to let the man be understood.

'Take it out,' begged Moss around the gun, his eyes beyond negotiation above it. 'Take it out, it's . . .' His body strained hugely, choking him off. 'Cramps,' he gasped, eyes rolling back under fluttering lids. 'Nnnnggh. Jesus! *Uh-uh-NNNGGHHHH! Fuck! Fuck!* O jesus please.' He rolled in the ropes like a chain ferry in a swell as the spasms rode him. Decker watched with one eyebrow raised, keeping the muzzle mashed against his lip. When he finally quietened, Decker flapped his free hand at Olsen, who was standing back against a wall, wincing at every fresh convulsion.

'Do it,' he said.

Olsen went over to the other side of the bed, reached out a hesitant hand. The base of the thing was the size of a hockey puck, moulded to stop it going in irretrievably. If that was possible, Olsen considered, as he raised his fist.

He brought it down sharply on the base, the heel of his hand connecting with his forearm following through behind it. Moss reared up like a wave, almost lifting the bed from the floor, his body rolling as primal spasms racked it. Decker had to pull the gun away sharply to prevent Moss leaving some of his teeth in the barrel. When it subsided he was glistening, running sweat; his breath coming in short, frantic gasps as he strained helplessly against the ropes. Decker crouched again.

'Now,' he said, reasonably. 'You can answer to me or you can answer to the Boss. Which is it to be?'

'Anything,' gasped Moss, 'whatever you want. Got coke, few AKs, couple tec-9s, some ordnance . . .'

'Ordnance, huh?' said Decker, taking a shell from his pocket, holding it up for Moss to see. 'You got any more like this?'

When they let the girl out of the bathroom, she stepped warily around Moss, still hogtied on the bed, his eyes bulging cold fury, his nostrils flaring over the duct tape across his mouth

'You going to let him go?' she said as she picked her dress from the back of a chair.

'Would you?' said Decker reasonably.

She stepped into her dress, hitching it over her hips to her shoulders. 'And did you know the CD is louder in there?' She jerked her head to the bathroom. 'Speakers either side of the tub. The *echo*.' She shuddered. 'You are two cruel, cruel men.'

'And you're, what, Mother Teresa?' said Olsen, handling the sex toys gingerly as he packed them away for her. She looked impishly over the bed at him.

'Sister of Mercy to some,' she said, taking the proffered bag from him. 'You want a piece, sweetcakes?'

Olsen flushed red. She chuckled and took a card from the pocket of the bag.

'Here,' she said playfully, holding it out to him. 'You got the look.'

Decker laughed out loud, and Olsen had to take it, show he could take the joke.

'Gimme a call sometime,' she said, eyes flashing mischievously. 'But you might want to leave it a while. Something tells me I'm taking a little vacation.'

Decker pulled out his wallet and extracted five soft hundreds. 'Buy yourself a sunhat,' he said.

'Maybe I will,' she said, making the money disappear. 'Us strawberry blondes can't be too careful.'

'Speaking of which,' said Decker. 'If you could wait five minutes before you leave, we'd be grateful to you.'

'How grateful?' she said, pushing it but still playful. Decker gave her another bill, and it disappeared the same way.

'C'mon,' he said to Olsen, still holding her card in his hand. 'Save that for your hope chest. Let's go.' Olsen snapped to it, slipping the card in his pocket, gathering up their stuff. They moved towards the door.

'What about him?' the girl asked Decker as they passed. 'You think I should take it out?' she asked.

They considered the Boss a moment; an unfortunate matter, but one for responsible expedition.

'That,' said Decker, 'is up to you, miss . . . ?'

'Mistress,' she corrected. 'Mistress Dion.'

'Mistress Dion,' Decker agreed, shooting Olsen a look as he returned her smile. 'I wouldn't want to tell you how to do your job.'

6

THE SHADOWS WERE LONG but the city baked on, releasing the heat it had stored since dawn in one long burst; pumping it back till morning, when the cycle would start over again. The edge of the city turned cooler as the day wound up but the powder-blue Merc pushed on, tracking from the red through the orange of the weather-channel thermoscape, cooling itself as the traffic thinned and the road opened up. Decker was intending to lose Noff's tail the only way that was sure: by heading out to the open dark, taking to high ground, and seeing with his own eyes that his dash pulsed the only light for twenty miles around. In the meantime, with too much to talk about, they weren't.

It could start any time and Olsen knew he'd need to be ready for whatever the other man had to say. But Decker did not brim over with social skills at the best of times, and with the day catching up on them both he seemed content to drive in silence. Olsen held back himself, needing to get his options clear before he had to commit himself either way. He was dog-tired, not from the specifics of the long day but from running five senses overtime through it, covering his ass every which way every moment, recalibrating his position a hundred times a minute. He was not used to this, preferred it when the lines were drawn clearer and his function was a binary hit the target or miss it. For now he had to fight the fatigue, the rhythms of the car on the clear desert road towards the border, keep his head straight and ready for when the guy with his hands on the wheel spoke up.

He glanced over furtively, not wanting the movement to trigger response. Decker's eyes were fixed on the road, his hands at ten o'clock. They'd got what they wanted today, found the mouth of the tunnel that led through to the light maybe, and Olsen was prepared to forget about Segotta and what he could take him for. What Moss had given them had been better, and the getting it had been easy. All they had to do was do it again with the next name in the chain, then the next and the next till they got to the Contender. Take him out and they'd be top of the tree, undisputed heavyweights, big guns for hire who could wait for the work to come to them. Set up a pyramid, maybe, contract out what they didn't need themselves, take a percentage and stash it away. He'd set a figure and get out when he reached it, not get greedy, take the money and run like a smart fucking man. One year mountains, next year the ocean: keep it fly, keep the dust off him. Set some of his money to work meanwhile, provide for the future. Could be sweet.

Except for sourpuss here. Olsen knew already what Decker would say when he finally spoke up. Regardless of what Moss had given them, he'd want to play it by the book, wait for orders that wouldn't be coming. Olsen didn't think the Contender had gone to ground: most likely the guy had problems of his own to take care of right now or they would've seen him. If he was top of the tree too, like Decker said, he'd have a schedule to maintain, a stove with a pot on every burner, and as far as Olsen could see it, they should move while he tended whichever pot was boiling over on him right now. They should get on his case while his eye was off the cast, have him look up from the stove to find two guns in his face.

They passed another mile marker, into triple figures for ninety minutes now.

'Another hour or so should do it,' Decker said.

'One of the drops was flagged today, wasn't it?' Olsen couldn't help saying it like he didn't want to hear it.

Decker checked the odometer. 'Let's think about what Moss gave us first,' he said.

Ninety miles later, they were parked on high ground half an hour from any highway. The car cooled and ticked in the dry breeze, the dust-settle on the hood already thick enough to write your name with your finger. Decker erased a patch with the edge of his hand, propped himself ankles crossed, arms folded.

'You sound like a horse,' he said.

Olsen grunted, concentrating hard as the backed-up fluid drained out of him. The problem with getaways, there was never time to take a post-stress whiz when you needed one. Finally he finished, hitched himself up, walked back over buttoning.

'So what now?' he said. The sky was alive above them, angry rashes of light.

'You think Moss was telling the truth?' said Decker.

'No skin off his nose,' agreed Olsen. 'I mean, maybe some, but in the circumstances.'

'You pick the pain that's less immediate.'

'Guys like him, every time. We better believe him.'

'That's one option,' said Decker, noncommittally.

'You ever hear of this guy Kentrelle?'

'Doesn't sound made up, does it?' Decker admitted. 'No, I didn't. But I don't spend much time around backwoods militiamen.'

'Where's Humboldt County anyway?'

'North of Napa,' said Decker. 'Dope country. Terrain's like

106

the lost world, Indiana Jones. You grow what you like there, no one's gonna find you, much less close you down.'

'Good place for a training camp.'

'Is what I'm thinking. This guy Kentrelle ordered this pile of hardware, I'm betting he's got plenty more up there. But cut-down Steyrs with pumped-up rounds: they're turkey-shoot weapons, not what you use to hold off the ATF. Not his style.'

'He could've been hired to do it.'

'I don't think so. What you saw with the Postman was a pro job. Militiamen aspire to be soldiers, not cleaners. I can see them doing it for money but if it was me holding the purse I wouldn't hire a bunch of beardy backwoods misfits. The Postman was code three. You don't mess around.'

'So this guy Kentrelle, he's a conduit for the weapons?'

'Or a lure for us,' said Decker. 'There's the problem. He's a link in the chain but that's all he his. And first we'd have to find him, commit ourselves in that terrain. It's not gonna be like working in a city. Anything could go down, any time. With Kentrelle or the Contender or anyone else's toes we happen to step on up there, and believe me, there's a lot of guys working things in those woods who don't welcome company.'

'Speaking of shy guys,' Olsen said.

'He's already headed Napa way,' said Decker.

'And we're not?'

'I think we can make him come to us.'

'While we do what?'

'Business in the city.'

'The drop wasn't just flagged, it was serviced, wasn't it?' Decker bit his lip pensively and nodded.

'Which one?'

'The stump.'

'The one with the roots or the one with the hole?'

'The one with the hole,' said Decker. 'I think I found us an ace in it.'

The night air smelled of dry dust, of hardpan baked back to the stone age all day then wind-skimmed raw each night.

'There's ace in the hole and there's fire in the hole,' began Olsen carefully.

'You think the Contender serviced the drop?'

'You don't? C'mon, he leaves instructions there and we follow them, he can put us where he wants us.'

'These were seven-day drops. Today was day seven, and if the guy knows anything, he'd know that.'

'So?'

'So I went on my own,' Decker said. 'If it was him filled the drop, he would've been watching for us to pick up. When he saw I was alone, he could've dropped me from two hundred yards while I was in the open: not have to worry about you getting behind the car with the first shot, then coming out firing. He could've cleaned me up no trouble, got on with his life.'

'Say he wasn't ready. Say he had other stuff on his plate today.'

'Be nice, wouldn't it?' said Decker sourly. 'If he's setting us up, then it's with Kentrelle by way of Moss. It's been too easy.'

'You call today *easy*?'

'Yeah, I do. I call today pretty damn good. Options are clear now. One hand, we can go up to the backwoods, take on a bunch of crazies. Option two, we've got my postman's next job and fifty Gs cash.'

'Whoa, whoa, whoa. Fifty grand?'

'Forty now,' said Decker, jerking his head back to the car. 'Had to put down ten to drive her off the lot.'

'We split the rest?' If Olsen was faking, he should've been off Broadway. He looked like a man who hadn't seen new cash in a long while.

'Cool your jets,' said Decker. 'This is fighting fund, not pay day.'

'I need stuff,' Olsen complained.

'We keep it,' Decker said firmly, not about to budge on this one. 'You got any access to other funds? Neither have I till this is over. We keep the bulk of it intact till we need it.'

'Or until we're sure we don't need it,' said Olsen, starting to feel like he could hold his end of an argument with this guy now. 'Come on, man, we got what we wanted today, let's move on it.'

'It was too easy. You're letting a little success pump you up.'

'You're letting it hold you back,' argued Olsen. 'What've you got against good luck? 'Cept this is not even about luck. Whoever hit your postman used a team, and that compromised him. You can't hire six guys like you, you have to hire six guys more like me. Guys who don't give a crap long as they get paid and they walk away. I know you can't admit anyone in the same business as you could be so unprofessional, but welcome to the real world, man. We're not rocket scientists, we're killers. Only difference between us and the guys we switch is we get paid less. We've got a target and we ought to move on it right now.'

'What if Moss warns him?'

'You kidding me? "Oh, hi, Kentrelle, this is your man down south, two guys bust in on me wanting to know all about you and hey, I'm sorry but I had to tell them 'cos I was taking it like a bitch at the time." You crazy? Jackboys, you can't even cuff 'em in front of their women because they don't take losing face. Ol' Moss is gonna keep this quiet, forget all about it, believe me.'

'There's a lot of ifs and maybes in there,' said Decker. 'The way I work, I try to avoid those when there's an option, and there is. The drop gave us orders and resources. If we pass it up, it's not going to be offered twice. Someone out there's looking out for us.'

'Someone out there's setting a trap,' said Olsen. 'And you want to walk right into it. We've checked the drops every day. Anyone was watching us, they'd see where they were, could leave whatever they liked for us to find.'

Decker shook his head. 'I use a password for pickups too,' he said. 'Anything dropped has to come with six digits from a sequence only me and the Postman knew. It was there today, with the money and with the orders.'

'So he got it out of the Postman before he killed him.'

'Did it look to you like the Postman was tortured first? If it did, you've taken your time to tell me.'

Olsen looked away.

'Then we're set,' said Decker. 'First light we go back to the city, scope out this next job of mine. If my postman bid for it, the Contender did too. As far as he knows he got the contract, and it's plain he's content to leave it till he's good and ready, till he's finished with me or both of us. So when we don't go up after Kentrelle he'll figure we got ourselves killed already. Unlikely, but it happens. He'll come back down, and we'll be in the last place he expects us: doing his next job for him.'

'Which is?'

'Put it like this,' said Decker, gesturing to the orange sky over the western horizon. 'You think Thin City would miss one fat lawyer?'

Thin City it was. Olsen knew from Discovery there'd been a time when fat meant rich and you wore your weight, if you had it, like guys wore Versace today. Now fat told the world your life was Jerry, junk food and jacking off if you could still reach your hand to it. Anyone who meant to go places in this city was thin as a whip, broadcasting to whoever was listening their shameless, blameless lifestyle, their superhuman life expectancy, and how much they'd sunk into their backhand and their background meanwhile.

The lawyer had sunk a lot. If Charles P. Travers had been born above a gas station and spent his twenties chasing ambulances, he'd been born again at thirty-five and the only thing he chased now was campaign funds. At forty-two, he was a lawyer who spent as much time in the chat-show chair as in court, expounding his theories on many things, but on welfare reform in particular. Teenage mothers deserved no handouts, unless they could prove they were raped. Steel-fronted crack houses in no-go ghettos were armoured and fortified with taxpayer money. The reservations were petri dishes for that family-wrecking virus of gambling: the Indians were laughing at us from behind their bottles. If the varnish on him needed a little powder to take the edge off the gloss for the cameras, then the viewer at home neither knew nor cared. Travers knew what he was doing, and that was setting himself up for office over the next five years. Mayor, state governor and then who knew? The Consensus knew, the way Decker told it, and they didn't want him getting there.

'What if he doesn't?' Olsen said, as they followed Travers's car on a long tail through morning traffic.

'What if he does?' said Decker. 'The guy is part of the circus, understand? You take a career politician, they learn to play the game if they're good. But this guy runs the game already. He's not going to be told what to do, come the day.'

'So the day doesn't come.'

'Even if it did he wouldn't last. We have a fine tradition of blowing mavericks full of holes without anyone giving orders. Our communal immune system, maybe. Rock the boat too much and the culture throws up a psycho with a carbine.'

'Or a couple of mailmen in a powder-blue Merc?'

'No, we do it for money,' Decker said dryly. 'Look in the glovebox.'

Olsen opened it and took out a buff folder. Inside were copies of numbered-account transactions, telephone-call sheets, seven-by-fives of a younger, thinner Travers at restaurant tables, on golf links, in a tux at a wedding.

'This is a paper trail,' he said, handling the photographs like they might bite.

'We haven't done anything yet.'

'But even so.'

'The guy's a civilian,' said Decker as Travers's Jaguar pulled over towards the Intercontinental. 'And true, if you're a soldier you shouldn't care. But the Consensus have been doing this long enough to know that if you keep making a guy switch civilians and you never tell him why, he goes bad.'

'So this tells us?'

'That Travers here's been a popular guy. The pro-life snipers, the Auschwitz deniers, the racial purists: fatboy tied the bib on with all of them. Didn't use a long spoon either.'

'He's still in bed with them?' Olsen flipped his eyes right without moving his head as Travers's car disgorged the man himself.

'If we could prove it, we wouldn't need to worry,' said Decker, switching into the fast lane.

'So we leak these to the *Times*, get it ready to blow,' said Olsen, leafing through the seven-by-fives once more. 'Then the guy's found with his head opened up and a nine in his hand, no one asks too many questions.'

'Yeah, if we wanted to risk everything we've all ever worked for,' said Decker, not taking his eyes off the restaurant across the street. 'No paper. No trail. Not ever. It's done sometimes, but by guys who that's all they do. All they've ever done: blow whistles, know everything there is to know, all the angles. But they weren't given this job, we were.'

'But someone's gotta ask questions, public-eye guy like that. However we do it,' he added quickly.

'Not if you answer the questions there and then.'

'So we do what? Plant stuff at the scene? Finger someone else?'

'We tell them a story,' Decker said.

'A story?'

'Like Elvis.'

'Let me know when I'm supposed to get this.'

The guy was trying, despite his mouth, Decker could see that. There was no gain in pushing at each other like a couple of locker-room jocks, but this was a learning curve for Decker too.

'You remember in *Deep Throat*?' he said.

'Deep what?'

'*Deep Throat*, jesus. Linda Lovelace? Biggest grossing porn flick ever.'

Olsen frowned. 'I thought that was Pam and Tommy,' he said. '*Deepthroat*. That's what, European?'

'Never mind,' said Decker, feeling his age. 'What happens, you can guess from the title. But I had a girl once, a working girl, show me how you do it. You press in under the jaw here –' he demonstrated – 'and it suppresses the gag reflex. She used to hit guys extra for it, but I bet it was the best hundred most of them ever dropped.'

Olsen mentally measured back from his mouth. 'All the way?'

'Gross, unless you're doing it,' agreed Decker. 'But guys like us, we learn the hold, we can fill a client's throat, then let go. He starts choking and, 'less you give him the Heimlich, that's probably it.'

'Man,' said Olsen, getting it. Just put a gun in his face, your thumb under his jaw and a fat wedge of Whopper in his mouth. No ligatures, no signs of struggle.

113

'Open him up, all you find is hamburger,' said Decker, 'and there's the killer. You'll notice our friend here could stand to lose a few pounds.'

'Yeah,' said Olsen with distaste, watching the man close a pudgy hand around his water glass.

'And the hungry childhood's already part of the guy's mythology,' Decker said. 'Every chat show, every magazine spread, there it is. The American dream and doesn't he know it.'

'So he chokes on a Wendy's . . .' Olsen began.

'And everyone nods sagely, chooses to believe that's all it was.'

'Like Elvis.'

'Like my ass,' said Decker. 'Elvis was so full of speed, they hadn't cremated him, the Graceland worms would've excavated Tennessee. But they leaked the choking thing so people could say it was the hungry kid inside that killed him.'

'You can take the man out of the ghetto but you can't take the ghetto out of the man.'

'Reads the headline, and no one asks any questions. Make it into a story, make it look like the ironies of fucking fate, you can walk away from anything.'

Olsen looked at the guy with new eyes.

'Except with women, of course,' said Decker. 'You're inclined that way, you can press under their jaw on the QT, suppress their gag reflex. But the day I find the button turns off their bullshit detector, I'll be a rich man.'

Olsen returned Decker's smile, without thinking about it for once. Maybe he could do this: he felt like he was getting it now, and that felt good. He'd never been much of a student, but now he saw why the geeks put up with the rough-house from guys like him in high school.

'You said it there,' he said easily.

*　　*　　*

'So where's *your* hungry kid?' Decker said casually as the centers squared up for the fourth quarter. Travers sat courtside a dozen rows below them, shouting occasional advice to the Lakers' troubled guards like everybody else.

'How do you mean?' said Olsen sidelong. *'Put it down the line! Down the christing line, man!* Ah, jesus, you believe that?'

'Guy's got a heavy chin,' Decker agreed. 'You don't have to talk about it if you don't want.'

'About my hungry kid?'

'One thing about this business, it doesn't recruit Richie Cunninghams.'

Olsen looked blank.

Decker cast around for an update. 'Mentos kids. Mom, Dad, matching sweaters at Christmas.'

Olsen watched the play a moment. 'What do you want to know that for?' he said after a while.

Decker kept his eyes on the court too. 'Just, y'know. There's a lot of weight we carry as it is. You don't get much chance to talk to a person carrying the same as you.'

Olsen watched the game.

'Though I can guess,' said Decker under the crowd noise. 'You got into this because the way you were brought up, someone offered you a break, you took it and were grateful. Am I right?'

Olsen didn't answer.

'I'm only saying because that was me too,' coaxed Decker.

Olsen wanted to say. He really did. He wanted to tell how very much Miller had seemed like the big time; and how, by the time Olsen got the chance to see what Miller really was, he had enough on his hands trying to find some way out without thinking about whether taking every opportunity that came his way mightn't be the best game plan to use. Those six months, christ, finding out hog heaven was a pen full of

115

sucking muck, no way out except down into it. Miller's death had brought a backhanded kind of relief, mixed in with the horror.

But he had a half-sister alive somewhere on the east coast. He didn't know where, but it wouldn't take anyone who had a mind to do it long to find out. Long as she was alive, he came from nowhere.

'I can't talk about it,' Olsen said, and turned his head. 'You understand?'

Decker held eye contact a moment. Poor little schmuck. He'd fallen out of the world of gym and poker games and the bar where everybody knows your name: the place you were supposed to wind up when the army was through with you. Decker had expected to end up there too, a long time ago.

'Your call,' he said and reached into his coat. 'You want Cracker Jack or milk duds?'

Sitting in the parking lot later, waiting for Travers to come out of the meet-and-greet VIP lounge.

'You see a white Neon tonight?' asked Decker.

'Like the one passed us at lunchtime?'

'Yeah.'

'Uh-uh. Was looking for one too. Wasn't there one down the street from old Moss?'

There hadn't been. 'I don't recall,' Decker said.

'I'm probably mixing it up.'

'It was a tense time. You always remember mixed signals.'

'You got that right. Turns my gut just thinking about it,' said Olsen. 'I mean, who could . . . y'know? How can . . .'

'Don't go there,' said Decker, hands resting on the wheel at twenty of four. But Olsen seemed to want to talk tonight.

'I mean, okay: I've watched some tapes in my time, some far-out stuff,' he said. 'And most times you're reaching for the remote, you know what I'm saying? But once in a while you can be like, okay. Maybe. But, *man*. I mean, jesus fucking wept. You ever see anything like that?'

'You'd be surprised,' Decker said.

'What, really?'

'I could tell you stories.'

'In the line, of course,' Olsen teased, looking sidelong.

'Naturally,' Decker said. 'You see it so often you're more shocked when it's not there.'

'Yeah?' said Olsen, interested.

'Oh, yeah,' Decker said. 'Certain types of guys. They make it: they get the houses, the cars, the wife, the mistress. Everything they see, they can have. But they finish the day, they've only got one belly and one dick.'

'I read there's this restaurant, megabucks only, they eat swan and shit. Eagle.'

'To impress each other maybe,' said Decker, rolling his head to stretch out the neck muscles. 'But chilling, different story. One thing with rich guys: you look in their icebox you got pot roast, you got cold cuts, you got a gallon ice cream and some sodas, same as the rest of us.'

'You do a lot of rich guys?' Olsen said.

'Poor guys don't wind up with private armies,' Decker said shortly.

Olsen accepted this, considered a moment. 'So what you're saying: if you can eat what you want, you eat what you ate as a kid.'

'Seems to be the story. They don't get tired of it.'

'But they do get tired with sex.'

'Like I said. Could tell you stories.'

'You mean, stuff like that? Back at Moss's?'

'You're pretty interested.'

'That's natural, isn't it?'

'Thought it turned your stomach.'

'You know what I mean.'

Decker conceded with a hitch of his shoulders. You thought about what you couldn't have, even if you didn't want it exactly.

'It's the one thing you can count on, if you're frisking some hotshot's place. Box of whatnot in the closet. Some of them have special rooms.'

'For pain?'

'For things that seem to drift that way, yeah.'

'Man,' said Olsen, reflecting. 'I had it made in the shade, I'd have me a different buncha honeys every night. And I tellya, it's not me who'd be squealin'.'

'Yeah, so you'd think. But the evidence says otherwise.'

'You saying I'd be into that type shit? Ol' Moss the Boss?'

'I'm saying,' said Decker, 'that guys who've got it easy seem to enjoy a little pain once in a while. A little fear, maybe.'

'Reminds them of the old days.'

'Seems to be the idea.'

'But if you never got out of the old days?'

'He's coming out,' said Decker, gunning the engine. 'C'mon, put your belt on.'

That night Travers was at a fundraiser at the Palisades and so were they, watching the tuxes file in.

'Those guys, most of them be into that weird shit?'

Decker groaned inwardly, wishing he'd never mentioned it. 'It seems to go with the territory, yeah.'

'So how does this fit with what you were saying about that Dorky guy?'

'Dawkins?'

'Yeah.'

'How do you mean?' Decker had been explaining the beauty of the itch-scratch reflex, the way it removed any irritant on the skin while stimulating a combative blood flow to the area.

Olsen screwed his forehead up, staring at the dash. 'Well, if these rich guys are the top of the pile, the survival of the fittest, okay? Then how come they're not just, y'know, using their johnsons to make babies? Isn't that what their genes oughta be telling them to do?'

Decker should never've started this. 'There's the problem,' he said. 'Or the solution, depending which way you look at it. You take the un-American view, you could say that the rich get rich from fucking the world over. You could say that this is nature's way of making sure they're just a temporary blip on the timeline. They don't reproduce successfully 'cos they're too busy getting golden showers to fertilize anyone. And the kids they do manage to produce either go Menendez or Columbine.'

Olsen nodded slowly, chewing it over. 'The way I see it,' he said, 'if ol' Dorky is on the money: the better you are at humping, you know what I'm saying? The more satisfaction you get from straight sex, the more reproductions you'll have. So put that over a thousand years, and the only people left will be the ones who really – I mean *really* – get off on just good ol' dick and pussy. All the perverts and shit, they die out. And everyone that's left, they come like a fuckin' freight train every time 'cos it's in their DNA to. That's why they're still on the planet.'

'That's one way of looking at it,' Decker said. He knew he should be grateful that Olsen was making such an effort to find a level between them. Sometimes he wondered if it was better to find things out for yourself and know the truth of them, rather than be told them and take assumptions on trust.

'Man, I tellya, my genes ain't dying out,' Olsen said absently, glancing at a cat outside the window. 'I love to fuck.'

'Yeah?' said Decker, irritated. 'Who're you planning to have kids with? You're gonna, what, take a baby stroller on jobs with you? Lock your wife in Fort Knox where no one can whack her?'

'Whoa.' Olsen held up his hands. 'I was just talking.'

'Yeah, well, think what you're talking about,' said Decker, surprised at his own short fuse.

They sat in silence for a moment.

'I apologize,' said Decker.

'I was just tryna, y'know. Take the ball and run with it. I mean, I appreciate your telling me this stuff,' said Olsen.

Decker felt weary. 'I didn't mean to . . . y'know. Snap.'

'Forget about it,' said Olsen. 'Just the tension coming out.'

'You got that right.'

'Okay.'

They were quiet another moment.

'You tense 'cos Travers is a, y'know. Civilian?'

Decker shrugged.

'You mind me asking?'

He shrugged again.

'Because the only jobs I had so far were, like I say, jackboys and whatnot,' Olsen went on. 'Me or them. I guess it's different when they're not shooting back.'

'You could say that.'

'Is it better that way? I mean, less to worry about?'

'That's one side of the coin.'

'But the flipside . . .'

'As you say. You want to sleep at night, you've got to know why you're doing it.'

'Prevention better than cure.'

'Is the way you have to look at it. Switch some guy now, and maybe in twenty years you won't have to commit a combat unit to switch a hundred. Or a thousand.'

'And that's enough? A maybe?' Olsen looked over.

'If it isn't, you're in the wrong business,' said Decker, warming to it. 'Miller told me something once, not long after he took me out of the ranks. If you could time-travel, would you go back to Vienna, switch Hitler when he was still painting crappy postcards?'

'Sure you would.'

'But we can't time-travel. We can't have the hindsight that makes you sure. So in the absence, you've got to be sure another way.'

'Miller said this?'

'Yeah, he did,' said Decker. 'And the only way you can do that, you've got to want to keep things the way they are. You've got to appreciate the value of the way things are. Miller said that's why it's possible – why it's a good thing, even – that we live this way. No women, no kids, no security. I mean, we have to, but there's a bigger reason too. We get to know the value of the ordinary – we get to see why it has to be preserved – by being denied it.'

Olsen was quiet a moment. Poor little fuck, thought Decker. Miller'd been too far gone to give Olsen what he'd given Decker.

'I guess nothing's the way you think it's going to be,' Olsen said after a while.

'I guess not,' said Decker gently.

'Do you regret doing it? Getting into this life?'

'What is this, twenty questions?'

'I mean, on a personal level. Forgetting what you just said. Would you do it again? If you knew then what you know now?'

'That's a dumb question. You can't know till you do it.'

'But if you could go back somehow, like you said. Time-travel. Just for the sake of argument.'

'You mean would I choose to be sitting in a car on stakeout with an empty apartment to go back to? When I could have a wife, kids, a pension?'

'But the satisfaction. Keeping the peace.'

'Sounds like horseshit sometimes,' said Decker. 'But what Miller told me made sense at the time.'

'But then look at how Miller turned out,' Olsen said sharply.

Decker thought a moment. 'Maybe the millionaire Bruce Wayne only put up with being Batman because when he changed out of the costume he was the millionaire Bruce Wayne.'

'They say you don't miss what you never had.'

'They say a lot of things,' Decker said, a little unnerved at how it came out.

'You had a girl once,' said Olsen quietly. 'Didn't you? I hear you in your sleep. There was a woman once. Before this.'

Decker's silence spoke for him.

'You loved her?'

'It was a long time ago,' Decker said.

'Man,' said Olsen, looking at him in a new way. 'I thought you were the Tin Man.'

Decker shrugged, looked away. So had he, once.

'What was it about her?' Olsen persisted. Decker didn't reply. 'I mean, I'm interested. I never met a woman, there wasn't a part of me thinkin' about the day I was stagging it again. Must've been something pretty special about her.'

'I guess she was pretty special,' Decker conceded, her face popping into his consciousness through a quarter of a century.

'But what in particular? I mean, was it in the sack or, like, you could talk to her, or what?'

Decker shrugged. 'This guy told me once that you can't tell what makes a woman attractive once you're in love with her. Before, it's easy: you can say great ass, nice personality, whatever. But once you're, y'know, in over your head: then it's too late. You can't tell any more.'

Olsen chewed this over, and they sat in awkward silence for a while. You started talking on stakeout, it always ended like this, thought Decker.

'C'mon, there's no one else here,' he said. 'Let's call it a day.'

'And do what?'

'Whatever normal people do,' Decker said, turning the key in the ignition.

They went to bed early that night.

'There he goes,' Decker said, a little relieved to see it next morning. Not a white Neon today but a blue Camarro, pulling out from a side street by Travers's racquetball court and following the man's Jaguar as it turned out of the lot into traffic.

'It's a different guy,' noted Olsen. 'Got forty pounds on the last one.' Decker put the Merc into a basic troy config with the Jag and Camarro as the three cars joined the freeway: the traffic was too heavy for anything more sophisticated. Twenty minutes later the Camarro was relieved by a grey Cavalier outside Travers's press call downtown. The Cavalier was driven by a different guy again.

'Three stooges,' said Decker, circling the lot as the Camarro headed for the exit.

'I don't get it.' Olsen frowned. 'These guys are serious, what're they doing in kiddy cars?'

'Let's see where Curly here calls home.'

The Camarro pulled out into traffic and they followed him on the freeway up to the valley, to a Dunkin' Donuts where they had to wait while he read the paper, ate two with sprinkles and took a lengthy rest stop somewhere in back. When he came out they followed him through Van Nuys to a neighborhood strip mall where he parked, got out of the car and entered a blind-fronted office next to a nail salon. Star & Frost Security was written on the window in white adhesive block letters. Two units along was a coffee shop.

'Get me a cappuccino, skim milk, no chocolate,' said Decker, proffering a ten.

Olsen took it and got out, putting on his sunglasses as he

crossed the lot. While he was inside the coffee shop, the Camarro guy came out of Star & Frost with a padded envelope and some papers in his hand, stopped inside the edge of the shade to consult what appeared to be a fax. He looked like a cop, late thirties maybe, forearms ropy with muscle below the cuffs of his Polo shirt. Olsen came out of the coffee shop with a takeout bag, crossing in front of the guy, and Decker watched closely but didn't see anything that looked like recognition. He was still watching when Olsen opened the passenger door, letting a blast of hot air into the cooled interior, but the guy was heading back to the Camarro, head angled the other way.

'Nothing,' he said, handing Decker his coffee. 'Counter, waiting area, office behind. Couldn't see into it.'

Decker unpeeled the dribble cap, took a sip. 'Man,' he said, peering mistrustfully into it. 'Even the coffee you *buy*.'

Olsen took a Mountain Dew from the bag, sweating already from its short exposure to outside. 'You want some of this?'

Decker shook his head, took another sip, eyes on the blank office door. 'Make it last,' he said.

At one o'clock a woman appeared, five-nine, dark hair, one-ten, twenty-seven or eight. She was dressed Gap-smart, short-sleeved blouse and cotton trousers, but she was inside the coffee shop before they got a chance to check her too closely. They had to wait another four hours for that: promptly, on the stroke of five, she locked up Star & Frost, headed over to a vintage red Beetle parked on the shady side of the lot, unlocked it manually and gunned the engine.

'Break me off a piece a that,' said Olsen appreciatively as Decker started the Merc, his shoulders popping with the sudden activity.

'Sweet car,' said Decker, following two vehicles behind. They tailed her through the rush hour to a condo building a few blocks shy of Valley Plaza where she parked, collected her mail by the door and disappeared inside.

'Want to go in?' said Olsen, one hand on the door.

Decker shook his head. 'Just get a name.'

Olsen walked briskly over, scoped past the bank of mail-boxes, rang a bell that got no answer, came back.

'Lauren Reese,' he said, getting in.

'Like the candy or the golf clubs?'

'The candy.'

'How about the car?'

'Duct tape on the driver's seat, decals worn off the instruments. Needs a paint job like, bad. New gearshift and headlamps, though.'

'Working piece by piece as she can afford it,' Decker said. He didn't get a single part of this.

'She's what, a secretary?'

'Something like that, I guess.'

'Then where's the boss? Star or Frost?'

'Vacation, maybe.' Decker shrugged. 'Doesn't matter. If someone's hired their team to scope out Travers, she'll know who. You want to know something about a business, ask the secretary.'

'You want to go bust in, see what we can find?'

'Not yet,' said Decker. 'Let's see if Miss Reese here has a life or not.'

He sent Olsen back to the apartment in a cab, stayed put in the Merc half a block from the condos. He was grateful for the lumbar seats but had spent almost eleven hours straight in the car nonetheless: even though he stretched where he sat every hour or so, his shoulders were up around his ears by seven. At eight she came out wearing shorts and a backpack, her dark hair tied back: he followed her to a gym a mile away, then sat in the car park wondering what the hell to do.

125

He honestly didn't know, and he had to have a plan by the time he went back to the apartment. Olsen had taken staking Travers with relatively good grace, but he was itching to get back on the gun trail, north after this Kentrelle guy. Decker knew Travers was the better bet: whoever had filled the drop was telling him so. But Star & Frost? Some *Yellow Pages* custody-battle dirt-diggers? It didn't make sense.

After fifteen minutes he got out, went round to the trunk, took a pair of nerdy steel-rimmed specs with clear lenses and a Dogers cap from inside. Thus attired he entered the gym, filled out a membership application at the desk and requested a brief tour of the facility from the harried-looking girl at the desk. A personal trainer named Mike appeared after a short wait, and they began with the yoga studios, where classes were in progress. She wasn't there. Decker expressed a preference for upper-body over new age and Mike took him up another floor to the main suite, two thousand square feet of busy treadmills, Stairmasters and Hoist machines, MTV screens overhead and a Naya water machine in one corner. He saw her immediately, on a spin bike on the far side, and instinctively lowered his chin, letting the bill of the Dodgers cap shade his eyes against the bright, no-nonsense fluorescents overhead.

'You trained before?' said Mike.

'Not for a while.' Decker grinned inanely, rounding his shoulders and pushing out his gut to hide his physique. Mike led him over to the first machine, a tricep dip, and long-sufferingly began extolling the properties of each machine, working clockwise.

It wasn't until almost halfway round that he could scope her safely: working hard and focused on a StarTrac, her back to him, moving fluid and easy against the resistance, sweat darkening the back of her sports bra, loose tendrils of hair sticking to the olive flesh above her shoulder blades. Decker noticed he wasn't the only guy in the place checking her out. But Mike, meanwhile, was doing his job, demonstrating the Glute Master, face down; and Decker muttered 'Yeah' and 'I gotcha' in the right places, watching her out of the corner of his eye. She spent a lot of time here, that was evident – she was no hardbody, no Madonna; there was plenty to let you know she was a woman, though Decker doubted there was an ounce of her that she could gain by losing – beneath the sleek lines, the warm flesh that soaked up the harsh gym light and bounced it back as Cancun sunset, every muscle was like pulled caramel under her skin. She wore black high-top sneakers, an inch or two of soft white sock rumpled above, and Decker only snapped his eyes away when he became aware of Mike asking him if he had any lower back trouble.

'No more than the next guy,' he said and grinned like a car salesman, but Mike was looking at him like he was a pervert just come to check out the flesh through his Coke-bottle glasses. 'Listen,' he said, 'I gotta be somewhere. Thanks for your time, guess I'll see you around.'

'No problem,' Mike muttered distrustfully, but Decker was already turned on his heel and heading out. He glanced into the wall-mirror just before he got to the door, saw her working as before. But when he let the door close behind him and sneaked a peek back at the mirror through the porthole, her head was ducking back as if she'd glanced up and over. By the time Decker was back in the Merc, he'd already decided he'd imagined it – wishful thinking – and tried to think instead about what the hell he was going to suggest to Olsen now.

After all, what would a girl like that look at a guy like him for? Especially in his dorky disguise.

Olsen was stripped to the waist, doing one-arm push-ups on the bare cement floor, when Decker got back. He'd spent the two hours after the gym back outside Lauren Reese's building, waiting to see if she went out or if some guy – who, oddly, he expected to look like Olsen – dropped by.

None did. Instead she'd come back from the gym seventy minutes after Decker had left, carrying a grocery sack and looking like she was just getting through a run-of-the-mill weekday evening. It'd consoled Decker somehow to see the blue play of light from her TV against her window; consoled him that even women as young and vital as her – women who ought to be safely on board the gene train, tickets good for the long ride to the end of the line – didn't spend their free time so differently from him. On one night of the week, anyway.

Olsen finished his reps and wiped himself down with a sweat towel as Decker filled a jelly glass with water from the faucet, chased an acidophilus gel cap with a mouthful, then dumped out the rest.

'Anything?' Olsen said from the door.

Decker shook his head, filled the glass again, turned and offered it to him. Olsen took it and drank it off in one, waiting expectantly for Decker to point the next turn.

'I don't know,' he said. 'You find anything?'

'I ran her through a couple of stalker sites on your notebook,' Olsen said. 'Her home phone, social security and credit record are saved on the desktop.'

'She look real to you?'

Olsen turned down the corners of his mouth, shrugged. 'Much as anyone.'

'And Star & Frost?'

'*Yellow Pages*,' Olsen said, 'and AOL. Insurance, matrimonial, bona fides. No job too small. Your One-Stop Shop.'

'So what do you think?'

'I think it's bullshit,' Olsen said. 'I have to say it. We could spend a month digging down and find some nut at the bottom, hired S&F 'cos he thinks Travers is boffing his wife. And when they find out he ain't, he hands over another cheque and tells them she's moved on to Geraldo.'

'I hear what you're saying,' Decker said, rubbing at his eye. 'But I don't like coincidences. We get a contract on Travers and whoa, someone else is scoping him too.'

'We took a straw poll of dick shops, I tellya, we'd find every celeb in the book has some loser paying for 'veillance.'

'Yeah, I hear what you're saying,' Decker repeated.

Olsen knew better by now than to push it. 'You think the Contender's using the nut angle to have these jokers do the legwork on Travers for him?'

'I know how crazy it looks.' Decker shrugged, shaking his head.

'Why don't we just pop him?'

'Travers?'

'Collect the dough and get the next job.'

'I don't think that's what they want,' said Decker ruminatively. 'I think whoever gave us this, whoever's looking out for us: they gave us it because it's the Contender's job, not ours. And maybe he's on to that. Maybe he's using Star & Frost so he can watch us watch them.'

'Lot of maybes in there.'

Decker shook his head, eyes on the floor. 'Yeah, you're not wrong.'

'But the gun trail . . . man, we don't have much on Kentrelle, but we know where he's at.'

'Only to the nearest fifty miles,' corrected Decker.

'But if we don't move on him he could move himself,' finished Olsen. 'Labor Day last week, remember? Fall's closing in. Maybe whatever he's got up there moves south for the winter. And if we get up there and he's gone, well. You want to wait till next spring?'

The guy had a point, but Decker had spent twenty years playing his head against his gut.

Olsen read his expression. 'Tell you what,' he said. 'We got money. I could fly up to Oakland, drive to Garvil: 101 north from Santa Rosa, shouldn't take more'n a day even with the redwood traffic. Scope the place out, be back inside a week. This Kentrelle's running a camp, he's gotta buy supplies somewhere: shouldn't take longer'n a couple days to find out where. Meantime you work on S&F, see who hired them to stake Travers.'

Decker went to the refrigerator. 'You went shopping,' he said.

'Somebody had to.'

Decker took out an iced tea, popped the top. 'Do you understand why I can't ask you to go up there?' he said and took a swallow.

Olsen thought it through. 'You think the Contender's set up this surveillance on Travers to throw us?'

'Is the size of it,' Decker said, wiping his lip and offering the beverage. 'He hasn't moved on us yet: that has to be 'cos we're looking out for each other. If he can get us apart . . .'

'By putting a fork in the trail?'

Decker nodded resignedly. Olsen took a swig, swallowed.

'I think Kentrelle's for real,' he said. 'I mean, okay, he's running some asshole outfit, bunch of gun-happy misfits left over from the millennium. But if the Contender hired them to wipe the Postman, he did it for a damn good reason: anyone in the business'd have to be crazier than a shithouse rat to want in on a play like that. You've said it yourself.' He handed the bottle back. 'So look at it from the Contender's point of view. Upside: he got a team stupid enough to do it. Downside: they were assholes, doing it for money, didn't give a crap if they left shells lying around for us to find. But they weren't gonna tell the guy who hired them that. The Contender doesn't know about the shells – if he did, Moss would've been dead long before we got to him. If he's setting us up it's with Star & Frost.'

130

'What if he heard about our visit to Noff?'

'That loser?' said Olsen. 'C'mon, we made him look like an asshole. When he finds ol' Moss is still alive, he'll think this is some play from Detroit for his territory. I tellya, he's not gonna be shouting our names from the rooftops.'

'But that doesn't change the fact –'

'I'm in on this as much as you are,' Olsen interrupted, not a little surprised to find that he seemed to mean it. 'If there was a time I coulda walked away from this, then it's gone now. I want what you want: let's get out of this mess and get back to work. We show the Consensus we can fight our way out of this, they'll be fighting each other to use us.'

Decker bit his lip, feeling like a heel. Instead of being pleased at how Olsen had come along, at the effort the guy had put in, all he felt was tired. The last thing he wanted was to come out of this and be back at the top of the for-hire list, he realized.

'Okay,' he said. 'You want to check things out up north, I'm not gonna stop you. Just look out for yourself, okay?'

'And you'll check out Star & Frost, see who hired them to watch Travers?'

'Till I hear from you,' said Decker. This could be a mistake, he knew it, but he was too tired to argue. 'The moment you find anything, I'll come up.'

'Meantime you'll work on that Lauren babe?' Olsen's eyes crinkled at the corners.

'Yeah, I guess,' said Decker. Thinking, In my dreams.

7

B UT IT WAS OLSEN'S sleep she invaded. He woke with a
start, realizing, as he settled back into his body, that it
was only his seatbelt that had kept him from his feet. His
seatmate grunted, rattling his copy of *Time*. Olsen blinked,
glancing up and down the aisle. Lauren Reese had been
leaning over him, in a stewardess uniform, and he'd been
checking her cleavage as she poured coffee; but as the pressure
built down below another pressure had joined it: that of a
muzzle pressing into his groin. He'd looked up into her green
eyes and she'd said . . .

What? It was gone already. All he could remember was the
gun in his crotch and the mischievous look in her eyes. It didn't
matter: dreams don't mean anything. He sat back, pits slick
nonetheless, his shorts bunched damply at the top of his
thighs. It wasn't like him to sleep on planes, especially a short
hop like this. But then a lot of things these days weren't like
him.

Having direction, for example: that was a new one. For the
first time in his life, he knew what he was shooting for. This
was some kind of test, a real test, not an SAT, and he'd been
waiting for it all his life. It had been what he'd dreamed of,
atop the loft-conversion stairs in his mission-control bedroom,
between his piles of *Soldier of Fortune* and the flight sims on

his computer. Downstairs his parents had conceived tests for him, dreaming them up while they rolled joints on non-glossy, rough-paper magazines: vacation tests, cookout tests, tests of talking, of emotional diarrhoea, of hippie-wilderness mind-fuck; everything that the America outside their house screamed was irrelevant. On the wall by the raw-stone fire-place, above the bookshelves full of spaced-out South Americans and guilt-tripping Asians, had been photographs, black and white, of their own great-grandparents, cold off the boat from the other place, staring set-jawed into the week's-wage-a-shot camera. They had looked like people who had tough choices to make. They had looked like adults, aged twenty-two. At forty, Olsen's parents had looked like children, had lived like children with their hiking, their barefoot lazing, their lying dozing in a three-hundred-dollar rainbow-coloured Mayan hammock. Babies in a big crib, sucking on a water-pipe pacifier. They apologized for everything, and apologized for nothing; they felt bad, but had found that feeling good helped them forget it. Olsen had distanced himself and waited, plying the night with his computer while they practised wholegrain sex below; finding for himself the stray of white-dollar America – and god, did he find them, lines of text progressing like cartoons across the screen in front of him – wanting as bad as he did, but holding back, even inside their arcane BBS platforms, like they felt they were being watched.

Finally, the recruiter had come to his high school. Olsen had seen him in the parking lot, had felt instant kinship with the hard eyes, the tall walk, the shaven jaw set like a man's rather than a sub-woman's. The absolute self-belief of military hierarchy had swallowed him up like a true womb, enveloping and bathing and protecting. In a way the recruiter had failed him – or other recruiters, blindly making up quotas – by permitting faggots and jokers and bleeding hearts into the ranks; his gave Olsen responsibility. He'd made sure that these fake men didn't stay in his unit, and someone had noticed, pulling him out for evaluation. His mother had died slowly of breast cancer and his father had clung to the tofu, the roots and leaves and seeds, until pancreatic took him twenty months later. Only in their last weeks had their faces set, drawn and hard-eyed, into those of adults, but Olsen hadn't seen them. He'd signed up with the dud Miller, deep cover and no way out, within weeks of his mother going into the last battery of chemo.

But that had been a test too. The shadowy figures that Decker called the Consensus – and Olsen loved them while he feared them, whoever they were – those guys had been watching then, and were watching now to see who came out on top of this. Maybe they'd even set it up, put Olsen with Miller to see if he could ride that bad wave; then pitted the Contender against Decker to see if the guy still had what it took, see if he deserved to be top of the tree when the cards were on the table. To the winner the spoils, and Olsen, having survived his own test, wanted a piece of that. Decker would come out on top, he'd see to that: but Decker couldn't do this for ever. When the time came, when the order came – as Olsen didn't doubt it would – it'd be time to put Decker out to graze. And he'd pick up the keys to the kingdom, be the big swinging dick men called on when they needed someone fucked: that was all he wanted. That was all he'd ever wanted, even if he'd only come to realize it lately. He could be the best that he could be.

He didn't doubt the Contender wanted it too. Lucky son of a gun, getting picked for this. Maybe he'd had his own Miller to weigh and find wanting, maybe he'd gone through the same hoops. It occurred to Olsen, for the first time, that maybe his luck had sucked so much because the Consensus was manipulating it; maybe he was as much the Contender as this other guy. In this psych tests the guy had wanted to dwell on his fucked-up family, on the trauma, the hurt. Well, there was a world full of hurting people out there and if you didn't get what was going to fix you yourself, then no one else was going to do it for you. Now that he could see the way the land lay from the vantage Decker had given him, Olsen guessed what'd put the Consensus on to him: he was trained, after all, had sat through Miller's lock-picking class, his comms-security class, his field-guide-to-the-poor class, his car-boosting class and a score of others, seeing the use of this information to a guy like him, whatever he wound up doing. Decker's tutorials had only seemed to confirm that the man had lost his mission somewhere; but what he said about the Consensus rang true if you understood the military, and military guys were the only guys Olsen had ever had time for. How he'd envied army brats! The life, the rules, the dress uniforms hanging in the master-bedroom closet; a father who could teach him to strip weapons and respect values, a man who had a Code. Miller had probably figured he could play the missing major for Olsen, and looking back, that'd probably been the way it was, Olsen could admit it now. At the time he'd thought he was being given the break of his life – special ops! Deep cover! – because of his record: the hazings, the beatings, the seizing and deployment of authority and discipline within the shrunk world the military had given him. Looking back now, Olsen could see that his record had been no better than any of the other guys who made it into his Seals squad. They'd all done good to get there, and they'd known it: but good was all it had been. Now Olsen had a shot at something more, and he meant to take it.

When they landed, he picked up a Cherry from the Hertz lot, found a tire lever in the trunk and dug out the airbags right there. Turning down the air-con and cracking the windows for the first time since spring, he drove through the cooling maritime morning, north-east from Oakland towards the Concord base where he'd been on a three-week language course once. Bored and aching to cut loose, he'd picked up a deactivated Glock nearby one evening for a crazy sixty dollars, and after a half-hour's service conversation the guy had taken it in back and reactivated it. The shop was still there, as was the stripes-struck guy: fifty minutes later Olsen walked out with a retooled Sig Sauer, a .44 mag, a .38 snub and enough shells to get out of even the worst-case recon in the woods up there.

It was a little after eleven on a Thursday morning. His options, as he saw them, were to head back to the Bay, get some lunch and maybe a little tattooed waitress from one of those coffee shops, then drive up that night: or head up there directly and cruise for college-girl hikers, up to commune with the redwoods. He'd give them a trunk to hug, you betcha. It wasn't a sure thing but then neither was the waitress: however much they flirted for tips, in his experience, all they wanted at the end of their shift was to get off their feet and that didn't necessarily mean on to their backs. He drove towards the 707, a mile to the turn-off, keeping to the slow lane while he tried to decide.

A third choice came back to him from the plane. Digging through his pockets for a stick of gum to keep his ears open during descent, he'd come across Mistress Dion's card, grown frayed and grey in his pocket since they'd bust in on her business. At the time he'd enjoyed a brief, dawn-horny reverie there in his plane seat of doing to some girl what she'd done to old Moss, but now it returned to him as a serious option. Why not? He could head back to the city, be down on Geary Street by two, ten twenties in his billfold, leave the rest in the dash. Two hundred ought to buy him enough weird shit for a taster. One problem with being a soldier, the world changed on you while you were working and usually in a way you wanted a piece of when you got back, as the guys in 'Nam had found out. There were all kinds of sex going down out there, he knew: two or three of the women he'd had since coming out had promised to take him to clubs some time, but he had never quite managed to call them again. That had had more to do with the women than the idea, but in retrospect he wished he had picked up the phone. To think that all kinds of guys were doing stuff that he wasn't, guys any woman would choose second to him, made him feel like he wasn't trying. He was coming to it a little late in the game but that just meant he needed to make up lost time.

But two hours later and still blocks from the Pyramid, his brain took over again. The traffic on top of the night flight had given him a five-bell headache and he'd been so preoccupied looking for rat-runs out of it that he'd barely been scoping for a tail. Now the queued lanes behind him could've held a dozen pairs of eyes fixed on his Cherry for all he knew. Where was he gonna find a hooker who'd let him tie her to her cot and do her with a snub in his hand? Hooker, crap. They never let you do as much as regular women did anyway. He didn't know what he was doing, thinking of hookers at all. It was Decker's influence, messing with his mind. He swung a U at the next light and headed back the way he'd come, cursing himself for the wasted miles. He had a week away from the guy, he ought to make the most of it, start living like himself again. He came up to another light, thought, Screw it, and jumped it just for the kick. There: Decker would never've done that for no reason, he thought. It felt good. He sat up over the wheel as he cut in front of a PG&E truck, pushing the pedal, looking for competition before he ran out of city.

Decker was about to pull into the space eight cars from the Star & Frost window when a Filipina woman in a Honda full of kids appeared from nowhere and looked hopefully over her dash at him. He waved her in, backed up and cruised on, seeing the last free slot towards the far end of the lot. He was making a responsible speed towards it, looking out for stray toddlers or cats, when some Dodgers-capped tube-sock of a guy in a Ford Probe arrowed into it out of nowhere, laying rubber on the asphalt as he took the ground.

Decker pulled up as he was getting out, wound down his window to remonstrate; and the asshole flipped him off, standing square in the sunlight there, waiting to see what this cardiac candidate in his pussy Merc planned to do about it. Decker was out of the car before he knew it, about to kick the jerk's ass into the middle of next month, make him cry like a woman and scream like a man, when the fatneck said, 'Yeah? You want a piece?', and brought him back down with a bump.

What the hell was he playing at? He was on stakeout, for chrissake, and he'd been about to give some no-account loser the *antipasti*, *primi* and *secondi*, with maybe a couple shots of espresso for the road, in clear and present view of the target premises. Decker held out a palm and turned it sharply down, the old West African screw-you that had travelled the world over, and got back into the driver's seat, armpits pricking as the jerk's jeering laughter rang in his ears. Exiting the lot, he joined traffic for twenty yards, then turned in next door, a chiropractor/dentist/Subway/copy shop lot that had four spaces free. He took one on the Star & Frost side, cut the engine and released his safety belt.

Her Beetle was eight vehicles and one median strip away from him. The sudden sweat was freezing on his skin in the air-con, and his underwear was bunched up around his ass. He tugged at it furiously, ripping something in his pants, and they were good fucking pants, his comfortable pair: he gripped the wheel hard enough to make the tendons on his neck stand out like rods. For the space of ten seconds he was through with this shit, absolutely, positively and for here and ever after, fuck it all. Fuck them all. If a single fucking one of them shitheads out there appreciated even for a single fucking second what they had, and at what fucking price, he'd gladly do it for ever, John D. Decker, half dead and half alive, on the fucking rack, world without end: no life, no love, no children, no friends.

But did they? Not for a second. And even if they did, they wouldn't care; they'd say they deserved what they had and believe it, and that nothing was wrong with the world save for that affirmative action crap giving the good work to the wasters. Fuck 'em all. He could start with the shitter in the Probe, then drive over to Wal-Mart, watch them piling up the crap, stuff they didn't need, stuff they didn't even want, stuff they'd throw in the closet, then buy a bigger house for more closet space, more room to pile up more stupid fucking crap. Oh, yeah. He'd watch them for a second, take a good long fuckin' look, just to feed it, just to be sure. Then he'd start emptying magazines. He was no high-school fuck-up, he was code fucking four, the best in the business, could keep going for days, weeks, whenever, till they had to ground-zero the mall he'd holed up in and he'd welcome it. Because then they'd know – every last one of them would have to listen to the only language they understood – the story of his life, of his *pincha* fucking *vida* . . .

She came out. Lauren walked out the door of Star & Frost, locked it behind her and walked along to the coffee shop, swinging her purse. He watched miserably. She was young and alive and so full of successful genes she almost left a trial of them on the concrete behind her. And he had to fuck her over, arrive in her life, something she never asked for, deliver a situation she might never bounce back from. And in the meantime he'd just sent Olsen off to probable death: one fulla-come young piss-streak against maybe a dozen night-fighting bile-feeders if he was lucky; against one mean mother-fucking hitman from hell if he wasn't. And that was just if things worked out for Decker: chances were he'd signed his own death warrant too by sending away his backup, his extra pair of eyes, putting himself back where he was when the Postman died – or when he found out about it – isolated, alone and running for his life. The guy from the Probe was in the coffee shop too now, there at the counter with his shit-eating grin, saying something to Lauren Reese while she waited for her sandwich: *Fine-lookin' lady like you oughta eat more fer lunch 'n that, gotta give that sweet chassis ya got there sump'n to run on, yuck yuck yuck*; and she was laughing too, saying something back.

It was a mind-fuck, that was all, and the Contender was playing him for it. Decker had to hand it to the guy: he knew the life. The life wasn't blazing backdrops, Grand Guignol or a Beretta holstered under a tux: it was running, it was hiding, it was filling your pockets with burger-joint ketchup packets to make soup. A soldier's war wasn't elegant excision or blockbuster bombastics, it was lice and diarrhoea, boredom and deprivation, a life lived down in the dirt. The very banality of a suburban security set-up made it a fitting snare to catch a soldier, if that was what it was.

But there was the kicker. Announcing his presence, then holding back so completely, was masterly if it wasn't an accident. For all Decker knew, the Contender was dead, one of his own past jobs caught up with him while his attention was focused on Decker. For all he knew, there was no other code four: no guy just like Decker whom they played off against him, keeping them apart so one could never lead an enemy to the other. Which was what he'd been told from the start: maybe it was bullshit. Yeah, and maybe the Contender hadn't planted that in his head. And maybe he hadn't and maybe he had and maybe and maybe and maybe.

The one thing he could be sure of was that he was sick of it now, gut-shot sick. Ropes of colon spilling on the sidewalk while he tried to gather them up sick. If the Contender was him, he would never have done it this way. He tried to avoid unnecessary cruelty – but was this unnecessary? If he, Decker, was taking on a US code four, wouldn't he try to level the field by wearing him down? He hadn't discussed that with Olsen: it was hard enough articulating to a sceptical young man what'd become like drawing breath to Decker, putting what had come to seem instinctive and natural to him into words, and seeing the words stand alone, casting shadows, like desert monoliths whose exact purpose has been forgotten and can only be speculated upon. Was this his world any more? Was he a soldier still, or was it slipping? No one went on for ever, not in the old world, not with the old certainties. If this had happened ten years before . . .

He watched her with the guy in the coffee shop, the guy's grin getting wider, nastier, as she spoke, her back to him, the brown bag in her hand now. Decker watched her, feeling out of his league. And then she came out of the coffee shop, turned to exchange one last pleasantry with the Probe guy and Decker saw her smiling mouth form the words, enunciating them slowly so she wouldn't be misunderstood: 'Kiss my ass, you cheap cocksucker.' There was no doubt about it, no window in the way this time. The Probe guy snarled, then turned to take it out on the girl making sandwiches. Decker watched Lauren safely back to her office, then got out, stretched his shoulders in the sunshine. It was a beautiful day, and he had work to do.

It was a grey afternoon, and Olsen owed himself a couple hours off. Plainly there wasn't much to Garvil, dark or light, and he figured that even if he didn't get out of bed until noon the next day he could have the measure of the place before lunch: a one-strip town, bars, gift shops and rest stops stretched along five minutes of US 101 for the convenience of tourists heading up to gawp at the redwoods.

Though a few of them had plainly stopped a little longer this week: a banner hung over the main street read GARVIL FALL COLORS REGGAE FEST: HAVE A LEAF-BURNIN' FALL, FOLKS! Endorsed by the Chamber of Commerce, if you could credit it. There were covered stages set up in parking lots, red, gold and green posters: the whole town seemed to be shut down so tourists could smoke weed and buy earthenware bongs. Decker had told him this was the center of the Emerald Triangle but he hadn't imagined they'd be so brazen about it. What the country was coming to, jesus.

Rows of shining Harleys stood outside the bars as he cruised the main street, banker bikers in tailored leathers strolling around admiring each other's custom paint jobs. Olsen despised them but he was glad to see them. One thing he'd learned his last civilian summer, frying tempura in Colorado resorts: where there were guys with money for leisure-type stuff there were women too; high-maintenance women, but the kind didn't mind getting it from a frycook once in a while nonetheless. What the frycook had over the guys in four-hundred-dollar sweaters was that he actually liked to fuck, and women went for that. Most guys didn't like to fuck, and women knew it as well as Olsen did. Guys don't mind getting a blow job from time to time but mostly they like to get shitfaced. Olsen had listened, watched and learned. If you wanted a woman, you stayed the sober side of pie-eyed and when you were the last guy standing, you were the guy who got laid. If the trick here was dope, not booze, it didn't matter to him. Just needed to kill a few hours, get the lie of the land, see where the women were. He parked on the main street, entered the nearest bar and ordered a lite beer at the counter.

He saw her before it was half drained. Honey-brown hair, high cheekbones, mouth built for a BJ; playing pool the other side of a wall of sweet smoke with a couple inbreeds. Wrong side of thirty but nobody was counting this festival afternoon.

He gave her the eye a couple times and before his beer was done she was zeroing in.

'You're not stoned,' she said, sliding on to the stool next to him.

'How can you tell?'

'You were, you'd be grinning at me,' she said. 'That Dutch-cheese number.' She demonstrated and in return he gave her the teeth, all-American but not full of himself.

'That's much better,' she said, returning it. 'What've you got to smile about?'

He tilted his head, cocked an eyebrow that meant *you, maybe.*

'Lemme see,' she said, ignoring it. 'Clean-cut young guy, nice clothes, haircut. Up for the fall colours?

'You got me.'

'You gay?'

'No, ma'am. Just takin' time out from the ratrace.'

'How are those rats?'

'You know them?'

'Used to,' she said, and took a swig from her beer, leaving froth. 'You gonna buy me another of these?'

'Whatcha got there?

'Hemp beer. Try one,' she said. 'It's not so different from regular save for the leaf on the label. Max.' She caught the barkeep's attention and held up two fingers. Olsen put a ten on the bar, picked up the beer when it came and left the change.

'Not bad,' he said, swallowing. 'It doesn't . . . ?'

She licked froth from her lip. 'But the tourists like it.'

'Tourists like a lot of things.'

'You're not a tourist?'

'I like to travel.'

'But where'd you like to wind up?'

He held eye contact, letting the smile play around his lips till she broke it.

'Pick up your change,' she said, tossing a ten on the bar. 'Unless you came in here for the beer?'

She didn't expect an answer and she didn't get one.

'Twenty-five hundred, best I can do,' the guy at Vee-Dubs said, sucking his teeth as he ran his eyes over Lauren's Beetle one more time. Decker knew he could get more – the points and plugs he'd found under that ass-backwards hood were new, and the ports polished off to a high gloss – but he knew the guy knew it was stolen. Besides, he didn't have time: he had to get back to Star & Frost before Lauren came out for lunch. He slid a deck of currency from the calfskin wallet in his hip pocket, collected the keys to the green '72 California coupe and drove it straight out of the showroom, unnerved at first by the deafening VW growl from behind the back seat but getting used to it and the chunky transmission as he skirted the business district.

He switched cars in the lot next to Star & Frost at quarter of twelve but getting into the Merc he saw that over the way the blinds were down. When he dialled the number stencilled on the window, it rang, agonizingly, five times and he was turning the key in the ignition already, trying to think which precinct she'd most likely have gone to, when she said:

'Star & Frost, Security and Surveillance?'

He snapped the phone shut and exhaled. Close call. He'd meant to steal her car much earlier in the morning but the lot had been half empty till well after ten. It'd looked like he'd be waiting till after lunch and he was inclined to chance it, given that her car would take all of five seconds to bust into and wire and she'd parked right by the door the previous day and might do so again. But then a nice big laundry truck had pulled in next to her Bug, between the car and the window, and while the driver was getting his coffee-and-two he'd boosted the

Beetle and been in traffic before the laundry guy's sprinkles hit the frosting.

Now all he had to do was wait for her to notice it was gone. There was every reason she wouldn't when she went along to the coffee shop to buy lunch, but it turned out Decker's luck was in. When she was past the laundry truck, she glanced back and saw the empty slot where her Beetle had been; took two more paces and did a double take. He felt bad when her face crumpled – shock usually came before sorrow – and he saw how much she'd loved that car. He hated to see a face like hers sliding in sorrow, but it was good that she was broken up: made it easier for him to do what he had to do. This was what he told himself as she went back inside, only emerging thirteen minutes later when her cab arrived.

He thought she'd go straight to the police station but the cab took her home first, idling outside while she went in. She came out with what he guessed were her documents in a buff envelope, and then the cab took her to the cops. He parked two blocks away from the tow zones, gave her a good ten minutes to negotiate the foothills of auto-theft registration, then strolled in himself. Sure enough, he found her at the appropriate desk having the appropriate argument with the guy. He stepped up next to her, waited politely and didn't begin reporting the disappearance of a late-model powder-blue Merc until the uniformed drink of water behind the desk gave her the clipboard of forms to fill in. Decker put up with the desk cop's attitude long enough to get his own clipboard. She was still halfway down her second form when he began to write, filling out the first few lines but feigning puzzlement at the fifth box.

'Previous owner,' he murmured, tapping the chained ballpoint on the paper.

'You just put "Unknown",' she said, not looking up.

He glanced at her close up for the first time, telling himself, You're a guy who just lost his car, don't overdo it.

'Thank you,' he said.

'Uh-huh,' she muttered, and didn't look up from her writing till she was done. He felt her eyes on him momentarily, but then she was leaning over the desk, looking for the guy who'd given them the forms. He'd slunk off in the back somewhere.

'Shop,' she called. When it got no response, she pressed the buzzer set into the counter, then pressed it again, loud and long. After a full minute the desk monkey reappeared with a cup of coffee in his hand, set it down on the counter and commenced shaking out a Sweet 'n' Low while he studied a fax that was feeding out of a grubby Canon to their left.

'I'm done here,' she said, pushing the forms towards him.

'Just a moment,' he grunted, reading the fax as it ground through.

'Is that it?' she said. 'Do I go now?'

'I said I'd be with you in a moment, ma'am,' said the cop, taking a swig of his coffee as he waited for the fax to sever itself.

Decker skipped the last two boxes and signed the bottom of his form with a flourish. The cop picked up the fax and tossed it underneath the counter. Then he picked up Decker's clipboard and began to read.

'The lady was first,' Decker said. The cop looked up.

'Excuse me?'

'I said, the lady was here before me. Perhaps you'd like to deal with her complaint first.'

'Perhaps you'd *like* to let me do my job here,' the cop muttered long-sufferingly, used to this sort of thing.

'Perhaps you'd like to do it,' Decker agreed. He was very aware of Lauren looking at him.

'Listen, buddy,' began the cop, a goateed little asshole who looked like he wanted to be a wife-swapper when he grew up.

'You got any idea how many complaints come through this desk a day?'

'Do you know, I don't care?' said Decker. 'You should treat every single complaint as if it was your first.'

The cop narrowed his eyes. 'You want to do my job?'

'Do you want to for much longer?' Decker said and pulled a black leather wallet from his breast pocket, showing him the badge inside. The cop looked at it, looked up.

'I apologize, sir,' he said, and began running a pen down the columns of Decker's form smartly.

Decker turned to Lauren with an apologetic smile, relieved her of her clipboard and banged it down over his own.

'I said the lady was first,' he barked. 'And if we're done here, which I think we are, you might like to tell her that she's free to leave and will be contacted if there are any developments.'

The cop turned to Lauren, flushing red. 'I apologize, ma'am,' he said. 'You're free to leave. The department will contact you if there are any developments.'

'No kidding,' said Lauren dryly, and Decker smiled at her as she shouldered the strap of her purse. Then he turned back to the desk clerk.

He found her waiting for a cab in the lobby, as he'd hoped. As he walked towards the payphone, she caught his eye.

'You didn't have to do that in there,' she said, and for a moment he thought he'd blown it: should've let her have the option to deal with it her own way. But she was looking at him like she wanted him to say something.

'*I* apologize,' he said. 'I didn't mean to jump in with both feet.'

'You're a cop?' she asked, a little playful, looking him up and down.

'Was,' he said. 'Some days I miss it, some days I run into guys like Mr Charisma in there and thank the Lord I'm out.' Too much, damn. He backpedalled. 'People have lost their

147

automobiles here, they've had enough inconvenience without getting attitude. Reporting this kind of incident is the most contact that ordinary people have with cops: it's important that they're dealt with courteously and efficiently. They read enough bad things about us as it is. Guys like him let us all down.'

'Us?' she said, still that playful fender to her voice. 'Thought you quit.'

'You sound like my wife,' Decker said, and saw her glance to his bare ring finger. He let it hang in the air for a couple of beats. 'Excuse me,' he said. 'I better call a cab.'

'Where you headed?'

'Van Nuys.'

'No kidding,' she said. 'Want to split one? It's already ordered.'

'You're very kind.'

'So were you,' she said. 'Besides, we're in the same boat here.'

He accepted, thanked her, and they stood in silence a moment, staring out the glass doors at the bleached white concrete outside.

'So what did you lose?' she said, to break the silence.

'Old man's folly,' he said. 'Powder-blue Merc, two thousand on the clock.'

'Ouch.'

'Insurance'll pay,' he said. 'How about you?'

'Young woman's folly,' she said. 'I've been restoring the first car I ever owned.'

'Bigger ouch,' he said. 'I'm sorry. I guess that's something you can't replace.'

'I was hoping you'd say vintage cars have a better recovery rate.'

He made a sympathetic gesture. 'You never know.'

She took that on the chin, glanced out to the street. 'You

148

never do. I was burglarized once, had to go to a recovered-goods warehouse to reclaim my mountain bike.'

'Aladdin's cave,' he said, glad to change the subject.

'Had some great stuff,' she said, looking at him like she was checking if she could kid him. 'I ever get married, I'm gonna have my wedding list there. Those druglords have some neat stuff.'

Decker chuckled warmly, then looked pointedly over her shoulder. 'This us?' he said, indicating the cab that had just pulled up.

'I guess,' she said.

She gave the driver Star & Frost's address and he added six blocks with his own instruction as he opened the door for her, glad to get out of there. Pulling a fake badge on a cop was never the best idea, and as the cab drew away he thanked god that the LAPD appeared to have run an Affirmative Action for Assholes programme at some point in the last few years.

'So tell me,' she said, turning in the seat next to him. 'You gonna let me have a look at that badge? I never saw one.'

'Glad to hear it,' he said, keeping it easy as he reached inside his suit coat for the fake ID.

Olsen had the usual story ready to trot out over the token coffee – hippie parents, commune, serial abuse, bootstraps, high school, software sales – but she didn't seem to need it. It wasn't yet six when they reached her apartment but she was ready to go. After she came for the sixth time and lit a cigarette, she looked at him like it was time he got back to the bar, but he'd shot twice and wasn't going anywhere for a while. He felt like telling her that if she wanted to smoke she could take it outside, but instead he closed his eyes and rolled over while she finished her cigarette. There was a tense moment after she stubbed it when he thought she was going to try and wake him up, but after a moment she left him alone in the bedroom, and he heard the fall premiers come on the lounge TV.

He tried to nap but it didn't happen; it was too early for him. After a while he turned over on his back, irritated with himself for having moved too early. Normally it wasn't a problem; you got them in the sack around midnight, slept a few hours after and got out while they were still asleep. But if he got up now he'd have to go in there and talk to her, even though he was hungry. They got touchy about you rooting around in their refrigerators, he found, liked to make you wait to be offered food, which meant talking first. But if he stayed in here she'd want him out when she was ready to sleep herself.

He weighed it up, staring at the ceiling. Nice room; she'd spent some money on it, even if it wasn't to his taste – ethnicky doodads scattered on the bare floor, muslin drapes hung from the ceiling over the bed, some kind of tapestry on one wall with itty-bitty mirrors sewn into it. It looked bad: kind of woman who'd be full of herself, which was fine in the sack and on the way there too, but afterwards was just a pain. If a woman was a mess – and frankly, any woman who'd fuck a guy ten minutes after meeting him had some pages stuck together in Olsen's experience – then he'd sooner she didn't try to cover it up with this empowered BS, make a guy take a bunch of attitude when all he was interested in was the door. He should've taken her to a motel, he rebuked himself, as he wearily swung his legs out of bed, found his pants puddled on the floor and checked that his wallet was still in the pocket.

When he was dressed, he hesitated inside the door. She'd barely said a word before the fucking, which meant he was probably going to get an earful now. Even the nastiest of them wanted to talk after, try and dress it up into something it wasn't once it was done. He tried to think of an excuse for leaving abruptly that'd tally with the story he'd given her

150

earlier, but the best he could come up with was that he needed to get to his motel before the desk closed at ten. He thought of Decker, wondering if the man was enjoying his first night alone in two months: Olsen would bet fifty that at this precise moment, he'd still be trying to kid himself he wasn't going to get a hooker and a hundred that he'd pick up the phone by eleven. That was unless he was watching that Lauren bitch undress through night-vision glasses. Now there was one who'd want to give you an earful, he thought as he pasted a boyish grin across his features and pushed open the door to the den.

It didn't take long for Decker to get her to a bar – two strangers joined by misfortune, the cocktail hour upon them – but he'd been out of the game too long to know whether her ready acceptance of his suggestion was normal now or not. Last time he'd had much call to ask women for drinks it hadn't been any big deal, but that was in the seventies; now he wasn't even sure if women drank on dates. In movies lately, he'd noticed that they ordered drinks but didn't touch them; he guessed that was what it was all about now, showing that you could even if you didn't want to.

But Lauren wanted hers. The lone waitress in the Lazy-A Lounge and Grill had barely set the drinks down when Lauren was lifting her sidecar and toasting Decker across the banquette table.

'To crime,' she said. 'And making the bastards pay.'

'Amen to that,' said Decker, still playing the ex-cop, clinking the neck of his Miller's Draft against the rim of her proffered glass. She smiled and took a sip, smacked her lips with satisfaction.

'Good,' she said, surprised, looking around with new eyes. 'I never came in here before. You think the food's okay too?'

Decker glanced around at the worn scarlet velvet, the

sprung-seated banquettes. 'These joints,' he said, 'you get lucky with what you order, best quit while you're ahead.'

'I guess you prefer cop bars,' she said, sipping again. 'What's that place, O'Tooley's, downtown?'

'Once in a while,' Decker said, trying to keep it easy, not look at her too obviously. 'Though I was never LAPD. Chicago's finest, eighteen years on the north side.'

'Long time,' she said, and he saw her do the arithmetic, find at least ten missing years. 'What brought you west?'

'My wife,' he said, but lightly. 'Two decades of Chicago winter was a lot to ask a California girl to bear. She did, and she didn't complain, not once. But she always talked about moving back one day. So when the time came, we did. To Diego,' he added, wondering if he'd dropped the wife in too early.

'So you're up here for business or pleasure?' It was hard for Decker to tell if the flirtiness was still in her voice.

'I live here now,' he said. 'My wife passed two years ago. Diego's nice, but –' he shrugged – 'you know. You work a big city half your life, you miss it.'

'Is that all you miss?' She watched him over the rim of her glass as she sipped. 'My job, I meet a lot of LAPD guys like to stay in the game. They say if you've been a cop, you never really retire.'

'This one did,' he said, trying to find a way to lighten this up. 'But if I'm being honest, a shell through my shoulder here did most of the deciding for me.'

'I'm sorry,' she said.

'It's no problem,' he said, thinking, You're talking like some lonely old loser in a bar. 'Stiffens in the cold a little, but that was another reason to move here. How about you? You move here too?' It was a lame link and it hung there. But,

'Does it show that badly?' she said, like she was trying to help him pull the mood back. 'I was raised in Washington State, little logging town. Nowhere you'd know 'less you lived there. Too cold for me.' She gave a little shiver to illustrate, and Decker was reminded of the two blind dates he'd been on, years ago but the memory still clear: how hard you both try to break through the awkwardness, to find a level that feels natural. He was grateful to her for a moment, as he'd been to his dates decades before; then had to remind himself that this was work, that he was working, and that she was a woman from now, not twenty years ago.

'Was this the first city you moved to?' he said.

'I did my diploma in Seattle,' she said. 'Worked as a PA at Bechtol there for three years, my first job.'

'Didn't want to get too tan too soon, huh?' Lame again, but her expression made him remember how it was the warmth, not the words, that women seemed to listen for.

'Had to work up to it,' she agreed, smiling with her eyes. 'So. Two coldbloods moved to the hothouse. You think you'll ever go back?'

'To Chi?' he said. 'I don't think so. I have my life here now.'

'You don't have family back there?' Meaning kids.

'My wife had an early hysterectomy,' he said, wishing he'd thought of something better; he hadn't considered what a downer his cover story would seem to a stranger. She was looking concerned now, too. 'Listen,' he said, 'I apologize. It's a long time since I talked to a girl in a bar, and I guess most guys my age, there's a little more downside to tell than there was twenty years ago. I promise that's the last depressing thing I have to say.'

'Listen to him,' she said easily. 'It's a long time since I talked to a guy in a bar too. And if you were depressing me, I wouldn't be ordering another drink. You'll have one?'

'Sure,' he said, surprised and grateful at once as he watched her turn and raise her glass towards the waitress. Maybe women hadn't changed so much after all, he thought.

*   *   *

Just once, thought Olsen as he drained the rice, if they could be different just once. But they never were. Either you got out the door fast and they yelled stuff down the hall after you, or you tried to be nice about it, in which case they made you pay. Made you pretend you were their fucking boyfriend, some regular guy who liked to sit down and eat with them instead of some stranger who just popped over their chest ten minutes before.

'Could you bring a little cayenne through too?' she called from the other room. 'On the rack, left of the stove?'

'You got it,' he called back, pulling a sour face at her prim little spice rack. What the christ was he doing? Jesus, barely eight o'clock yet. He ought to be out there, settling in for the night, counting his options. He dumped the rice in a bowl and forced a dumb-ass smile as he pushed through the rough hemp divider.

They ate in near silence. Her apartment was above a taxidermist on the main drag, up brown-carpeted stairs through a side door. It had high ceilings, house plants, small rooms leading into each other. Kitchen to lounge to bedroom, windows cracked to admit the evening breeze. Her yard-sale furniture had throws, crocheted patterns in dull colours, things that didn't match, but if she'd ever noticed she didn't seem to now. She was forty the summer before, she said between forkfuls of brown-rice tuna salad, showed him a photograph of her on a balloon-ride. There weren't any pictures of her ex, or if there were they weren't out. There were things from vacations on the bookshelves – corn dollies, carved elephants – placed on the strip of wood between the ranked spines and the edge, too many to take a book out without moving them.

'Are they to keep the books in?' he asked her, trying to make conversation as they ate. She didn't say anything, just looked back at him as she tore off a chunk of bread, something impish in her eyes as she broke off a corner and popped it on her pink tongue. He looked down to his plate.

'I sure do thank you,' he said when they were done. 'It sure was good.'

She let her blond hair fall in her eyes as she unbuttoned her shirt and took it off, looking insolently at him all the time; unclasped her bra, showing him the welts it left on her shoulders. She reached behind her, took a japanned box from the dresser and set it on the table between them.

'You got any room left for dessert?' she asked.

'We ought to eat something,' Decker said, and she nodded, suddenly serious. Two drinks before she'd said, 'One more of these and I'll switch,' but she hadn't yet. The hum of voices, the fizzy smell of wet beer on polished wood, drifted over from the bar.

'I didn't mean to drink that much,' she said. 'You prolly think I'm some kind of a lush.'

'Two's my usual limit,' Decker said, lifting his fourth beer. He wasn't used to it, was breaking a cardinal rule of his here. 'But it's not every day you lose your car.' Or meet a woman like you, he was about to add, but she cut in.

'Like losing a part of you,' she said vaguely, looking away again. 'These last two years I put more work into my Bug than I did into myself.'

Decker heard it through the rapidly tightening beer muffs and fell on it. 'Bug?' he said, leaning in. 'Like a VW Bug? A Beetle?'

'Yeah,' she said dejectedly, face down, twisting her glass by the stem. 'Some lucky sonbitch'll be buying a '74 California tonight. If they didn't already.'

'Helen drove one,' Decker said, as though it'd come out before he could stop it. It worked; she looked up.

'Your wife?'

155

He nodded, picturing Isabella Rossellini to get the right expression on his face.

'She told me to find someone who'd love it like she did,' he said, with a hint in his tone of *mea culpa*. 'But I never had the heart to sell it. Been garaged these last three years down in Torrance. I keep meaning to advertise but . . . you know how it is.'

She looked down at the table, twisting her glass again. 'I don't mean to sound pushy,' she said, looking up shyly. 'But I got to know my way around a Bug pretty well these last couple of years. If she's – I mean, your wife's car – if it's been garaged . . .'

'I'd like that,' he said.

'I'd love it,' she said, and held eye contact, lips parted; he saw what it would be like to kiss her. He had to get out of this fast.

'But we both had a long day,' he said. 'And, no offence –' she dipped her head to show none was taken – 'but we're old enough to know that evenings which start in a bar before five don't always end so well. Tomorrow . . .'

'Is another day,' she finished. 'You're right.'

'I could drive it to meet you some place,' he said, before the mood went. 'She runs pretty good.'

'I could come to you,' she said. 'I mean, if that's . . .'

'I'd like that,' he said, the sincerity coming unbidden.

'Then let's finish up here,' she said, nodding as if to confirm the decision to herself. 'You think that cab of ours is still waiting?'

'We don't have cabs here,' she said, looking over the joint at him as she licked the paper.

'Just, I ought to get to my motel,' Olsen said, 'check in.'

'Where you at?'

'The Red Roof,' he said, eyeing the reefer. Had to be a Red Roof around here somewhere.

'In *Willits*?'

'Yeah, Willits,' he said, remembering passing through another one-strip town an hour or so before Garvil. 'I only came up to, y'know, see what was going down. With the festival. Used to listen to a lot of reggae in college.'

'Won't get back to Willits tonight,' she said, ''less you drive. And I don't want to sour you on my town but the CHiPs keep a keen eye for drunk drivers during the fest.' She passed the tip of the joint between her bee-sting lips, looking at him, pushed it all the way in and pulled it back out.

'I'm not drunk,' he said.

'You're not,' she said approvingly and lit the reefer. 'Because you knew there was something better to come.'

He looked at her through the sudden wreaths of gray between them. 'I'm not much of a smoker,' he said. He'd barely seen it since he'd left home. Some guys had used pot on maneuvers, ratty-ass homegrown to pass the time, and if he hadn't wanted to get a rep he would've turned them in for it.

'Try it,' she said, flipping the joint over in the clip so that the roach was towards him.

'That's okay.'

'Local specialty.' Her arm stayed extended. 'You never had anything like this before.'

Ordinarily he would've thrown back 'I never had anything like you before' and changed the subject with his hand where it shouldn't be. He didn't drink, didn't smoke. But damn, he was away from Decker for a night, away from the heat. And frankly he'd fucked all he could for one day: if she sucked him one more time this side of sleep he'd be coming blood, if anything. He saw himself drifting off in front of the porn channel in a motel somewhere, but his natural instinct to escape was countered by the weight of food in his belly now. She was still holding the reefer out towards him; one more

157

second and it'd be awkward, would force a decision. What the hell, he thought, and took it.

Two hours later he was up on his arms above her, all thoughts of what he was doing there forgotten, staring down in disbelief as she bucked against him, busying her hand between them as he pounded into her. He was there all right but somewhere else too, fishhooks of itching delight snagged deep in his flesh inside her, snagged all over his body, never felt anything even close to this before, fighting for breath, arching his back, dragging the last reserves from his muscles, anything to keep going. The fishhooks bit, the lines tugging taut behind them, lifting him up and pulling him down till roaring, pounding, slamming, he came inside her again; and again kept going, pushing her up over the crest of her orgasm again and taking her there, spilling her over and dumping her down like a wave till she cried enough and he fell back, rolled over, her sweat on him and his on her. He turned his head and she was gazing at him with that faraway-too-close look and he almost told her he never had anything like that before; but instead he reached for the roach clip from the nightstand ashtray, lit it and sucked it down before she got to it first.

Next morning Decker was up at five, in a cab to Star & Frost by half past, back at the apartment with the part-exchanged Beetle by six ten. He parked it in the street and looked it over, wondering how to make a car that'd just come from a used showroom look as though it'd been garaged three years. He couldn't think how but got a better idea instead, went back up to the apartment for some black coffee to spot the gray carpet with. When he was done he got on the web, found nine realtors serving the area he'd said he lived in, called and left his current cellphone number with four of them. He doubted if even the hungriest of them would be picking up their messages much before seven thirty so he called another cab and went to pick up the Merc before Lauren got to work and maybe saw the powder-blue late-model sitting across from her office. Three realtors called him on the way, and he made appointments to view for later that morning with the two who had vacant possession. The traffic was thick now and the round trip took double what it had ninety minutes before.

Back at the apartment, pushing nine, he barely had time to crap before he was back out in the Merc, keeping the date with the first realtor. The place, a condo, wasn't right: a neighbourly neighbour said hi and smiled as they went in; she might say hi and smile to Lauren too, Decker figured, if she ever came there; might let it slip that the place had only been rented the last couple of days. The second, forty minutes later and eight blocks away, was better: a top-floor walk-up, own stairs and entrance, raw brick walls, basic furniture and appliances that he could add to. He paid the bond and first two months' cash, bull-headed the realtor into taking up references later ('I'm giving you my money and trusting my possessions to this place – with respect, ma'am, shouldn't I be taking references from you?'); he got the keys there and then, cranked up the air-conditioner to lose that stale smell, and drove straight to the neighbourhood Safeway for groceries, the K-mart for house-plants, picture frames and linen. As he scooted round with his cart, he thought about taking the blue line out to Acres of Books at Long Beach, but figured he'd break his back trying to hump the quantity he needed; he couldn't just go to the nearest Borders because the damn things had to look used, and to get out to Long Beach'd take him most of what was left of the day to drive. Queuing to pay, the best he could think of was the paperback place on Wilshire; wouldn't have the art books he needed but those were the ones that could look new. He filled the Merc's trunk, sweating hard already, and headed out of the Valley on the 405 towards Santa Monica.

He didn't catch his breath until after three, when the plants were in place, the books on the shelves, a snapshot of him and his last girl at a fairground in 1979 framed on the bedside table. He'd picked up an old camera and some developing trays four doors along from the bookstore, to make it look like he had a hobby, a life: he remembered clothes, he'd have to bring some over, shoes too. He didn't have much of a wardrobe, had never been a clothes horse, and there wasn't time to go and become one now. He took a good look around, then swept the apartment for anything she might conceivably come upon that would give him away: empty drawers, broken fixtures he didn't know about. Only then did he sit down, get the feel of the unbelievably uncomfortable couch – he made a note to tell her he'd bought it deliberately, to stop himself turning into a potato – and kick his shoes off for a couple of minutes. It wasn't the first time he'd had to assemble a life with a few hours' notice, and he didn't think he'd done badly. He would've preferred a less elaborate cover story, but it hung okay with what he'd been able to put together: ex-cop, widower, living on pension and life insurance while he got his head together for being alone, reading books, thinking about maybe improving on his high-school certificate but not sure he was ready yet. The widower part, that was the only smart thing: would excuse the short-term feel to the apartment when she came here later. She'd just think, new start, he must've thrown everything out and started again after his wife died. She already knew he was weird about it: she'd picked up on something in his tone as he gave her the story, asked, 'Why don't you like talking about yourself?' He'd said that this was the first time he'd talked about himself to a woman since he met his wife, and then had to spend the next half-hour reassuring her that he was surprising himself, how easy it was to do with her.

Lying to women was harder work than it was worth, he decided, opening a can of tomato soup, spilling some on to the stove and burning it on. Guys who do it routinely must enjoy the anxiety. Maybe he should've at least thought about giving this part to Olsen: a younger man didn't have to come up with so much back story, so much complication. Lauren's résumé, even with prompts and questions, had taken ninety seconds to his six minutes: took a PA course after high school, three years in Seattle, four years here, nine months of them at Star & Frost. Her work was a means to an end for her, nothing more, she'd said; it came with the territory for PAs, they were hired guns, brought in when needed and then let go, blamed for everything that went wrong in the meantime because they were new. She'd taken the Star & Frost job to get out of temping and all the crap that came with it, but she wasn't interested in the work the firm did at all. She said PAs rarely were: day-to-day it was pretty much the same, didn't matter if you were working for the police or a pornographer.

She didn't seem to like talking about it – he guessed she was tired of trotting it out in singles bars – and had changed the subject. But he needed to get back on it tonight, maybe try to get back to her apartment rather than his. Which reminded him. He called her machine and left the address so she'd know where to come to, reading it off the back of the junk mail he'd found in the box, trying hard to sound the way he'd sounded the night before and not doing bad, given the day he'd had. He turned on the shower before he'd even hung up, unbuttoning his shirt with his free hand as he spoke, forcing his face into a smile though it was the last thing he felt like doing.

8

OLSEN KNEW HE SHOULD'VE got a shower at her apartment but he hadn't wanted to risk waking her. Instead he'd collected up his clothes, for the second or third time since he met her, and stumbled around in the pre-dawn gloom trying to get his sore limbs into the right holes. He'd damn near humped the muscles off his bones before they passed out; he figured she'd be feeling it too when she came round. Unbelievable. It wasn't just a case of the second time with her being better than the first; that was never true in any case. It was the weed they'd smoked. She'd called it Sensey and he thought that was a pretty good name; it'd dragged senses out of him he never knew he had, turned the rest up to double what he usually got. She was a good-looking woman and he'd always harboured a sneaking preference for older meat, though his pride usually made him pass them up if there was anything younger available for the same effort; but he'd had plenty like her and he knew for sure that this was something else, and that had to be the pot. He didn't pretend to understand it – weren't smokers the ones who never got any? Just sat around eating Cheet-os? – but he wasn't going to argue with it. He found the little lacquered box in the living room where she'd left it, and slipped a good pinch of the skunky green weed into his wallet to try later, see if he couldn't replicate the effect with a motel porn channel. Then he slipped out of the apartment, located his Cherry on the main drag and bought coffee and donuts from a convenience store four doors along from a burned-out T-shirt shop. There must've been a fire overnight, he figured as he passed it a second time, tracking across the wet sidewalk, catching the stench of oxidized compounds unknown to nature, floating out from the charred shell like bad breath from a derelict mouth; seems I wasn't the only thing smokin' last night he thought and smirked.

He didn't think anything more of it till he was halfway into his breakfast and he saw the CHP cruiser mooching down the main drag towards him. He took a swallow of coffee, watched it pull into a slot four down from him and then sit there: fat cop in a tight uniform slumped in his seat like a sucked cock, head turned Olsen's way as he spoke to his dispatcher on the shortwave. Olsen ate and drank, staring doggedly straight ahead, knowing he should just put the Jeep in gear, let the cop tail him to the town line then write him off as someone else's problem. He would've done it if he hadn't just had a woman but he had, and he was going to sit and enjoy his breakfast like anyone else. What he thought of – without humour – as the Miller time had left him with a taste for payback, for getting all the things a working man was entitled to. He turned in his seat, met the cop's gaze and held it as he brought the cup to his lips and drank.

Which seemed to tip the balance. The cop stared back, either chewing or talking into the receiver held up by his mouth, it was hard to tell; then hung it up, put on his aviators, got out. He took a moment to straighten his belt before waddling across the blacktop to draw himself up by the Jeep's window. Olsen wound it down.

'Help you?' he said.

'See your license, sir?'

163

Olsen dug out his wallet, flipped it open and held it out the window. The cop pulled a notebook from his hip pocket, jotted down the number, put it back. Olsen put away the wallet and looked expectantly up.

'This a rental?' the cop asked.

'Yes, sir.'

The aviators hid any reaction. 'You mind telling me where you've been this morning?'

'Just passing through,' he said, indicating the donut tray on the passenger seat. 'Stopped for breakfast.'

'Vacation?'

'Yes, sir. Up to see the redwoods.' Olsen smiled, easy; they liked to get you talking, small town like this, see if you were nervous about anything.

'Where'd you stay last night?'

There was no point trying the Red Roof on him. 'I drove up from Oakland, left around three this mornin' to beat that traffic. Is there a problem?'

The aviators shone his smile back at him.

'Step out of the vehicle, please.'

Olsen didn't move. 'Is there a problem, officer?'

'This vehicle was parked outside Shirelle's along the street here from five last night, I'd say that was a problem,' the cop said. 'You want to come along to the station, give me an account of your movements, or you want to do it here?'

Olsen tried his best to look contrite, put some man-to-man in his tone. 'I'd like to help, officer, but I can't.'

'And why would that be?'

'I was with my girlfriend.'

'Where?'

'I can't tell you.'

'Why is that?'

'She's married,' Olsen said, pleading a little, guy to guy, raising the centre of his brow. 'So am I.'

The cop looked away, used to this sort of thing. 'Would you step out of the car, please?'

He put him in the town tank's holding cage, took his belt and shoelaces away, bagging them along with the pinch of weed from his wallet. That hadn't been smart, Olsen could admit it, but such a pathetic amount had to be a misdemeanour, especially in a town that held reggae festivals, for chrissake. He sat it out, waiting to be charged so he could pay his fine and forget about it, but the cop – Sheriff Richard P. Monk, he gathered from the electoral posters stuck around the walls – seemed to like playing games.

Olsen wasn't worried yet, just irritated. He had no doubt he'd be out of there as soon as the cop tired of it, though he was aware this was going to make looking for Kentrelle a little awkward. He'd just have to switch assignments with Decker, that was all. But he knew he'd be on his way – would have to be – as soon as the hick badge out there made a couple of calls. The driver's licence, along with the name he'd volunteered, had been given him by Miller, and they were one thing that he knew his dead boss hadn't been jerking him around with: they identified a real guy with a real social-security number, real paid-up health insurance and IRS history, who lived in a real apartment in a real building that had real accounts with real utility companies, paid direct from a real bank account that Olsen made sure to drop a few hundred dollars into whenever he had it to spare. The first money he'd got from Decker, that'd been the first thing he'd done, or one of the first things, anyway. Decker himself had looked the license over, grunted and handed it back. The good sheriff didn't have enough to occupy him, that was all.

He was not run off his feet, that was certain. If Olsen scooched up against the far side of the cage he could see a slice of the front office through the door, see a glorified receptionist with a badge tapping away at a PC. The phone rang twice all morning. At one the girl from the desk came in with a waitress dressed in a pink diner uniform to bring him lunch – a tuna melt with plastic cutlery – and he took it without giving either a hard time. When she came back at three forty and said that Sheriff Monk was out on a call this afternoon, did he want to order dinner from the diner's menu or just go with the special, he tried to look like the bemused, fed-up guy he was.

He took the special, local venison in a chestnut sauce, wondering if this was preferential treatment or just the way things went in rural lock-ups. He'd recommend this place to Decker, he thought; the man liked eating at twelve and six like a hick too, he'd love it here. When he was done he drank the lukewarm coffee she'd brought, watched the clock tick to six fifteen and then pass it. Decker would be tearing his hair, he knew: Olsen'd been supposed to make a touch-base call on the clean Radio Shack cellphones Decker had bought expressly, but he'd been relieved of his when they slung him in here. The only option was to sit it out, find out what.

It was after seven and dark outside before he got the chance. Monk was wedged into a leather-back swivel chair behind an old desk that was clear save for a photo frame and a brown and cream switchboard telephone. Olsen didn't sit down. When Monk first brought him in he'd played the frightened college boy, the one who'd read a few too many stories about what backwoods cops did to longhairs; but now he figured he was on firmer ground, had a right to be pissed off after a day in the cells. Plus, this was the guy's office, not his interview room; that had to say something, Olsen figured.

'Sit down,' Monk said, looking a little more human without his aviators; but not in a good way, in Olsen's opinion.

'You gonna tell me what this is about, please?'

'Soon as you tell me where you were last night.'

'I believe you need a reason to keep me here.'

Monk shrugged. 'Tees and Vees burned down last night. This morning I find you sitting outside, telling stories about where you've been. I'd say that's reason enough.'

Olsen shook his head disgustedly. 'Some crappy T-shirt shop burns down at the end of the season and you need to look for the person who did it? Why don't you call the insurance company, get the name that was on the claim form they got first post this morning?'

'Why don't you tell me what you're doing here?'

'I spent the night with a married woman,' Olsen said. 'I'm married too. Why is this tough for you to understand?'

'I don't see a wedding band.'

'It's in my glovebox. I took it off while we fucked.'

'You had sex with the woman in your car?'

Olsen looked him in the eye. 'That is correct. Then in her apartment.'

'Is that what you came here for?'

'I'm on vacation, like I said.' Olsen sat down, ran a hand through his hair. 'It's like this. My . . . lady and me, we've had a few problems. I came up here to straighten my head out, give her a little space too. I didn't intend to meet someone else but . . . two lonely people. Lasted a few hours and didn't mean anything. Is that so strange?'

'You going to give me her name?'

'Do you understand why I'd prefer not to?'

'I can't say that I do.'

Olsen exhaled, brought his head down to rub his temples.

'Listen,' he said, looking up, talking straight. 'I'm not proud of what I did last night, but it happens. I'm not proud of having a little weed in my wallet either, and I'll gladly pay whatever fine you have around here. But you look as though you've been in enforcement long enough to understand that people do things all the time that they can't explain to a stranger.'

Monk shrugged. 'Can't say I haven't found that, no.'

'Then would you please tell me why you're holding me?'

The cop looked at him, level over the desk, for a good while longer than Olsen found comfortable.

'I have to tell you,' he said eventually, 'I ran your license number. I made a few calls: checked your credit record, your social security, your IRS file. You want to know what came back?'

'Nothing,' Olsen said, exasperated. 'I file my returns on time, make all my payments, make sure my accounts are in compliance. You didn't find anything.'

'I didn't find anything,' Monk agreed, 'you're right. Every inquiry I make returns a 3-17, account cancelled. I never saw a 3-17 code in twenty years, had to look it up to find out what it was. Cancelled: not deceased, not emigrated; cancelled. You existed, Mr Peterson, until three months ago. You going to tell me why that is?'

Compounding your mistakes was what got you killed, Decker knew that, but knowing didn't seem to help tonight. He raised his glass when she did, smiled, drank, and left the smile on his face while she gushed some more about the Beetle he'd offered to sell her. Something bad happened, you let it cloud your judgement, and it cleared the way for whatever had your name on it: chances were, some asshole with a cheap gun who would never know how lucky he'd been that you were off balance that day.

'I guess we all know the truth of that,' he said and gave her a slow smile, the George Clooney grown-boy kind that he knew ought to work with most women. She took it as a reassurance, a green light to continue talking about the first car she'd ever owned, and he leaned forward, watching her eyes and her mouth like he was supposed to. Olsen was dead. Six minutes after their touch-base call had been due, Decker had flipped open his phone to check it was charged, to confirm that he hadn't gone crazy. He couldn't begin to guess how Olsen'd contrived to get himself killed so quickly: there was no way he would've made a move on Kentrelle so soon. So that left, what: car wreck? Gay-bashed? Like most young toughs, Olsen did look pretty gay. Motel fire? Any one of which would have made at least local news up there, but AP, Reuters and the primary Bay Area wholesaler had had nothing like that. So at the end of a day when all he would've wanted to do – even without finding out about Olsen's demise – would've been to get in a hot bath and go to bed, he'd had to shower, shave for the second time and dress for a date, something he hadn't done in twenty years.

'Must've been a tough call,' he said, frowning and nodding almost imperceptibly as she went on.

He'd had to have dinner with women in the line of the job, of course, maybe as many as a dozen of them over the years. The difference was that they had all been closer to the target than this, implicated in some way: players, who had some idea of the consequences of a wrong move and were trying not to make one. Lauren was a civilian, and he'd never done this before.

'Unlike the Rabbit,' he said, and they both laughed because that was the way to move this on. The waiter, who'd been hovering at a discreet distance, saw his chance, moved in and gave them their menus. Decker glanced over the top of his at her just as she did the same: they both smiled, one of those moments that seal intimacy more than any words can, and looked down again, both knowing from that glance that this evening was heading more in one way than the other now.

It was mostly cut fish but he spotted a bluefin *carpaccio* and then a risotto further down – easy to eat, no distractions with bones. He pretended to give the menu further attention, to win himself a few extra seconds of neutral ground. Apart from the two visits to the men's room that he reckoned he could get away with without looking like he had some kind of a problem, this was going to be all the space he got for the next few hours, and he took the opportunity to empty his mind, just clean it right out, find a balance and come back into the scene. He'd rehearsed it often enough for it to happen almost unwilled, and when he closed his menu and said, 'So how did the second guy lose the pink slip?', she backtracked into the story and took it away towards the opening he'd seen, giving him at least forty seconds before he had to say something else.

He used it just to look at her, now they were in the next level, now she was showing more than she'd permitted herself before. What he saw was that he could take this as far as he wanted. She was following the basic pattern of dates – risk a little, get reassurance rather than rebuff; risk a little more, and so on – and it told him that she didn't do this very often. After the waiter came back and took their orders, he reminded her where she'd been up to in her story.

'And it feels more like working out together than making love,' he said, pouring more wine. 'You know? "You want me to spot you?"'

He lifted his glass as she went on, sipped, decided that if he was going to feel sorry that Olsen was dead, then it was going to come later; now, all he felt was a kind of relief. He'd needed him badly the first week or so, more than he'd been prepared to admit; the respite he'd got from having what amounted to a bodyguard, albeit a truculent and semi-trained one, had given him sorely needed space, let him put 10 per cent of his consciousness on recharge even while the rest barrelled on in overdrive. But now his usefulness had passed. If he'd been able to find Kentrelle, then fine, Decker would've been prepared to use that; but since he'd got himself killed – there was no other explanation for the missed call, unless he'd been thinking about running and having Decker track him down and kill him – then Decker was on his own again. There was a certain relief to that.

'I think scars are beautiful,' he protested. 'One girl, a working girl on my buddy's beat back in Chi, she had a –' he traced a jagged line with his finger from his temple to under his earlobe – 'like a lightning strike. Kind of flaw that makes a face mesmerizing instead of just pretty.'

'But I got mine from slipping in dog-do,' she said, and they both laughed, warmly, looking into each other's eyes. As the waiter placed the plates before them he wondered whether the Postman had ever felt about him the way he felt about Olsen, and pushed it swiftly out of his mind.

'I take it that whatever you're here for, I'm not gonna be consulted on,' Monk said, watching Olsen closely. 'But you're in my office now and I'd like you to listen.'

Olsen tried to keep still in the chair. Miller must've known he was about to go down, so had shut off everything that might point back to him when he wouldn't be around to manage it. Olsen should've thought of this, should've got some new ID. Too late. The reason he'd been locked up all day was to give Monk the time to think how to handle this, but now he could use a little more time himself. 'I don't know what you're talking about,' he said.

'I've served this community for twenty-five years, Mr Peterson, if that is your name,' the sheriff said. 'I don't expect you to compromise your orders, but I do expect a little respect for my office here.'

'I am a private citizen,' Olsen began.

'I took a look in your trunk this afternoon: you know what I found, so don't ride me,' Monk said calmly. 'Reactivated weapons, Mr Peterson. Those budget cuts I read about, they must be biting harder'n I thought if you guys're buying your shootin' irons at yard sales.' He tilted back in his chair. 'Unless . . . naw, that couldn't be right, could it? You couldn't be up here on the type of business calls for untraceable weapons, could you?'

His tone was that of a man who'd seen most of everything over a quarter-century and who wasn't scared of what he hadn't.

'You need a reason to hold me,' Olsen said quietly. 'Either charge me or don't but let me tell you this: either way, the moment I'm out of here, I'm gonna have your fucking badge.'

'You are, are yuh?'

'I know what's going on here and so do you. I don't have anything to add.'

'Then let me tell you a couple things,' Monk said. 'I don't care which agency you're with, you are not quote going to have my badge. I am the elected representative of this community. You understand that? Elected. I do not answer to Washington, I answer to the people of this county. And if Washington wants to make the way we live here part of some vote-grubbing crusade, then there are people out in those hills gonna give you all the headlines you want, sir.'

Olsen stared blankly back, the way he'd used to with teachers riding him in high school.

'Is it "sir"? You going to at least tell me your rank so we can address each other correctly?' Monk said. Olsen stared back; Monk shook his head. 'Okay, have it your way. They teach you fellows common courtesy wherever it is they train you?'

Olsen sat mute.

'Fine,' Monk said, with something more than resignation in his voice: it occurred to Olsen that the man was embarrassed, though why was beyond him. 'You're sticking to your orders, I have to respect that,' Monk went on. 'You don't make 'em, you just follow 'em: fine. But since I'm on the ground here, yet no one saw fit to take intel from me, I'm gonna talk to you and

172

you can relay it back. I don't have a choice in how we do this, but I'm going to have my say. To you, right here, right now. Okay?'

He looked for a response, wasn't surprised when he didn't get one.

'Listen,' he said, 'have the courtesy to reply, huh? I'm a public servant same as you. Our pay, such as it is, comes from the same pot. I'm just trying to do my job here.'

'Why're you holding me?'

'Because there must and will be dialogue between a federal agency three thousand miles away and us guys on the ground here,' Monk said, standing his corner now. 'I know what you think of us back east but let me tell you something, we're talking about a plant grows commoner'n crabgrass here. That seems alien to you, I can understand that; but when you got it growing of its own accord in your back yard, you look at it a little different. People here, they figure that if God put it in the ground, then it's good. You all watchin' LA gangbangers on CNN, you can think it's the devil's own scourge, but we live on the land, you understand me? And a man who finds his living from the land learns not to argue with nature. If it grows, and if it has a use, a man is going to utilize it. Back in Washington you c'n take your cues from Pfizer Pharmaceutical and its so-called duty to its stockholders, but folks out here, we see a higher power everywhere we turn our head.'

He was over his head here, Olsen didn't doubt it now. Stories he'd heard about what happened to guys in boondock lock-ups suddenly seemed a little less far-fetched. No one knew he was here except this mad fuck and him. He tried to think, fast. What would Decker do here? It didn't matter: Decker didn't get his ID from Miller, wouldn't be in this stupid hole. He sat poker-faced, the path of least resistance, waiting for the guy to give him options.

'Now I'm not gonna contend there aren't some characters

out in those hills I wouldn't like to see off my turf f'rever,' Monk was saying. 'But there're some four thousand voters on my register – and that's my low estimate – came here to treat their symptoms in peace. Not with the half-assed crap the health-insurance/chemical corporation complex try to push on them, but with the stuff that does the job. I'm talking glaucoma, MS, the big C here, stuff you don't fuck with. Most of 'em are dying, but they're people like you and me and, sir, I hope you never have to contend with a half of what they do.' He put his elbows on the desk. 'But should it befall you, then you'll know the truth of what I'm saying. They deserve to die with a little dignity, with the appropriate care for their symptoms, and that's something you boys want to deny them. You're only following orders, sure, but those orders come from bribe-taking corporate-puppet politicians and the whole damn country knows it. You gonna dispute me on that?'

Olsen shrugged.

'I don't envy you, y'know.'

Olsen didn't need to shrug again. Monk looked at him like he genuinely felt sorry for him.

'So you're free to go,' he said. 'I could book you, call in the ATF to have a little look at your armoury, but we both know whoever runs you would get you out before the door swung closed. I'm not wrong, am I? No, guess I'm not. But I want you to think about what I said here tonight. And I want you to understand the kind of men who're out there. People here take their Constitution for what it was meant for. You go out in those hills, you're gonna find the right to bear arms is enshrined for a reason, and that's to permit the citizen to defend what God gave him against your sleazy Capitol fucks when they commence to make a mockery. You've come here with arms, my friend, tooled to your teeth: so I ask you to remember Chechneeya, Ireland, Afghanistan, 'Nam. Remember the lesson: when your career politicians vote up a guerrilla war in terrain they only ever saw when they looked out the window from club class, then the poor grunts they send in get their nose bloodied good. You can go back east and tell whoever sent you that if you bring your war on drugs up here, you're gonna get your ass spanked. You're not gonna win, this terrain will make sure of that. And me, I'm gonna get twenty years of work try'nta find a balance here flushed down the bowl overnight.'

He stopped, breathing hard now, but Olsen still didn't have anything to say.

'So go,' Monk said resignedly. 'Go do whatever it is you came here for. I'm probably only about half as dumb as you think I am, but I'll tell you this: I'm not so dumb I don't know that if I try to impede you I'll be wasting my time and my budget. But if you're good enough to be working deep cover, then I know you're an intelligent man. Remember what I've said here. And if you won't, then you better hope you never get sick, boy. You better hope you never get old.'

'The equivalent for guys is hitting forty-five,' Decker smiled, pushing around what was left of his entree. She'd said that the one thing women never told each other was how having a baby ruined you; he'd come back with the only comparative he had. 'No one warns you about that. You don't think you're a vain guy, in fact that's the last thing you think about yourself; but one day you look in the mirror and think, those aren't my eyes any more. That isn't my face, y'know? Jesus, every time someone looks at me from here on in, that's what they're going to see, not me. Not the me I know, anyway.' He chased up a forkful of risotto from the rubble on his plate to cover the awkwardness of honesty, but paused with it halfway to his mouth. 'I think that's all there is, but maybe there's more round the corner,' he said to defuse it. 'I'll keep you posted.'

'I might hold you to that,' she said, and somehow the

playful seriousness in her voice made it okay again. She was good at that.

'You don't want to listen to an old man,' Decker teased her.

'You'd be surprised,' she said, tilting her head to catch the soft music – Buena Vista, piano and voice – a little better. 'You hear these guys? I'd sooner listen to an old man sing about love than a young one any day. Young guys, it's all pain and misery and I want you and I need you tonight. Old guys sing about women, they're like, sure: men have died and worms have eaten them, but not for love.'

'I like those old guys,' Decker said, 'the ones in southern Italy, you know them? Sit out on the street all day in their picnic chair. The widow from down the street sitting out in hers too, everybody easy with each other. They make you feel like, even if nothing else works out, at least one day you'll know the score.'

There'd been a moment when he could've wound this up without letting her down hard, but that'd been half an hour ago and he hadn't taken it. In an ideal world he could have just broken into her office, stolen her hard drive, ransacked the filing cabinets, and found an invoice with a name and address on it; but this world was far from ideal, and he was more than sure that whoever'd hired Star & Frost to surveil Travers wouldn't have left a paper trail. When there wasn't a paper trail, the best you could hope for was a memory trail – something someone had seen, something that meant nothing to them but might mean everything to you. You found the anchor where the chain met the ground, then followed it up from there. She was the anchor, and if she didn't know the information he needed, she could lead him to someone who did.

'Maybe I'll be the widow from down the street,' she said. 'Pitch my chair next to yours, you'll be too old to complain.'

'There's something to look forward to,' he said. 'People in

here look at us, probably think I'm your father. But when we get much past seventy I guess age gaps stop mattering.'

'I don't want to think about seventy.' She said it unselfconsciously, like she'd never seriously thought of it before.

'With your figure? Us guys in our nineties, we'll look at you and think *jailbait*.'

'That's where you plan to be? Italy?'

'If I am, I'll save you a picnic chair.'

'Better make it a wide one,' she kidded, seriously. 'My family, the women run to the tushy end of the scale.'

'Are they still up north? Your family?'

'Oh, yeah,' she said, and changed the subject. She kept doing that; but there was probably nothing to it, he conceded. She'd worked hard to get herself down here, there had to be a reason for that.

'You don't want to be some hired help who's there one day and gone the next,' she was saying. 'You want to be something more. But if you try to be a person, people use it against you. I worked out of the same agency as this girl once, used to go for coffee together when we took our timesheets in. Her mama got bad bones after the menopause, couldn't get her groceries up the stairs any more, so she used to go over at weekends, take her to the market first thing. This supervisor guy was plaguing her, trying to get her to come rock-climbing with him Saturday mornings – losers never ask you to dinner, they ask you to kayak, or jetski or whatever. So she blew him off saying she helps her mama Saturdays, didn't think a thing more about it until a few months later, this big overtime push comes up: a real tough tender they just poached from the competition, three hundred more in your paycheck for a couple of months if you got picked for it, plus the chance to get your hands on stuff that you'd never get near during the week. She pitches hard for it, but it goes to people don't need the money or the experience. She found out later the rock-climber told everyone she had to go nurse her mama on weekends, couldn't be relied on to show up.'

'Rock-climbers are perverts anyway,' Decker said. 'It's just an excuse to have a big box of ropes and clamps in the bedroom.'

'But you get so you almost wish you never saw the salaries,' she went on, like she hadn't heard him. 'Honestly. Leaving parties are the worst: someone heading off after fifteen years, and you're only there for six weeks but they think you'll be offended if they don't invite you. So you go along, sign the card, drink the Chard'nay, and before you know it you've spent thirty bucks, it's late, it's a twenty-dollar cab fare home and you'll be dry-mouthed and tired in the morning. When all you wanted to do was go home at six, eat salad, soak in the tub and get your good eight hours.'

'Why don't you get out of the short-term?' he asked, knowing better than to kid now.

'Why doesn't anyone?' she said, looking him in the eye. 'Same as with sleeping around in a small town. You get a rep for not letting the grass grow, people think you're a bad bet for anything longer. But listen to me bitching. No one made me do this.'

'You bitch all you want,' he said, pouring out the last of the wine. 'When you've been married twenty years you get a taste for it.'

'Well, don't say you didn't ask for it,' she said, watching him put the bottle in the bucket.

'C'mon, it can't be that bad,' he said. 'You must meet plenty of guys, at least.'

She pulled a sour face. 'Guys who know they'll never have to see you again, the moment your contract's up,' she said. 'I meet plenty of those.'

'How about this place you're at now? The security company?'

'Actually, that's the best thing about it,' she said. 'They're ex-cops, like you. Seen enough life to know that a quiet one's all anyone wants in the end.' She played with the stem of her glass.

'Amen to that,' he said, tentatively.

She looked up, smiled. 'Maybe – I mean, if you'd like it – they have a poker game Thursday nights? They're always trying to deal me in and I always cry off, but I could go with you. If you'd like it.'

'Sure,' he said, 'I'd like that a lot.' It was what he'd come for, he reminded himself: to get an in with those guys, find out what they knew, who they thought they were working for. 'Now, don't tell me you don't eat dessert. You gotta work on that tush if you're gonna keep the family tradition up.'

'I'm a traditional girl,' she said, and took the dessert card from its stand on the table.

The note under the Jeep's wiper read *None of my business but let me know yr okay* with a phone number. Common sense told him to go, point the grille to the hills, or maybe back towards Willits. But it was late, he'd have to chance finding a motel with its office still open. When he dialed the number from the note, she said:

'You were parked all day where you left it last night, I was worried.'

'I woke up early, it was a beautiful day. I went for a walk in the woods.'

'That was what I was worried about. Tourists walk off into the woods, next day Sheriff Monk has to take the dogs out.'

'I'm not a tourist, I'm a traveller,' he reminded her.

'So where you travelling tonight,' she said, her voice pitched where it was when he met her.

She gave him black-bean stew and bread she said she'd made herself while she gave him a chance to call before she dialed mountain rescue.

'It's not the week to be walking in the woods,' she said, rolling a joint the size of his johnson while he ate. 'The smoke comes up, you can get lost before you know it.'

'What smoke?'

'From making this stuff,' she said, nodding to the bag of green weed as she licked the paper. 'Sensimilla.'

'They smoke it? Like a ham?' He pushed in another forkful.

'The fall equinox was Sunday,' she said. 'Equal day, equal night. Pot only gets strong when there's less day than night. For regular pot you harvest the male and the female plants about two weeks from now, before the daylight goes and the temperature drops: but I think you noticed this is no regular pot.'

Damn right he had. He flashed back eighteen hours: her climbing the wall with her back, him straining up underneath her, feeling like he could disappear up inside her if he kept on pushing.

'They cut down the male plants and burn them,' she said, making final adjustments to the joint with a licked finger. 'Fifty, maybe sixty thousand eight-foot plants: one hell of a bonfire. When the smoke settles down, the female plants go, huh? Where did the guys go? There's no pollen of a sudden, you see. So they go into overdrive, trying to signal the boy plants to fertilize them, pumping out their pheromone – which, lucky for us, is the stuff that gets you stoned – and, bonus, they coat their buds in extra resin to pick up any pollen that's in the air. It's like reducing two sauces, putting them together, then reducing them again. Sensi is what you get: extra-strong pot, double-infused with THC.'

'Sounds pretty smart,' he said, chasing the last of the stew with a hunk of bread.

'Sounds pretty cruel, if you think about it,' she said, watching him. 'They take the boys away and the girls pine for them; just pine away.' Olsen had the feeling the joint in her hand wasn't the first of the evening. He swallowed his bread, and the noise brought her back from wherever she was.

'Did you see the smoke from the fires today?' she asked.

'I can't say I did,' he said truthfully.

'Then maybe I'll show you them tomorrow,' she said, picking up a lighter in the same hand as the joint. 'You want to do the honours?'

'Thought you'd never ask,' he said.

'Shall I pour?'

'Go ahead,' Decker said. Lauren reached for the small china teapot and held the lid with one hand while she poured with the other.

'So it's like I said,' she went on as he sipped from his cup. 'A guy's version of optimism runs like this: he meets a wonderful woman, she falls in love with him, they set out on the long-term, okay? Her thinking she's as safe as she's trying to make him feel. But all the while he's just expecting it to go down in flames: might take five months, might take fifty; but he's expecting it to be doomed from the start, and the best he lets himself hope for is to be pleasantly surprised. Which isn't going to happen, not when he's been expecting it to be broken from the beginning. He thinks he's buried this deep inside him – guys like to think they can hide their feelings, but they never do. It comes out all the time, in everything they do, from the presents they buy to the vacations they take, and the woman gets her nose rubbed in it from day one. You can't live with that pressure, and it ends badly. And all the guy's friends think, I'm right to expect it to be doomed, and take it into their relationships. You see what I mean?'

'There's probably more truth in that than I'd care to admit,' he prompted, and she went on.

He listened only as far as he needed to. He needed to get to the poker game, nothing more: give him five ex-cops to work on, all missing the life and ready to talk, and inside an hour he'd find out who hired Star & Frost to stake Travers. So he listened to what she said only enough to say the right things back. That was what it was all about: listen, remember, ask the questions they want you to ask.

While she talked, he watched her: good-looking woman. Good mouth, nice shape to her head. When she worked her eyes in time with her mouth, she was probably beautiful, he thought. Someone had once said to him, you can only tell what makes a woman attractive until you fall for her; then you can't tell any more . . .

'But what can you do?' he said, filling the gap.

'Exactly,' she said. 'You're not about to go back for more, not after that. There was this one time . . .'

He was pretty sure she'd come out of this okay; it might even do her good, he thought through his headful of red. It might take a few days to get her to the poker game, but he'd make sure she was a different woman at the end of it. She was too smart to be a temp; he could help her snap out of this rut she was in, stop wasting her life, look at what she'd got and make the best of it. Whoa, silence, playing with her teacup . . .

'It seems to me – and tell me where to get off if I'm wrong – but from what you're saying, Lauren . . .'

He talked. Talking was easy when there was a crisis; and she'd just lost her car, the thing she'd put more time into lately than herself. Being a sensitive man every day was hard, and he was glad he didn't have to do it; being a sensitive man in a crisis was easy, and his mouth toiled away on automatic. Blah, the part of you that you don't let anybody see, blah; can't let decisions you made when you were backed up into a corner direct the rest of you life, blah. Talking was something he knew how to do; every job there were a hundred people to get past, one way or another, and the easiest way nine times out of ten was with talking, and listening, and talking some more. He knew how to talk; his mind was running away, talking; but even as it did, something inside of him tripped. The function that professional soldiers call drift sense – developed and exercised over a lifetime of laying it on the line – kicked in. A neuron was woken somewhere deep in the vaulted caverns of his brain, and he gave it space, subconsciously, his life having relied on its function too many times not to. And it fired and grew and branched and connected, working quietly deep within him, even as his mouth chattered blithely on. Circuits activated and fired off bigger ones until at the side of Decker's consciousness a message appeared: *Something you need to check back here*. He kept on talking, but checked, and his pulse quickened a fraction with what he found. There was a pattern emerging in her talk. A pattern, like she was trying to tell him something, like she was waiting for him to click.

Competition, she was talking about. Young men and old men, and why the latter made better lovers. That was a type of competition. He raced back, four, six, twenty-five minutes, to after the entrees had arrived. She'd been talking about temps versus long-term staff, how the people who were nice to you on your first day were the people you'd spend the rest of your contract avoiding. That was another kind of competition. Next time there was a gap he said:

'You don't talk about your friends.'

She looked up. 'What do you mean?'

'The way you talk, it's unusual. Women pepper their conversation – illustrate it, you know? – with friends' stories, with family stories. You haven't once.'

'Bullshit,' she said, 'neither do you. And besides, that's like saying all black guys have got rhythm: may be true, but take that one step further and you're saying they're no good for anything else.'

He backed off, penitent, playing the old guy who's been out of the game too long, till she seemed to have let it slide. When it was safe again, after he'd asked for the check, he called her back on it. His mouth said, 'But I may be wrong. Probably there comes a time when you should stop trying to keep hold of the reins. I can't see it because I'm too close to it.'

But his eyes said, or tried to say, I'm listening. If you're trying to tell me something, if you're scared because someone's been talking to you about me, I'm listening.

He'd been in the job long enough to know that everything means something if you know how to read it. But she said:

'I don't think you'll ever want to let go the reins. And, for what it's worth, I don't think it'd suit you,' and covered his hand on the table with hers.

Olsen slid out from under the arm she'd thrown across him some time in the night, found his shorts on the floor, dragged them on and went through to the kitchen. He filled the kettle, found matches, lit the stove and set it down to boil. It was usually at this point – when he wasn't out the door already – that he commenced looking around for Alka Seltzer; but apart from the chilli she'd served him repeating a little already, he didn't need it. Incredible, he thought: no hangovers with this stuff. His throat felt a little sore from the smoking, but other than that he didn't feel dick. Hard to believe, he thought, going out for the paper, that something – some drug, not to put too fine a point on it – could take you so indisputably to another place, but leave you next day feeling like all that was wrong with you was not getting to sleep till you'd finished coming your brains out.

And blow his brains through his dick he most certainly had. The stuff was incredible. Was this what those losers in high school had been smoking? Man, he might have whaled on them a little less if they'd slipped him some. Till he met this woman – Courtney, she'd told him her name last night, indicating that he should shout it out with what breath he

184

had left while she came – he hadn't even known it existed. And he'd thought the sex they'd had before had been a one-off – man, anyone'd expect it to be downhill after that. Morning after the first time Jake Olsen could've died a happy man, but last night it'd been even better. He'd fallen on his feet here.

But then a girl went past on a bicycle, flashed a glance at him, and he was about to smile at her when he saw himself, saw himself as she'd see him: fetching the paper from the stoop in his BVDs, hair cowlicked up one side and his face puffy, skinny shanks below baggy white cotton; saw himself in all his glory and thought, What the fuck? What was he doing here? If he'd shouted some smart remark to the girl on the bike, she would've told him to get back inside to his wife. A husband was what he looked like, a partner, fetching the paper off the stoop in his underwear, not caring what other women saw because he was out of the game. He went back in, tossed the paper on the couch, still in its wrapper, and went back to the bedroom to get his clothes on and out of there.

She wasn't in bed any more and the bathroom door was closed. He tugged on his pants, threw his shirt over his shoulders and headed to the kitchen to sluice his head under the faucet. Had he lost his fucking mind? He'd missed the call to Decker, which put him right back where he'd been after Miller died: on his own, no one in the world knowing or caring that he existed except himself. All that time hunting the old man down; those nights out on the road, nothing to go on but Decker's license plate and description, a hundred motel clerks: '*Have you seen my father?*' He was snorting and puffing under the cold stream, rebooting his hair so he could get on out of there, when the kettle started to sing; he ignored it, splashing palmfuls of gritty water into his pits, then ducking his head right under to get the back, and it wasn't till he straightened up and found a towel held out under his nose that he saw she was there too, her head turbaned, a fluffy white bathrobe tied around her.

'You don't need to use cold,' she said, 'I would've been done there in a second.'

He smiled, taking the towel. 'Didn't want you to see my bed head,' he said. 'I find that's the way to scare a girl off for good.'

'I'll take your word for it,' she said and reached up to the shelf for a can of Folger's while he scrubbed himself dry. When he was done, coffee was already dripping into a pint mug; she was making some kind of tea for herself.

'You do drink coffee, don't you?' she said over her shoulder.

'Sure,' he said. It'd be awkward enough getting his tail out of here now; might as well get a cup of joe inside him first. Besides, look what'd happened last time he went out for coffee, he thought ruefully. 'Did you sleep all right?'

She lifted the filter off the mug, the corners of her mouth turning up a little. 'Nothing like wearing yourself out to get your eight hours,' she said, handing him his coffee.

'Glad to be of service, ma'am,' he said, giving her his midnight eyes as he raised the mug to his lips, sipped and swallowed. 'Good,' he grunted.

'Though you might need it,' she said, and before he knew what, his hands were tugging the towel from her head, spilling out her wet hair as his mouth found hers through it. He got her up against the counter, her robe coming open and his pants going to half-mast almost by themselves, and as she kissed him back, he thought, He doesn't know where I am. I know where he lives and I can go back when and if; but meantime he doesn't know where I am. He took a buttock in each hand and lifted, and she hooked her calves round his hams, pulling him into her.

It wasn't bad for morning glory, but it wasn't a patch on how it'd been with the pot.

*　　*　　*

186

Decker knew he should get up and at least check the street from her window, but he was spooned in behind her and, even if he did still have his underwear on, he hadn't done this since the Carter administration. Her hair was in his face (*capelli*, wasn't that a better name for it? Italians understood these things. Hair was what forensics found strands of on your front fender) and his arm was around her waist, his groin scooched up into her butt. He could've lain there all day, his mind chasing after his senses, the creamy yellow light filtered through the blind, the good bed smell of a woman, the kind you couldn't get in a hotel room with a two-hour visit.

It was only the thought of her waking, finding him awake, and assuming that he'd hung around in bed for sex, that got him up and into her kitchen. They hadn't fucked the night before. On her sofa a little after two she'd given him the green light with her eyes and her body turned towards him, but something had held him back, told him to check:

'Am I in the game here?'

'Do you want to be in the game?' She'd said it softly, looking into his eyes, pushing a strand of hair back from his forehead.

'I'm not sure I can remember all the moves,' he'd replied, meaning it more than he could tell her.

'I know them well enough,' she'd said, but there'd been something bittersweet in her voice, a timbre he knew better than he cared to admit. His drift sense had surged forward, screaming for attention: *She talks about the young pushing out the old and you ignore it? She talks about being a hired gun, all the accountability and none of the security, and you ignore it?* – and though he'd pushed it back down, he'd almost said it to her face: You're more like me than I want to know, aren't you? But he hadn't, and though it had switched the moment, sent their lips to each other's shoulders instead of their mouths, and turned what could've been a desperate, hungry lunge into a solace-seeking mutual embrace, he was glad of it. It hadn't been his drift sense; just his regrown virginity talking, he told himself, filling the kettle at the faucet, finding matches for the stove. It was only what anyone ought to feel at the end of a successful first date: You're just like me, aren't you? It was probably better this way: if they weren't lovers, then that meant they were friends, and once he'd got to the poker game and found out what he needed to know, it wouldn't hurt her too bad for her friend to have to go back to Chicago for a few months, then never come back.

He watched the kettle, the oxygen-hungry flame's persistence under it.

'I was hoping you'd stay in bed,' she said from the door.

He swung around, too fast, told himself to chill. 'Thought I'd bring you your tea,' he said. 'I thought you were still asleep.'

'I was, kind of,' she said, shuffling over in a towelling robe and matching mules. 'But then I remembered it's a school day. If I don't go answer those phones . . .' She reached past him to pull a mug from a hook.

'. . . the end of civilization as we know it,' he finished for her.

''Xactly,' she said, dumping a teabag into her mug. She looked up. 'I'm sorry. I'm not a morning person.'

'No problem,' he said, and decided against touching her cheek. 'Neither am I.'

She lifted the kettle off the burner, filled her mug, dunked the bag with her fingers a couple of times and took a sip without taking it out.

'I've got to get ready, John,' she said. 'I miss the eight forty bus, I'm toast. I wish I didn't but I do.'

'No problem,' he repeated, feeling like he'd fallen into a dream, right down to standing there butt-naked save for his Calvins. 'I shouldn't have drunk too much to drive home. I shouldn't be here.'

'I wouldn't say that,' she said, looking at him over the rim of the mug. 'I wouldn't say that at all.' And there it was, the face he knew from the sofa cutting through her morning mask. 'You're parked outside, right?'

'I could drive you,' he realized out loud, the world falling away as he touched it now, brushed her cheek with his fingers.

'Save half an hour over the bus,' she said, setting her tea down but keeping the face on, impishly turned up towards him. His hand hung by her face, didn't want to come back.

'You going to move that hand or you want me to do it for you?' she said. Her hand was on his, and moving it, before he could think to respond.

He scrubbed his balls with her loofah after she left, doused the red flesh with TCP to get the smell off, then sat down in front of the cartoon channel, holding himself in his hand, to think. No one knew he was there save for her and the sheriff, and Olsen already had a way round the cop. Sounded like he was on the side of the people rather than the WTO-NATO-Zionist coalition: he didn't need to break into the guy's apartment to know it'd be full of JFK books, Roswell, Waco, J18 and N30; open his browser and go straight to alt.conspiracy.black.helicopters. He'd swallow any story Olsen cared to give him, and a line from high school – Cliff's Notes? – surfaced from ten years back: the bigger the lie, the more the saps believe it. He could lay something on the cop about a daytime soap star, serial stalkings, erasure of all state records and creation of a new identity. He'd seen it on cable; like the WPP but for fag actors instead of snitches. The shitkicker would lap it up, and if he didn't want to, then fuck him: he couldn't touch him now he was out of his jailhouse.

Courtney wouldn't be any harder, if he played it right. If he fucked her whenever she wanted – and if she kept that Sensey shit coming, he'd have no problem with that – then she'd feed him, buy him stuff maybe. She had money: ran an organic meat business for all the old farts who'd come up here to smoke their last days away. He hadn't got it – if they were terminal-C anyway, what did they care about a few chemicals? – but she seemed to be doing pretty good out of it: the keys to a Mazda MX-5 hung next to those to her pickup on the rack by the door, and her bedroom had widescreen digital and a DVD. Olsen was thinking she spent a lot of time at home, but that only meant there was less competition here. He could chill a while, get his bearings, then load up his Cherry with her stuff when she was out and head wherever he hankered for, sell it and start again.

Before she left that morning she'd told him to use whatever he wanted, make himself at home. He'd felt he ought to say something so he pulled a pinch of thigh hair through his pocket to bring the shine to his eyes, looked into hers and said, 'Why're you being so kind to me?' He'd already let slip he was an orphan, etc., got it in soon as he could even if it'd seemed a little surplus to requirements. She'd said:

'I know that look in your eyes too well to miss it, babe. I was running from something myself once, but somebody helped me. You can tell me about it when you're ready, and if you don't get ready, that's okay too.'

It popped into his head from nowhere, and it almost came out – 'I just got the diagnosis, came up to get my head round it' – but then he figured he'd have to wear rubbers for ever with her after that and he was hoping that when her bedside box ran out (and he was giving it another eighteen hours, tops) she wouldn't be replenishing it: women liked to feel safe with a guy, he'd found, and that usually involved tossing the Trojans after the first few times. So he kept his mouth shut, gave her a look that was part gratitude, part incomprehension at her kindness; she almost visibly melted, saying, 'You don't need to worry 'bout a thing, you're safe here.' Touching his hair and kissing the corners of his eyes. When she was gone he found half a jay from the night before in the ashtray, lit it, and by the time it was down to the clip he was trawling the bookshelves for something to whack off with.

Even if they weren't morning people, they'd managed pretty well. When he pulled up to drop her off, he said, 'That was incredible,' and meant it.

'Try me after I've had my coffee some time,' she said, one hand on the Beetle's door. 'How about tonight?'

'I'll drink mine too.'

'Come round at eight. And skip the decaf,' she said, winked, and slipped out.

He waited, engine rumbling, as she scooted across the parking lot to Star & Frost, watching her keister move under the business skirt; he had to drive away before he got too distracted to be safe. But he couldn't resist turning his head as he pulled into traffic, caught a glimpse of her disappearing inside the office door. Man, she was a fine-looking woman. Not drop-dead, not at first; she was the kind you had to look at twice, but when you did you thanked the god that gave you eyes. And when she'd slipped her robe off . . . he had to pull into the turning lane and crawl along at twenty till it passed.

She'd been sweet, tender and sweet, no other way to put it. He saw the gym work in her body and kissed her between the eyebrows for the effort she'd made, waiting for someone who'd appreciate it and never giving up hope. Moving with her, against her then with her and then it was hard to tell, a warm breeze playing across them as they reached down inside one another: it had felt like being reconnected to life, dry ports suddenly sluiced with bandwidth, drinking up the data. She had a mole under one shoulder blade. Her hair smelled sweet at the roots. She had a full complement of pubic hair – not a porn-star patch, not a G-string wax, but something Decker hadn't seen in twenty-five years – and her whole body stiffened when she came. The Beetle's six valves burbled and popped behind him, the good warm wind tousled his hair. The Merc was still reported stolen, but he didn't anticipate the LAPD would be breaking out the overtime to find it; he'd drive it over by her place at six, tell her it was a loaner from his dealer; cab back for the Beetle, then hand her the keys. She'd try to give him money but he'd tell her to wait for the insurance; and then he'd be out of her life before her claim was even processed. Let her take a holiday with the insurance money, forget him; meantime he was going to show her – or remind her – what it was like to be appreciated.

Letting himself back into his own apartment brought him back down to earth. The poker game was Thursday nights: that was tomorrow, and there was no way she'd be introducing a man she'd met to her co-workers after only two days. He'd have to try for next week, which meant stringing her along for nine days; it'd take balancing, not letting her get too hooked on him but not risking blowing the deal. Once he was sitting at the card table he'd have what he needed inside an hour, no doubt about it: cops talked to cops, and cop he could do; but he had to get there first. He didn't like the thought, but there wasn't much about his job to like; *like* wasn't supposed to come into the equation. All that mattered was control, he thought, sniffing the milk from the refrigerator and deciding to take the coffee black, irritable bowel be damned.

So: nine days with her. This was all he could permit himself, even for a mad fling. He was endangering her by being around her, and he wasn't stupid enough to think he could give her what she wanted and be looking out for the Contender the way he'd do it if he was on his own. He should get her out of the city, drive way into the desert so he could be sure they weren't being followed. Wasn't that what people did? Went out of the city, to a desert spa, where the sex could happen on neutral ground? So by the time they came back to the heat there was a bond there, the kind you couldn't forge in city bars or in bedrooms that had work clothes hung over the back of the wardrobe door. That was what they'd do this weekend, he decided. If she didn't have plans. The sex had already happened, but the strategy was second-nature enough for her not to think it weird. In the desert he needn't be looking over her shoulder instead of into her eyes. It would buy him a weekend out of his life. Monday it would start again, but Friday night through Sunday . . . it wasn't enough. It didn't seem enough. Christ, was this ever going to be over? Yeah: it could end right now. He could walk out into the street without a weapon on him, and just keep walking until it happened. Then it'd be over all right.

The water in his eyes surprised him, stripping off his shirt for the shower, smelling her good smell on him. It wasn't for her, or for Olsen: fuck Olsen, if he was dumb enough to get himself in a car wreck or to have even thought about running. It wasn't even for knowing he had to walk out on her; it was for himself, and for what he'd let himself become. He let it come, his gut hanging loose, hands hanging useless at his sides, let it come to let it out. Then pick it up, start over again. It didn't matter if you were living in the world or if you were living in hell to protect it. It was what everyone had to do. Get on with it, man, he told himself and headed for the shower, turning the dial to blue. He was going to have to do Travers some time in the next month or so; better go and see what the lard ass was up to.

9

OLSEN WAS JUST LOOKING, that was all. Just checking his options, as he made a fast march up the dirt road, keeping to the baked part in the middle and avoiding the deep-rutted tracks on either side for fear of turning an ankle. He was sweating freely inside the fatigues he'd packed down south, and the webbing chafed his shoulders, but the late-September sky above him was the colour of an x-rayed lung. This confirmed him in what he was doing – if he'd left it a couple more days, this track might've become the streambed it plainly was for eight months of the year. But he was only looking, nothing more.

Eight-tenths of a mile up the incline the track branched, but there was grass – dead grass, but grass nevertheless – to the left, while the ruts were deeper on the right. So he turned right, rounded a bend, and soon he was climbing even steeper, between the ferns and briars and poison oak that choked the trees. Just looking, that was all. He'd just been looking when he booted Courtney's browser, connected, and gone searching for something to jerk off over. None of the sites he tried would accept Miller's credit-card details so he'd had to make do with some sign-up-to-see-more samples, Japanese schoolgirls tied up in sailor suits. He'd not been satisfied when he was done – the best he could find were thumbnails, and he'd had to squint to see them – so he'd trawled around her desktop to see if she kept any porn on her hard drive herself. He searched for .JPG, .GIF, .TIFF, .MPEG, and came up with nothing. Idly he opened her file manager to see if her bank details were on there anywhere. He ran a search for 'bank', then tried 'checking', then 'account'. A file labeled Delivery Accounts popped up in front of him: he opened it, and there was the name he'd come up here to look for or forget, in nine-point Monaco, forty folders or so down: Kentrelle. Barely able to believe it, he'd opened it, found a bunch of invoice numbers that meant nothing: but when he ran the numbers through her Find File engine he came up with delivery notes. Four sides of beef, four sides of pork, twenty pounds of chicken legs and wings, forty of breast . . . the man liked his white meat, evidently. When he scrolled down to the bottom, the instructions to the driver read:

(NB Pick up grocery order from Shirelle, pack with delivery, and collect four cases Wild Turkey from Ed Tookey.) Rural route 809, take dirt road on left 4.7 miles after the Jackson place. Turn left after 0.8 miles, proceed 1.2 miles and take right fork. DO NOT ATTEMPT THIS ROAD OCTOBER THROUGH APRIL – LEAVE CONSIGNMENT AT TURN, PICKUP HAS BEEN ARRANGED . . .

He had his hunk of .44 mag, his .38 Sig Sauer and his snub. He would've brought more if he'd known how much meat they got through up there – had to be eight men at least, allowing two pounds per man per day – but since he hadn't known, he was just looking.

He heard it before he saw it: distant popping sounds, shots spaced apart. He headed into the undergrowth, scrabbled through rotting leaves to the wet soil beneath, scooped a handful up and smeared his cheeks. When he saw it, a clapboard house covered in camo-net, the infra-reds surrounding it looked as childish as the twenty feet of razor-wire he'd cut through two hundred yards back. A quick recce found it full of stuffed and mounted trout, bare of personnel. A Quonset hut was pitched on the other side. The roof was painted in greens and browns, and its far side was leveed with earth as if it was being swamped by the soil. Rounding further, he saw that in front of the levee were targets on posts, cut-outs of cops, G-men, SWAT personnel. One of them had what seemed to be a colour copy of George Clooney's head pasted on it. The popping sounds came from two fat white guys in black fatigues with too many pockets, plugging away at poor George with firing pistols. Olsen screwed the silencer on the .38 and dropped them both where they stood without a space between his shots. They lay on the bark scraps, clutching at the wounds in their thighs, trying to stem the femoral flow as Olsen trotted over the cleared ground towards them, his Sig at high port.

'Forget it,' he warned the one on the left, who was reaching for his fallen Springfield Armories 1911, and kicked his arm. 'Where's Kentrelle?'

'Fuck you,' the guy said and kept reaching. Olsen shot his buddy in the head and stamped on this boy's wound, ground his heel in hard.

'Apply pressure to stop bleeding,' he said. 'Where's Kentrelle?'

He thought the fucker'd passed out for a moment: his eyes rolled back, lids fluttering, face whiter than a news anchorman's teeth. He put the gun in his face, seized his right earlobe and twisted as hard as he could without ripping it off. The guy's lids opened wide.

'Where's Kentrelle?' he repeated, pulling the gun back to two feet.

The guy's eyes searched his fatigues, looking for a badge.

The absence of one didn't seem to reassure him; he looked up into Olsen's eyes.

'Out,' he said, between panting breaths, 'back soon.'

'Alone?'

'With the rest of the team,' the guy said quickly, his free hand moving towards his face. 'Bad motherfuckers, man, I wouldn't –'

Olsen racked the slide, put the muzzle between his eyes.

'You were about to touch your nose, weren't you?' he grinned. 'You know what that signifies, Kentrelle?'

The Santa Ana winds were beginning to blow, and even with the Merc's air-con cranked it had been a long, headachey day. Travers had made three client visits, two press calls and one mistress come – loudly enough for Decker, in the next room at the LAX Holiday Inn, to hear even without his omni-mike. He'd followed the woman to Rodeo Drive, then home to a Spanish Mission-style gated community above Topanga Creek; by the time he was back out of the canyon it was pushing six and he drove straight into the Valley to his new apartment, showered there but had to run out to a Ralph's for shaving cream. It was almost eight, and he realized, as he buzzed up to Lauren, that he couldn't think of a thing to say.

He didn't need to. She let him in with a kiss, her hair wet and falling around her face. He wanted to take a handful of it, wipe the day from his face. Instead he said, 'How was your day?'

And it was as simple as that. She cooked spaghetti with tomatoes and *pancetta*, and he went out for a bottle of Bonterra. As he strolled back, not caring about the heat, he didn't feel that he was kidding himself to say that pornography and simple lack of contact hadn't, in fact, screwed women up for him. He didn't doubt that they would, to a guy who started out bad; but he'd been lucky with the girlfriends he'd had, decades before, and this woman – this normal, sensible, friendly woman – was putting him in touch with a part of him that he'd lost.

He wasn't getting any crazy ideas – this was going to finish in a week's time, the night of the poker game – but he was going to use this week all he could, use his time with her, and maybe at the end he'd be the better hitman for it. You don't miss what you don't have till it's there in front of you, but here she was: and with her came rest, recharge, the chance to be a man again before he went back out to do what he had to.

When she let him back up, he had to stash his guns fast while she tossed the spaghetti with the sauce. He put one by the bathroom door and one under a cushion on the couch; if she took him to bed again he'd tuck it into the back of his shorts, then palm it between the mattress and the headboard on what he knew was his side of the bed, the one furthest from the door. He didn't like doing it and it must've shown in his manner somehow as they sat down to eat.

She didn't let on, not while they were eating; not even when they were making out on the couch afterward, or when the making out turned serious. She told him after, when his head lay on her breast, his eyes closing despite himself.

'Guys think women are as clueless about men as they are themselves about women,' she said, out of nowhere. He opened his eyes, looked up. 'But they forget: few guys knew their mothers well but most girls know their fathers,' she went on, stroking his hair. 'I don't want you to worry, and I'm only going to say this once. My dad and me, we loved each other. He wasn't a good man, not always, but he showed me parts of him that I don't think he showed even my mother.' She put a finger on his lips to shush him. 'I know enough from him to see that you're running, John; I don't want to pry into what you had with your wife, or into your new life here either. But you look to me as though you're running, and I don't care if it's from yourself or whoever. I just want you to know that you don't need to run, not while you're with me. You can rest here with me for a while. Okay?'

He looked up at her and she looked back, still stroking his hair. He badly wanted to tell her there was no problem and mean it.

'Do you think we might go away this weekend?' he asked her.

'Yes,' she said, not breaking eye contact, keeping her hands where they were. 'Yes, I think we might do that.'

At noon the next day Olsen was parked across the street from the car that Kentrelle had told him about. Black Cadillac De Ville, the late model with the thermal-imaging camera built into the grille as standard: standard, that is, if you had the thirty-five thousand bucks to begin with. And this was just the car he used on jobs. Whatever this guy was into, he was into some genuine money here.

The guns that had killed the Postman – the guns that had come from Moss to Kentrelle to this guy – had been loaded into that sleek, ergonomic trunk over there. He didn't know what might be in there this afternoon, but his own trunk was packed for most contingencies. He'd taken an M-6o machine gun from Kentrelle's Quonset in case he met any trouble on the way back down the hill but'd had to leave it behind at Oakland airport. From the lot at LAX he'd stolen the green BMW he sat in – not his choice of colour but what could you do? He drove to Decker's apartment to find it locked. That saved him a scene anyway. He got back into the Beamer, drove down to Torrance, little place he knew, and bought a used Walther and a box of cheap rounds from a bearded guy whose fading NRA T-shirt strained over his belly; he didn't wish him a nice day as he gave him his change, just returned to the copy of *Soldier of Fortune* he was reading. Olsen went round the corner, loaded the Walther, then walked back in, put the barrel on the fat fuck who'd just sold him a firearm with barely a glance at his ID: this time he took him for a Mossberg pistol-grip shotgun, chromed with a laser scope, along with a .38 and a .9, both Sigs.

'And whatever cash you have in the register,' he'd said, cool as Christmas. Courtney's TV, sound system and computer had netted him less than eight hundred bucks and he didn't know how long it'd be till he found Decker. The gun-shop guy handed over six hundred bucks and change. Olsen told him to have a nice day.

He had barely slept since Courtney's the day before but he couldn't let this go. He'd had to drag Kentrelle, bleeding and moaning, into his house to have him find this address – the man must've been some kind of tight-ass accountant once, because he had his invoices 32-bit encrypted on his PC, every little job down to this one. Storing and delivering the guns for the Postman's hit had earned him twenty-eight hundred bucks, Olsen had noted as he'd pushed the barrel of his snub into the soft part above Kentrelle's nape, taking out the man and the monitor with one round. But what's it cost you, Kentrelle? he'd wanted to say, but the guy was dead and voided before it came into his head. He'd save it for another time, might even write it somewhere to help remember. Because there were going to be other times. Screw Europe, fuck Africa; he was on the trail here, ahead of Decker. He was close to the money.

When the guy came out of the deluxe condo block – a geeky middle-aged guy in an expensive sports shirt and running shoes – and zapped the locks on the Caddy, Olsen was cool. He was cool as he tailed him out of Hidden Hills across the Valley. He was cool when the guy pulled into a strip mall somewhere deep in 818. He was cool as he pulled into the space in front of Subway that gave him the best view of the sleek black De Ville. But he broke into a hot sweat when Lauren Reese got out of the tan sedan the Caddy'd pulled in next to, and got into the passenger seat.

Decker went to Saks as Lauren'd told him to, bought a swimsuit, sunblock, athletic socks; two pairs of black silk boxers, tennis shoes, a bottle of that modish new cologne that didn't smell of anything much. What present could he give Lauren, hide it under her pillow while they were unpacking tonight in their desert-spa suite? He settled on a pair of pearl stud earrings, thinking he could defuse the embarrassment of present-giving by saying she could wear those and nothing else tonight. On a roll with it, he added an ounce of Chanel No. 5. As the Saks saleswoman gift-wrapped his purchases, she told him that was one lucky lady he'd got himself; Decker replied that he was the lucky one. It came out gruffer than he'd intended, and he walked swiftly out of the store as soon as he was done.

But he swung the bag from his hand as he strolled past the windows. He knew she'd wear the earrings this weekend and never again. In a week's time, when he was gone, she'd be telling herself to throw them in the trash . . . but she had her head screwed on. The pearls would go into a doodad box and stay there, moving house when she did, not seeing the light of day till she was older, old as him maybe, sifting through her memories and happening on them. She wouldn't be thinking badly of him as she turned them over against the light. He would be just a time that happened once; the kind that happened all the time out here, he thought, or ought to. He turned to descend a wide curving staircase so as to feel the change of pace.

He was going to give himself this. It was irrevocable already, he told the rational part of him, the part that was yelling, *Are you out of your mind?* Twenty years ago – ten, five, two even –

it was the rational part of him that was getting the payback from everything he did. The rational part of him looked at his life and said *You're doing necessary work that most men couldn't do: take your satisfaction from that.* He had as far as he'd needed it. But now there was another part that was sitting up, begging to be fed: he guessed it was nothing different from the average fortysomething schmuck who wakes up one morning and thinks, Screw the Lexus, I want a Firebird. A red one. One weekend wasn't much – not after a quarter of a century of loneliness and hookers – but it might feed this need, wherever it came from, and then maybe it'd go away again. He saw himself by the pool, watching her swim, watching her body cut through the water, saw his own limbs moving under the blue . . . Forty-eight hours of time out, starting when he'd pick Lauren up at five: what to do till then? It was only just after one, his bag was ready packed in the Merc's trunk, he was too nervous to be hungry, and he couldn't think of anything more to buy.

An hour later he found himself in a movie theatre, his first time since the original release of *Grease*. It was an arthouse, showing a weekend of Al Pacino. Since when was Al Pacino arthouse, he wondered as he handed over his eight dollars: probably since a fleapit ticket cost eight bucks, he told himself, opting against popcorn, even if this was a special day. He didn't want to have gas later.

The flick was *Donnie Brasco*, a movie he'd read about with interest at the time but'd never managed to catch on HBO. He wanted to see how they handled the Johnny Depp character, the deep-cover cop who becomes more like his prey the closer he stalks it. As he stood up from the seat closest to the entrance two hours later, he didn't think they'd done a bad job with him. But the Al Pacino character wasn't so hot, he thought, narrowing his eyes against the sidewalk glare: the way he was watching TV in his sweats at the end, the nature show, the night he knew he was getting whacked. That was wrong. When men know they're fucked, they fuck their wives, a thief had told him once, and Decker believed him. When you know you're about to get pinched or worse – and you always know, the guy said – then you buy your wife flowers. You know you're not going to get touched by a woman again for four to seven, or ever, so you fuck your wife while you still can. This guy used to stop by the florist on the way back from a job if he knew he'd pushed his luck, because if he'd pushed it too far and they were coming for him tomorrow, then tonight was the time to buy the lady flowers. Maybe the director knew this, but had thought it was better to have Pacino watch the nature show, so he could put the gazelle and the lion on the screen as some kind of metaphor. He'd talk to Lauren about it tonight, maybe, if she'd seen the movie; and if it didn't seem like sailing too close to the wind. When he saw a spray of irises in a florist's window on the way back to the Merc, he stopped and bought a bunch: they'd wilt before tomorrow, but he could put them in a cup of water in the Merc's beverage holder for the drive.

Olsen followed the tan sedan back to Star & Frost on a long tail, watched her park in the lot next door and walk smartly over to her office. Then he didn't know what to do. There were too many unknowns here. Where was Decker? Did this mean he was switched already? Had she been playing them both all along? Was she the Contender? Then who was the guy in the De Ville?

Olsen tried not to look but he saw it now, the way the trail had been set for them. Leaving the rounds at the scene of the Postman's hit to begin with. Moss being easy like that. They should've seen it; but if he hadn't suspected, then Decker hadn't either, he told himself. Everything looked better with hindsight; it hadn't seemed so easy at the time. He had nothing to reproach himself with. Whoever she was – or whoever the guy in the De Ville was – the one thing they couldn't have planned was his finding Kentrelle through Courtney. But even if he'd never met her he'd have found the place in the hills soon enough, he conceded to himself. Blind man could have found it. Even the most whack unit needed supplies, and Kentrelle's little set-up was hardly whack, however much money he had to feed his anti-federal fantasies with. Courtney had hindered him, if anything, made him waste a couple of days there. He just hoped it wasn't two days too many.

As the digits on his dashboard clock advanced, his anxiety built, but still he sat there. He knew she'd leave at five or soon after – she had to maintain her cover, after all – and he didn't relish the prospect of sitting outside her apartment or wherever; but still he couldn't bring it on. He needed to do this now, he knew, while the adrenaline was outgunning the tiredness, but he didn't know if it was the buzz or the fatigue that was telling him that. He debated burning rubber over to Decker's, seeing if the old man was home, but she could go anywhere meantime. He gripped the wheel hard in both hands, hard enough to feel the steel beneath the perforated leather, and held it for a count of ten. It was four twenty-eight. Time to get this done, he told himself. Go, boy.

He didn't know whether she was alone in there or had backup but better safe than sorry. Taking his Reebok pack from the back seat, he dumped the dirty clothes on the floor, walked round to the trunk and opened it. He racked the Mossberg on the floor of the trunk and slipped it muzzle down into the pack so the stock was protruding; ran the action on the Sigs, loaded them and stuck them in his waistband; put the pack over one shoulder, slammed the trunk shut. The sun pinned him to the spot for a moment, the hot wind mussing his hair; a quiet Friday afternoon, cars coming and going, the week's trials done and the world winding down for the weekend. He was some guy with a backpack, that was all. He walked, armpits pricking, over to the door of Star & Frost, trying not to glance at his shadow.

10

MOST LOOKERS WEREN'T SUCH lookers up close, but she really wasn't bad.

'Put the gun away, there's no call for that,' she said.

'You listen to what I have to say and then we'll see,' he said, rounding the counter, the front sight on the Sig holding steady between her manicured eyebrows. 'Who're you working for? Who's the guy in the Caddy?'

'I don't know what Decker saw in you,' she said, resuming her typing at the keyboard. 'I was him, I would've dropped you like a dog.'

He halted six feet in front of her desk, flicking his eyes to the door behind it. 'Don't fuck with me. There'd better not be anyone back there.'

She looked up. 'You genuinely don't know if there is or not, do you, Olsen? Tell me, where'd Miller find you? On a dumpster?'

'Whatever you're working here, you can count me in, operative immediately,' he said, keeping his voice level. 'Is Decker dead yet? 'Cos if he isn't, I can get him here for you.'

'So we can do what?' She said it as if she was interested to know.

'Whatever it is you're playing him for,' Olsen said. 'Cut me in. I want in on this.'

She finished what she was typing, hit return.

'Get away from the desk,' Olsen said.

'Or you'll do what?'

'Stand up. Do as I fuckin' say.'

'Don't talk to me like that.'

He took a step forward. 'I said now, bitch.'

She rolled her eyes, but pushed her chair back and stood up.

'There,' Olsen said. 'Wasn't so hard, was it? Now, down on your knees, hands behind your neck. You know how.'

'Go fuck yourself.'

He grinned. 'Do *what* now?'

'You heard me.'

'Bitch, I don't think I did.' Olsen kept it cool; no call not to. 'Did it escape your attention? I'm the one with the gun here.'

'No, you're not,' said a voice behind him.

Olsen snapped his head round before he could stop himself. The guy from the Cadillac was moving inside the door, a slim Beretta trained on Olsen's head.

'Put down your arm,' he said.

Olsen kept it on Lauren. 'Who the fuck are you?'

'Your boss,' the guy said, moving along the window, getting away from the line of the door. 'Put the weapon on the floor, Olsen. Put the weapon on the deck and do it *now*.'

Should he give her the earrings now, or wait? He could buy her a sandwich for the ride, put the box inside the wrapper. Too cute? Yeah, probably. And he'd have to take them out of the gift wrap. Do it in the suite tonight. Put them on her pillow, say something about the tooth fairy. The long-in-the-tooth fairy? He'd think of something on the way.

Decker slipped the Sig Sauer .38 into the waistband of his pants, the muzzle down by his coccyx, the grip turned to the right. It would dig into the small of his back on the drive out, but it was the only good place. She'd hug him when he walked through the door over there, he knew it – their first weekend away, after all – and when she hugged him, her arms went around his neck while she pressed her chest up against him: if he was wearing a shoulder she'd feel it.

He walked across the lot towards the door, telling himself, Don't mess this up, be cool, be hers, don't mess this up, feeling the hot wind on his face, relishing it, wanting to remember every second, every last detail of the hours to come, starting now: this was all he was going to get, and he wanted to remember it. Passing a Caddy with tinted windows, he checked his reflection: not bad. Really, not bad. He'd been right to take the day off, chill, do normal stuff. He looked less tense than he felt. He looked as good as it got.

They were all looking at him when he opened the door and saw them.

'John,' said the Postman, not taking his gun off Olsen.

Decker stood rooted to the spot.

'You'd better come in,' the Postman said.

He couldn't move.

'I'm sorry, John,' said Lauren. 'But you'd better shut the door.'

He took a step forward, letting the door hiss closed behind him. Olsen's eyes flicked three ways, but his arm stayed where it was even as Decker's right hand crept around to the small of his back.

'You'll forgive me if we talk later,' said the Postman.

Decker drew on him.

A pulse beat visibly in Olsen's temple. 'Somebody better start talking,' he said quickly.

'Drop the weapon or die,' the Postman said, holding steady on him.

Decker's right arm panned, as if through water, to Olsen. 'Where have you been?' he murmured.

'Saving your fucking hide, man,' Olsen barked. 'She's in bed with this guy. This is Kentrelle's fucking contact man. This is the guy who hit your postman.'

Decker took a step sideways, and all three snapped their heads towards him momentarily again. As he steadied himself, he glanced at the Postman's fist curled around his pistol grip. The ring with the weird grey stone was on his finger. The thing in Decker's pocket, the ring he'd carried for three months, was a fugazi. The hit Olsen had stumbled on had just been a job, someone who had to go anyway; stage-managed for Olsen to find, and cleaned after he'd gone. Decker looked up, saw Olsen's gun on Lauren, felt everything else fall away.

'Drop the weapon,' he said.

'Do as he says,' the Postman barked.

'I mean it,' Decker said.

'So do it,' said Olsen, 'do it and watch her skull pop.' A red flush crept up his neck but his face was white beneath the tan. 'This little bitch's been playing us both. You all put your arms down or I take her, I swear I will.'

'Please, Jake,' Decker said. 'Please put it down.'

'You'll have to pry it from my cold fucking fingers, man,' Olsen said. 'It's her.'

Decker took a step towards him.

'What are we waiting for here?' the Postman said irritably. 'Blow it out of his fist, John.'

Decker put the barrel of the Sig on Olsen's hand, but his head stayed where it was.

'Do it,' the Postman said.

'Move and she dies,' Olsen hissed.

Decker's head turned slowly till he was sighting along the barrel. The front sight blocked on Olsen's knuckles. His finger tightened. Sweat trickled between his shoulder blades.

'I need the truth,' he said, and dropped his arm. He looked at Lauren, looked at the Postman. 'He's the only one who's been straight with me,' he said, his voice unsteady, not able to help it.

'Then how do you feel about training him?' the Postman said.

Olsen turned an eye to the Postman.

'Say what?' he said, lowering his arm a little.

'I'm talking to Decker,' the Postman said coldly, but lowered his pistol too. 'What do you say, John?'

'*Train* him?' Decker murmured. He saw Noff's face, Moss spreadeagled on the bed; the Postman's intel had found the weak links, built the chain up around them. Could *he* plan an op like that? Yes, he could. With a postman's intel, he could. His right arm sleepwalked back to high port.

'I've been watching you both,' the Postman said. 'But I've been watching him a lot longer. It's time to move over, John. I want you to train him.'

'No.' Decker's voice was hoarse but firm.

'Why not?'

Decker's mind functioned behind his senses somewhere. 'He's not made for this.'

'That's what I said about you twenty-five years ago,' said the Postman smartly. 'You made out okay. Olsen is of his time, just like you were,' he continued, lowering his weapon. 'Just like I was before you. What he is may not be pretty, but what we do isn't either. But it's necessary. Do you still accept that?'

Decker's silence spoke for him.

'Then say you're willing to take what I'm giving you,' the Postman said. 'Travers is rolling now: he's standing up, getting good clean dollars in his campaign fund. We go for him soon, or we miss the window.' He glanced over at Olsen. 'Put that thing away, boy,' he said, and Olsen did as he was told. 'This is where the rubber meets the road, John,' he said. 'You're ready. Let's go.'

There was a silence, the bad kind; and then Lauren let out a

210

long breath. Decker looked at her, still standing behind the desk.

'I'm sorry,' she said.

The other men seemed to fade as her voice cut to him. 'Is that what this has been *about*?' he said softly.

'I wanted to be sure you were ready for this, John. I owe you that.' His eyes dropped a second, then came back to hers; she held them so firmly that only her mouth moved as she continued. 'Guys in the Life can get too far from the life they're protecting. They get lost in the play until the rules of the game are the only rules. But you still know who we're working for.' Her eyes began to move a little as she searched his. 'You need to stop now,' she said. 'I saw it in you but, John, it's not a failing. It means you're ready for what's being offered.' Her eyes on his were like the grip of a hand on his forearm. 'Don't throw it all away. *Take* this.'

She was the one who did what he did, knew what he knew. He saw her walking along to the coffee shop, head in the air, not covering any bases; he hadn't been able to walk like that, even in his bedroom, for years now. But in hers . . . Lying in her arms he had dreamed the pull between them as gossamer strands, gathering on the heat they made together, falling across them both, connecting them: now he saw the heavy cable from like to like that had been there all along. It didn't matter. Whatever had happened had been the kind of time that happened all the time out there, nothing more. But she wasn't out there any longer, and neither was he.

The Postman's voice seeped into his reality. 'If I'd come to you with this three months ago you wouldn't have been ready, John, you know that. But now you've proved yourself. Now you're ready. So tell me and let's get on with our lives. Are you going to accept?'

He said it like there was an alternative.

'Do I get a say in this?' Olsen piped up, but Decker ignored him. A postman, he could be; a postman, running this guy. A postman, with intel and backup and a life.

'Where does she go?' he said. 'How does she come out of this?'

'As the new code four,' said the Postman, and shot Olsen in the chest. He flew back, hit the wall, sagged down. A flower of blood bubbles blossomed over the scorch ring on his shirt.

Decker cried out. His gun was up and on the Postman before he knew what he was doing.

'Little prick,' said the Postman, walked over and put his gun in Olsen's gasping face. 'Here's a gift from an old man. Maybe you'll take it now.'

He put the muzzle in Olsen's eye and fired. Lauren glanced at them, then turned her whole face on Decker.

'He tried to offer me a deal, John,' she said gently. 'He thought I was the Contender. He wanted me to cut him in.'

Decker looked at her, then back to the Postman and the boy on the ground.

'I was the only one who was straight with you,' she said. 'Put the gun down, John.'

He looked at her. You think we might go away this weekend? Yes, she'd said. Yes, I think we might. And when she said it, he'd seen them both, limbs flashing in blue water . . . His arm started to come down, but slowly. At forty degrees it stopped.

'We're all done here,' said the Postman matter-of-factly. 'You're a postman, operative immediately. Put the gun down, John.'

Decker stayed where he was.

'Toss the weapon, John,' Lauren said. 'And then we can start again.'

'Chrissake, Decker,' the Postman put in, holstering his gun without looking at it.

'We'll be good together,' said Lauren.

Decker's arm rose slowly, the pistol pointing off into space now. He looked at her, then from her to him, then back to her again. She was just like him; like all the other brave men and women who'd given up what we value. Gave it up, suffered prison and worse, so that victory could mean the absence of anyone's defeat.

'Let it go,' said the Postman.

'It's time,' Lauren agreed, looking into his eyes. 'It's your payback time now.'

'She's right,' said the Postman, watching Decker's arm rise until it stopped. 'That's the way, John. Drop it.'

'Please?' Lauren said. He looked at her. She meant it. It was time for the hard work to begin. His arm moved as though it was someone else's, as if it was moving through deep blue water . . .

And then for John Decker it was finally over.

A NOTE ON THE TYPE

The text of this book is set in Linotype Sabon,
named after the type founder, Jacques Sabon. It
was designed by Jan Tschichold and jointly
developed by Linotype, Monotype and Stempel,
in response to a need for a typeface to be
available in identical form for mechanical hot
metal composition and hand composition using
foundry type.

Tschichold based his design for Sabon roman on
a fount engraved by Garamond, and Sabon italic
on a fount by Granjon. It was first used in 1966
and has proved an enduring modern classic.